BREAKING FREE
A KIMBELL TEXAS SWEET ROMANCE
BOOK SIX

ANGEL S. VANE

BONZAIMOON BOOKS

BonzaiMoon Books LLC
Houston, Texas
www.bonzaimoonbooks.com

CHAPTER 1

N ATE

~

office of Bell Capital. David Bell leans back in his chair, shifting his feet onto the cherry wood desk as he smooth talks more millions out of another unsuspecting member of our family.

The sheep, he likes to call them.

The entitled, lazy, silent, limited partners who keep our family's private equity firm one of the top in the country. However, none of the hundreds of descendants of the great Kimberly Bell, founder and namesake of Kimbell, Texas, are more successful than David Bell's branch of the family tree.

The branch my small leaf flutters on in the wind.

If not for my dad, the Bell Family coffers would be stunted in the millions, existing off pathetic profits from rural banks across the southern US. But Dad had a dream that wouldn't be denied. With a business savvy that belied his privileged and spoiled upbringing, he demanded his inheritance at age nineteen and built a private equity business that dwarfs the legacy banks of the Bell Family. He was better than Midas. Everything he touched turned to platinum and diamonds.

As his only son, he expects me to do better.

To be better … than him.

This morning, at the Deal Sourcing Team's weekly meeting, I wasn't.

Didn't even come close.

It was a blood bath.

I walk past his massive wooden desk, scuffed and scratched from his cowboy boots—a testament to how many times he's adopted that exact posture to close a deal. I'm the only one allowed to move freely around his office. I've been doing it for as long as I can remember. Dad loves to tell the story about how I took my first steps right in this office, pressing my hands against the edge of his chair and demanding "Up."

That might have been the last time I did anything that made him proud.

If the story is true.

I stop directly behind his chair and stare at the window. Buffalo Bayou Park stretches in the distance across from Downtown Houston, but my reflection steals my attention.

The most noticeable reflection of how different I am from my dad. Coal black hair, deep-set brown eyes, striking cheekbones, square jaw, and olive complexion are carbon copies of my mom, a descendant from Ossetia, a mountainous region in Southern Russia. It's a place I know little about since she rarely talks about growing up there and has no plans of ever going back. But her lineage, etched all over my face, makes people wonder how I could've come from a sandy-haired, fair-skinned Texan with sky-blue eyes.

But the more profound difference lies in our drastically different personalities.

I'm not the smooth-talking, larger-than-life charmer who can make you feel good as he strips you of your business. My father can sell you a dream that turns out to be a nightmare, and you'd thank him for it.

My approach—outsmart, outwit and outlast.

I dismantle targets with detailed analytics, impeccable research, and an offer they can't refuse.

I don't waste time with coddling or relationship building.

What's the point?

They'll wake up from the dream eventually.

But will I ever wake up from this nightmare?

Chasing an elusive prize that keeps moving out of my reach.

After languishing in the bowels of the company for years, rotating through every single department, including janitorial services, I convinced Dad to give me real responsibilities.

He fired his long-time Executive Vice President of Deal Sourcing, my uncle Karl Bell, and promoted me to the role. I went from a lowly senior analyst to an EVP overnight, which left a target the size of Big Tex at the State Fair on my back.

Deal Sourcing is the core of our business—responsible for finding the companies we buy, improving their operations, skyrocketing their valuations, and selling them for a massive profit.

But private equity doesn't work if you buy the wrong companies.

The wrong target could plunge our business into the toilet and flush our billions down the drain.

Suddenly, this massive responsibility was mine.

And that didn't go over well.

Beloved Uncle Karl, King of the Water Cooler Gab, was much adored by our employees. They saw me as a nepo backstabber for taking his job. Not that he hadn't gotten it through nepotism, but that was beside the point in their view.

After stepping in, I made ruthless changes to the entire Deal Sourcing Team, which didn't win me any Boss of the Year awards. However, they did make the team more efficient, effective, and thorough in identifying the best companies to pursue as targets. Nothing got to Dad without my meticulous scrutiny.

But no one believes it's because of me.

Not the employees and not the market analysts.

Who gets all the credit?

Dad.

King Midas of Private Equity.

The man who hijacked the meeting with *my* team this morning.

Why didn't I move the meeting to tomorrow?

It's impossible for me to make it to Houston on time when my firefighter shift ends at 9 am. All the relaxed vibes and good spirits from spending the last twenty-four hours with men who are like brothers to me vanished instantly when I walked into the office. No memories of laughing and joking with Ronan, Wiley, Darren, and my best friend, Luke, over bowls of Coco Puffs cereal this morning in the Kimbell Fire Station break room could combat the instant sense of dread when I saw Dad sitting in my seat in the conference room.

My directors displayed rambling, lackluster, disorganized, sloppy, and embarrassing target company recommendations based on incomplete research and inept due diligence.

No wonder folks think I'm just a figurehead.

Dad plays the masterful role of Jim Henson, pulling all the strings and making all the moves.

But I'm no Kermit the Frog, Gonzo, or Fozzy Bear.

And one day, Dad and the whole world will discover I'm nobody's Muppet.

The phone slams onto the receiver.

I turn around and stare into Dad's ice-cold blue eyes.

It's time to face his wrath.

CHAPTER 2

L EELA

~

Trembling, I stare at the three missed calls from my attorney, Olivia Garnet. My appointment with her was supposed to be an hour ago, but my mother hijacked my morning again. Good thing Olivia isn't just my attorney. We've become sort of friends over the years she's worked with Sybille Organics. A fact I hope will stop her from being mad at me for missing our meeting.

"Leela! Come here," Mom calls from the hallway.

I grab my high-quality, fake black Chanel purse and slip it onto my shoulder. I have to leave and call Olivia back before she dismisses me.

Stepping back into the hallway, I close the door to the bedroom I've lived in since I was eight years old and turn to face her. I smile brightly before I respond. It's known that if you smile as you speak, people react more positively to what you need to tell them.

"Mama, I have to go. I've already missed one important meeting this morning. I can't miss another," I say, trying to brush past her.

She places a hand on my shoulder, daring me to continue walking.

As the dutiful daughter I am, I stop and look at her.

"Don't you own that little shampoo company?" She asks, raising an eyebrow.

"You know I do."

"If you're the boss, everyone's schedule should revolve around you. Whoever you need to meet with can wait," Mama says, then reaches her hand into her hair, pulling at two rollers. "My roller set cannot. You did these too loose. Come into the kitchen and do them over while I check the rest of them."

I open my mouth, debating whether to tell her I don't have time, then think better of it. The last thing I want is her to get mad and give me the silent treatment. When Mama is angry with me, Daddy always follows her lead and ices me out, too. Living at home with parents who aren't speaking to you is more uncomfortable than most people realize.

Plus, fixing a couple of the rollers in her hair will only take a few minutes. I follow her down the hallway, tossing my purse onto the couch as we enter the kitchen.

Mama pulls a chair from the table and plops down into it. She reaches and tugs at each roller I spent the last hour putting in her hair, meticulously checking the tension.

I redo the two she'd already concluded were too loose, rolling them as tight as possible.

"Just three more. The rest are good," she says, tapping at three more rollers. "Don't forget to stop by your cousin's salon and drop off more shampoo and conditioner. She's running out, and her clients like it for some reason."

"We never got an order from her salon," I say, focusing on the last roller. "And you might like my shampoo and conditioner, too, if you tried it."

"Child, I've been using the same products on my hair for over thirty years. Long before you were born and I like my hair just fine. No point in me changing now," she says, then tilts her head back at me. "Doesn't matter if your cousin didn't place an order. Remember she helped you get into that show in Atlanta, and that's when you said business started to pick up. You owe her. Give her a few boxes for free so your Auntie will stop pestering me."

The Atlanta show was over three years ago. I've given my cousin more than enough of my Botanical Essentials products to pay her back a dozen times over.

"Fine. I'll swing by there after work. But please try to tell Auntie that orders need to be placed and paid for in the future. I lose money giving away boxes for free."

Mama scoffs. "Tell her yourself."

I cringe. She knows I'm not going to do that.

"Don't forget you promised to pick up my shoes from the shoe hospital after work. I need those for church on Sunday," Daddy says, walking into the kitchen to replenish his cup of coffee.

"I didn't forget," I say, tapping Mama on the shoulders to let her know I'm done. She checks the rollers and seems pleased with my adjustments.

"And I need you to cover the light bill again this month. Money is tight," Daddy says.

"Can't you take it out of the rent I already paid?" I ask, hopeful.

"If I could, do you think I'd ask you to cover the light bill?" He snaps back. "Maybe if you weren't so busy spending all your profits from your little shampoo business on luxury clothes and purses, you could pay us what we deserve as rent."

Little do they know, I don't have any profits. Looking the part of a successful business owner means spending hours hunting through bargain deals at luxury brand outlet stores. Most of what I own is from several seasons ago and was bought at a fraction of the original cost. Thanks to my savvy sense of style, I can transform my finds into fabulous looks and convince people I'm more successful than I am.

He huffs, then adds, "Or move out and get your own place. You're twenty-eight years old, for God's sake."

"Your Daddy has a point. Harold moved out at eighteen and jetsets all around the world," Mama says with pride in her voice. "Oh honey, I got a text this morning. Harold has booked some new shows in Hawaii! Can you believe that?"

"That boy is a marvel. People worldwide pay big money to hear him play that piano. Can't wait for him to book some dates in Texas," Daddy says, sipping his coffee.

"Me too. Just hope it happens soon. It's been years since we've had a chance to see him," Mama says.

I resist rolling my eyes. My dear younger brother, Harold, is the gifted one. Child prodigy. Musical genius. Symphony composer at age five. And the most selfish and entitled person in our lives—not that my parents notice.

We all sacrificed to make sure his gift blossomed. Every extra penny went into his piano lessons, music theory courses, recitals, and competitions. While Mama drove him around and Daddy worked two jobs, I did my best to pick up the slack and make things easier for everyone—cleaning, cooking, and holding the family together. The moment Harold graduated from his fancy arts high school, he bolted. He rarely calls and never visits, but my parents still dote on him like he walks on water. And maybe it was worth it, seeing him succeed. Maybe.

Because of my dear brother, though, no one paid attention to the torture I endured at school. All I wanted was to leave behind the merciless teasing I endured as the fat girl with wild hair and too-small hand-me-downs. I just wanted to feel pretty, at least once—at prom.

I saved enough babysitting money to buy a dress and get my hair styled. I dreamed of walking into the dance with silky, straight hair reaching my waist. But that dream became a nightmare when the stylist, inexperienced with hair like mine, burned most of it off with a flat iron. I stumbled home in tears, pulling what little hair I had left into a bun.

I locked myself in my room and turned to social media, recording an hour-long, tearful diary about my salon disaster. That video led to a series chronicling my "Big Chop" and journey to restore my hair with natural, healthier ingredients.

Two years later, my hair was thick, shiny, and long—and about a million followers wanted my secret. From that, Sybille Organics was born with my first collection of shampoo, conditioner, hair oil, and styling serum, Botanical Essentials. Sales grew steadily, but so did expenses, and most years were losses.

But my new line, Herbal Root Essentials, will be a game-changer. The secret is in the extract from the rare calyxera root, which I discovered almost by accident. It has upgraded my products and driven stellar early reviews. This could be the big break I need—if my lawyer can help untangle the mess with the production factory.

As if on cue, the musical jingle of my cell phone fills the air.

"I have to go," I say, kissing Mama and then Daddy. I get a grunt in response as I rush out the door, answering the call.

CHAPTER 3

N ATE

~

"Sit down," Dad says, casually waving toward the chairs opposite his desk.

I do as I'm told. I adopt a casual, indifferent demeanor with my ankle resting on my knee. I don't dare speak or try to defend my team. That would be a foolish mistake. When David Bell has feedback, all you do is watch and listen. Swallow the tough medicine and slink out of his office with your tail between your legs. All of his executive leadership team members have been in this position. We all know the rules.

"Impressive job this morning," Dad says, his lips curling into a smile that falls short of his eyes.

"What? Is this a joke?" The words slip out, sharp, before I can stop them. My pulse spikes—waiting for the "gotcha."

Dad's eyes soften as his smile grows bigger and more ... genuine.

My heart pounds in my chest, each beat echoing in my ears like a countdown to something tragic.

"No joke." He raises his hands in mock surrender. "Handling your regular team meeting with me looking over your shoulder isn't easy. I recognize that. But you knocked it out of the park."

"So, this was some kind of test?" I warn myself not to get my hopes up.

"You've been running the deal sourcing team for two years now. I needed to know once and for all how much of the team's unexpected success was you and how much was them," he says.

"And your verdict is?"

"You were thorough and exacting in your assessment of the proposed targets. Quick with insightful feedback for the team. Gave clear details on the spot without mincing words. You decimated them for their incompetence, and it was beautiful to watch," Dad says.

"Well, I was hoping—"

"Don't go patting yourself on the back so fast." His smile fades.

I stiffen.

"You think I put you in charge so you could single-handedly be the deal-sourcing team? Every success that team has had since you took over has been because you're doing the work … yourself!" Dad's voice rises. His face burns red. "Your team? They're trash, and that's all on you. They're a reflection of your leadership. Or lack of it." He pushes up from his chair, almost knocking it over. "You think a strong leader steps back down to the bottom to do the team's work for them?" He demands, pointing a finger in my face.

"Of course, I don't—"

"Shut up! Don't talk until I tell you to," he snaps. "You've been cleaning up their messes this whole time. I've wasted millions on the highest-paid team in the company, who are a bunch of flunkies. You're too stupid to realize they are playing you. You're not in charge. You work for them."

I clench my jaw tight to hold back the response I want to give him. Hot burning rage races along my skin. I'm two seconds away from walking out the door and never looking back. A fleeting dream I'll never act on.

"That's unacceptable for someone who thinks he can be my successor. You're light-years away from being able to fill my shoes." His face gets redder by the second with each insult. "You put on a good show, but behind the curtain is a fraud. You're a doer. A worker bee. Not a manager and definitely not a leader … son."

He says the last word as if it's something disgusting in his mouth.

The blow stings, but I refuse to give him the satisfaction of knowing how much. My face remains passive, stone-like, as I match his gaze. A move that doesn't go over well as he stalks toward me.

His voice is a low growl now, trembling with rage. "You're a failure, Nate. A failure at leading. A failure at—" His words falter. He inhales sharply, eyes glazing over for a beat too long. His left hand trembles before jerking toward the desk, gripping it like a lifeline.

For a moment, I think he's just catching his breath after the tirade, but something's off. His face, already red from anger, seems to shift—his left eye twitches and his mouth contorts unnaturally, the left side of his lip dragging downward as if pulled by an invisible weight.

"Dad?" My voice is small, barely a whisper.

He tries to speak again, but what comes out is a jumble of sounds. His hand jerks up, fingers clenching at the air as if trying to grasp something.

"Dad!" I spring up from my chair, my pulse slamming in my ears. He's sinking—like a tower crumbling in slow motion. His knees buckle, his body collapsing toward the floor. I rush to catch him, but I'm not fast enough.

He slams to the floor with a sickening thud, his head just missing the corner of the desk. His sharp, ragged gasps fill the room, and his eyes flutter, one pupil larger than the other. A strangled gurgling sound rises from his throat as if he's trying to speak, but nothing makes sense.

The firefighter in me kicks in, instincts overriding the chaos. This isn't David Bell, my dad. Just another patient. Check. Assess. Respond. My hands move on their own—quick, efficient.

"Stay still. Don't move," I command, my voice steady. My fingers press against his carotid artery, checking his pulse—weak, irregular.

"Look at my finger," I command, moving it horizontally across his field of vision. He responds, but his left eye's delayed tracking and sluggish response are undeniable.

I rest my palms in his. "Squeeze my hands." Nothing from his left side. His mouth is still slack, drooping on that side. "Can you squeeze my hand?" I persist.

Dad opens his mouth to speak, but his words are incoherent.

I curse under my breath.

Face drooping. Arm weakness. Speech slurred. It's textbook. I've seen strokes before, but never like this, never from him.

"Now, who's putting on a good show?" I say, my words bitter and strangely unsatisfying.

He blinks at me, his expression a mixture of fury and fear. Even now, he's trying to stay in control, but his body is betraying him. He grips my wrist with his right hand. Part of a tattered, braided leather bracelet peeks from beneath his shirt cuff. I inhale sharply. Has he always worn this? Memories of my tiny hands painstakingly twisting the thin leather straps creep into my mind. Panic claws inside me, but I shove it down.

This is just another patient.

I glance into his eyes—eyes still burning with the same contempt. He hates that I'm a volunteer firefighter back home in Kimbell, even though that's exactly how I can save his life now. I move with practiced efficiency, loosening his tie and unbuttoning his collar as I catalog each irregularity in his movements.

I lean close to his face, my mouth near his ear so he will hear precisely what I say. "Don't think for one second you're dying on me before I prove you wrong. You hear me?"

"Is everything—" Susan, Dad's Chief of Staff, freezes in the doorway. Her coffee mug slips from her hand, shattering on the floor.

The dark liquid spreads like a stain across the marble. Words thick with emotion, she asks, "What happened? Should I call 9-1-1?"

My voice is steady and calm. "He's having a stroke. Grab the pilot now. Tell him we need the helicopter prepped for emergency transport. Hermann Hospital. Immediately."

Susan sprints from the room, her cries to Dad's bodyguards echoing off the walls as her heels click loudly down the hallway.

The bodyguards show up in seconds. I beckon them forward. "Grab the gurney from the emergency closet and help me get him onto it."

Within minutes, we stabilize and strap him down with restraints, securing his weakened left side to prevent further complications. I follow the men as they push Dad into the elevator. We ride in silence to the roof, me standing with my face to the doors as the bodyguards flank Dad on the gurney, giving him words of encouragement.

The doors open. I step to the side, allowing them to exit. As the bodyguards hoist Dad into the helicopter, I call the emergency room and give details on Dad's condition and the estimated time of arrival.

"You coming with us, Nate?" The bodyguard's question hangs in the air as the rotors whine to life.

I lock eyes one last time with Dad and see something entirely different in his blue gaze. Something I'm not prepared for and can't possibly handle.

Stumbling away from the helicopter, I shake my head. "No. There's something I need to do first."

CHAPTER 4

L EELA

I STEP OUT THE FRONT DOOR, BLINDED BY THE BRIGHT morning sun. The temperature is already ninety. Humidity suffocates me as my hand hovers over my phone. I close my eyes briefly, taking a deep breath, but it doesn't help. There's a weight on my chest that won't let up—like I'm about to drown.

I look at the phone in my hand. Olivia's name flashes on the screen. My stomach twists. If she can't help me, I'm not sure what I'll do. I'll be on the hook to repay a substantial advance from GrabHub, a major big box retailer, for failing to meet the terms of my dream distribution deal. It would be the end of Sybille Organics. I'd be bankrupt. The thought makes me want to curl up on the porch and ball my eyes out, but I don't have that luxury. With a resigned sigh, I swipe to answer.

"Olivia," I say, out of breath. "I'm so sorry for missing our call earlier."

"I'm a busy woman. Normally, I wouldn't bother tracking down a client who misses a meeting with me," Olivia says, a warning in her tone. "But we're friends, too, and you sounded so upset on your voicemail." She sighs, her voice softening. "What's going on?"

My fingers find the ends of my hair, twisting a strand nervously as I pace in a small circle on the porch. The words feel too big to say, but they tumble out anyway. "The factory botched the production," I say. My voice shakes. "I have two warehouses full of the wrong product. I can't send it to GrabHub. I can't sell it to anyone!"

"Okay, take a deep breath," Olivia says. "If your employees messed up the product, I'm not sure what I can do about that as your lawyer. As your friend, I can take you out for drinks to drown your sorrows."

"Raincheck on the drinks. I'm not sure I'll need that just yet. So, the products weren't made in my factory," I say, shaking my head as regret fills me. "I made a deal with a third-party factory to produce them. You reviewed the contract with GrabHub. The volume they want to buy is massive to stock my products in stores nationwide. We couldn't cover that in my tiny factory."

"So you arranged for a larger factory to help and didn't let me review that contract," Olivia says, a not-so-subtle rebuke in her tone.

My breath catches. I clutch the phone tighter, the smooth case digging into my palm. A bead of sweat trickles down my temple. I should've contacted her, but I was already delinquent on a multi-five-figure invoice from her for the GrabHub deal. I didn't want to compound that invoice with another one.

"Yes," I say, my voice barely above a whisper.

"And you're sure they created the wrong product?" Olivia asks.

"My production manager performed chemical compound testing to compare our formula to a sample from the production run. It's a standard part of our due diligence. It didn't match, so we tested a bigger sample, and all of them came back ... wrong." I'm almost hyperventilating as panic consumes me. "I don't know what to do. The

GrabHub shipment deadline is in three months, but I don't have any viable product."

"Not an ideal situation," Olivia says, remaining calm. "Send over the contract with the third-party factory, and I'll contact them to get an official response."

"Do you think we can force them to redo the products and ship new batches to me?" I ask, unable to dampen my sometimes unstoppable optimism.

"Only if their internal reviews indicate that it was their mistake *and* your contract has appropriate language to support that as a remediation action."

"So, it's possible …" I want to confirm as hope blossoms within me.

"This could take several months to untangle," Olivia warns, popping my tiny bubble of hope.

"If I don't meet the shipment deadline to GrabHub, they'll terminate the agreement," I say, feeling dizzy from the ramifications of owing massive funds to the store.

"I suggest you find another factory to start production. You can't wait for this situation to be resolved," Olivia says.

"But I don't have the money to do that," I whisper.

Olivia clears her throat. "You're a resourceful businesswoman, Leela. You got a deal with GrabHub when none of your competitors could even get a meeting with them. Don't underestimate what you can do. Get a loan. Find an investor. Do something. Do not lose this deal. I'll call you after I've had a chance to review the documents."

"Okay, thanks, Olivia," I say, then drop my cell phone into my pocket. I sit down hard on the porch steps, burying my face in my hands. My chest feels tight. Tears prick at the back of my eyes, but I force them back. Crying won't help.

The numbers don't add up. The money isn't there. And the walls are closing in no matter how hard I try to believe in this business. How did I get here? How did I let it get this bad?

But then I hear my mother's voice: "Little shampoo company."

And my father's: "Move out and get your own place."
I refuse to fail. Even if it feels impossible, I will find a way.

CHAPTER 5

L EELA

~

Before the Sybille Organics leadership team notices me in the doorway, I smile brightly and say in my usual sing-song tone, "Good morning, beautiful people!"

The hushed, huddled conversation abruptly stops, and they paste smiles on their worried faces. I place the breakfast goodies, my daily subliminal bribe to stay on their good sides, on the center of the table, then make the rounds to each person like I usually do. This meeting must feel normal for them, even if it's anything but.

"Sade, you're looking gorgeous as usual," I say to my sales manager as she stands and walks into my open arms. Bear hugging her, we rock from side to side as she giggles. "How's Denzel doing?" I ask.

"Well, he stopped peeing on my shoes, so I don't think he's mad at me anymore for abandoning him at the feline daycare when I went on vacation. But he's still playing hard to get," Sade says, giving an exasperated shrug.

I hand her the bag of donut holes and a vanilla latte with extra whipped cream. "Turkish angoras are notoriously aloof, but he'll come around." I gently squeeze her arm, then maneuver to Precious, who heads up the production team.

"Did you hear back from the factory?" Precious asks, grabbing the granola-topped yogurt from my hand, and she gives me a half-hug.

"I'll get to that, I promise," I say, handing her the small cup of black coffee. "But first, I need to check on y'all and catch up. How was your date last night?" I raise my eyebrows with hopefulness.

"Ghosted. Again," Precious says with a pout. "I'm not sure what I'm doing wrong."

"They're wrong. Not you. You think a guy who'd do that to a woman is the right man for you? No way. Keep swiping those apps. I heard a new one is getting results," I say, then pause, trying to remember the name. "Think it's something like country boys—"

"Yes! The Ladies Love Country Boys dating app. That one is good. You should try it, Precious," Faye, the head of finance, chimes in.

I hand her the extra large protein shake with whey powder, egg whites, and a dash of honey. "Those guns!" I squeeze her muscular bicep. "You look like you're ready for the bodybuilding competition already."

"That was the plan. Now, I just have to maintain. I'm so nervous," Faye says, hugging me.

"You'll do great," I say, then stop in front of Mischa, who gives me her customary scowl. "Are you bypassing hugs this week?"

"Don't I every week? You and all this happiness is not going to rub off on me. That's team too much in my book," Mischa says.

"Suit yourself." I give her a wink, then approach the table. "But I got something in this box that will brighten your day."

Mischa frowns. "What is it?"

"Lemon poppyseed muffins." I grab one from the box and wiggle it before her.

"Look at little miss sunshine playing dirty," Mischa says, snatching the muffin from my hand as she fights off the smile threatening to curve her lips.

Sipping on her protein shake, Faye levels me with a serious stare. "Please tell us you have good news. We need it."

"Why? What happened while I was out?" I ask, stalling for time. After the dire conversation with Olivia, I wracked my brain on the drive to the office for every option. There weren't many, but I settled on one that could work if I have even the tiniest bit of magic left that helped me snag the deal with GrabHub.

Sade clears her throat. "Orders of Botanical Essentials continue to fall. We're down another forty percent." She cuts a gaze at Mischa. "People aren't buying because they believe Herbal Root Essentials will answer their haircare prayers."

"And it will," Mischa says. "We've all used the new product. It's a game-changer. It was my responsibility to let the entire world know. That's why I flooded influencers with trial-size versions of the product to test. Have you seen the number of videos raving about it? Thousands. Literally." Mischa snatches a piece of her muffin and tosses it in her mouth. "My work here is done."

Faye says, "Your work has halted our cash flow! The GrabHub deal prevents us from setting up pre-orders for Herbal Root Essentials on our website. Customers are waiting to buy from their local stores, not us. Without sales of Botanical Essentials, we won't have money to cover our loan payment at the end of the month."

"Well, I'm the only one happy about this downturn in sales," Precious says. "Our equipment is so raggedy. There's not enough duck tape and gorilla glue to save it anymore. Calling for another repair would be a waste of money. We're down to about sixty percent capacity, just enough to cover those declining orders. Leela, you gotta buy new equipment. This can't continue."

"Wow," I say, then raise my hands. "Now, everybody, take a deep breath. Four count in and exhale slowly. Eight count out. Like you're pushing air through a straw."

The four managers follow instructions as I lead them through calming breaths. After the third round, I know there's no way I'm telling them the truth. I can't. They'd be devastated and afraid for their jobs and livelihoods. They would hate me.

There's still a chance I can right this ship. A Hail Mary pass, and there's proof that those can be caught when you have the right receiver in the end zone.

I smile at each one and say, "I spoke to Olivia this morning, and she's going to help with the factory mishap."

"Thank God!" Precious says.

"In the meantime, I'm working on securing funding to redo the product inventory," I say, hoping they won't ask for more details.

"Who would give us money?" Faye asks.

From looking at her and the others, it's clear that's not a rhetorical question.

I force my smile to be bigger, then say, "I met David Bell at the small business investor Symposium last week. He founded the private equity firm Bell Capital and was very interested in learning more about Sybille Organics. He gave me his card, and I called his office this morning to set up a meeting to discuss investment opportunities on Friday," I say, fudging the truth. Well, a lot. David encouraged me to reach out for advice, not to invest in my business. But that's an inconsequential difference. Now that I have thirty minutes of his undivided attention, I'll give him my best pitch anyway. What do I have to lose?

"Wow!" Faye says, eyes wide. "Bell Capital is big time."

"You never cease to amaze me," Precious says, shaking her head and looking relieved. "There's something to be said about sowing good into the earth and reaping the same back. That is you, Leela."

I can't help but smirk as their faces light up like Christmas morning. "Y'all, I know we're going through a few setbacks, but things are just one meeting away from turning around!"

The chatter in the room rises as we high-five each other and gush over the change in fortune.

I pray I'm not getting their hopes up.

Getting a loan from David Bell is nowhere close to being a done deal … and there's only one person I know who'll be honest enough to tell me if I've just made another huge mistake.

CHAPTER 6

L EELA

~

IT HAS TO BE A SIGN.

Getting fifteen minutes of Mr. Sabra's time on such short notice never happens, as his executive assistant told me twelve times in our five-minute conversation. Michael Sabra, my former cosmetology high school teacher, exploded onto the Houston hair scene after becoming the exclusive stylist for Basel Chase, Houston's own Academy Award-winning A-List actress. He's opened ten signature salons across the city bearing his name. With all the fame, he's never forgotten his humble beginnings. He makes time for former students when he can.

I'm more than grateful. He's the only person I know who can tell me what to expect from a meeting with David Bell. Getting an outside investor is the only way to save my company. My trip to the bank was pointless. The loan officer ignored my request and reminded me of the enormous debt payment due at the end of the month—a payment we don't have the cash flow to cover.

Without an infusion of cash from Bell Capital, I'm headed straight to bankruptcy.

Do not pass go.

Do not collect $200.

But Mr. Sabra has been down the investor road before. Basel's reality show chronicled his process of getting investors for his salon. If anyone can give me strategic tips to convince David Bell that Sybille Organics is worth investing in, it's Mr. Sabra. I know it's a long shot, but having a shot is always better than having none at all.

That's the only reason I broke every traffic law known to man, to make it from the north side of Houston to the Galleria in record time. Despite those efforts, I'm still five minutes late for the meeting.

Pushing through the revolving gleaming glass doors of Williams Tower, I race toward the last bank of elevators, feeling every bit like the outsider in the sea of serious faces milling about. The shimmering golds, oranges, and reds of my silk kaftan dress stand out like a flamingo in a sea of penguins. Nothing but charcoal suits, navy blazers, pencil skirts in shades of beige and black, shiny brown shoes, and sensible heels for as far as the eye can see.

One of these things is not like the others, for sure.

I ignore the strange looks and raised eyebrows as I hurry toward the last elevator door that's about to close.

With a high-pitched squeal, I say, "Hold the elevator, please!"

The dark figure in the corner doesn't move an inch.

I don't want to sacrifice my one and only Chanel purse.

Fine. The Chanel will be sacrificed. There's no other choice. And it's fake, anyway.

Holding the purse by its straps, I swing it between the narrowing gap. The purse bangs into the side of the door. The doors stop, then reverse, opening wide for me to enter.

"Oooh! I made it," I say, fanning my face as I inspect the purse for any oil or dirt smudges from its selfless gesture to get me on the elevator. The bag shows no wear or tear from its heroic efforts.

Glancing at the buttons, the floor to Mr. Sabra's floor is illuminated.

"Looks like we're headed to the same place," I say, smiling at the brooding figure in the opposite corner.

He doesn't respond.

Only I would step onto an elevator with Mr. Tall, Dark, and Rude. He's the corporate boss-type that I'd never be able to convince to help my business. Rigid, intimidating, with a jawline sharp enough to cut glass and a general aura of being too important to deal with someone like me. He'd turn down any pitch I make with one withering stare.

No words needed.

And that's if I was allowed in his office at all.

I sneak a glance at him through the mirrored elevator walls and suck in a sharp breath.

Sure, I see what I was expecting—the annoyed, "don't-even-think-about-talking-to-me" expression. A mouth that likely forgot how to smile around junior high school.

But there's something that I didn't expect at all.

The man is … stunning.

Not a pretty boy, but real man handsomeness amplified by a sexy scowl. He's tall and lean, dressed in a suit that costs more than my rent for an entire year, and fits him like it was sculpted onto his broad, muscular frame. Onyx hair, meticulously combed, but just messy enough to convey he didn't spend too much time on it.

He woke up like this.

Men of his caliber don't waste precious seconds of the day on their looks when there's money to be made. His eyes—dark as midnight and capable of swallowing me whole—stay fixed on the elevator doors.

I would've whistled if I wasn't concerned his frigid aura would freeze my breath mid-air. As the elevator rises slowly, I take the luxury of one last glance at him. Drinking him in, I appreciate the specimen sharing the elevator with me for the next fifteen seconds until …

My gaze reaches his eyes.

And that's when I realize he's been watching me watching him.

I'm vaguely aware that the usual elevator muzak is still playing—some mindless soft jazz track that doesn't match how my pulse is pounding in my ears.

His eyes lock onto mine.

Neither of us moves. The air in the elevator thickens, charged with a palpable heat that defies explanation.

A raw and undeniable thrill pulses through me, like I've touched a live wire. My heart skips a beat, then another, and I'm sure he can hear it echoing in this tight metal box. I feel pinned ... a butterfly on display, caught under his unwavering gaze.

He arches one eyebrow, a barely-there lift that feels like he's thrown down a gauntlet. My cheeks burn, but I can't bring myself to look away. There's a quiet daring in his expression, as if he's challenging me to break first. To surrender to the weight of this unexpected, electric silence.

I should look away.

That's what normal people do in elevators. They pretend to be fascinated by the floor numbers or remember an urgent email they need to read on their cell phone or feign a cough.

But for some reason I can't fathom, I'm not doing the normal thing.

Instead, I double-down on this game of chicken, studying the subtle shift in his expression. My move elicits one of his own. A slight quirk at the corner of his mouth. It's not a smile, more like the ghost of one that is threatening to be resurrected.

That one tiny movement transforms his face from unapproachable handsome boss to devastatingly gorgeous and interesting human being. The kind that makes you wonder what story hides behind those dark eyes, alive with a flicker of something I can't read but am dying to know.

Scientists call this chemical attraction—just neurons firing and hormones flooding. Nothing more than biology doing its thing. But biology has never felt like this. Like every cell in my body is aware of every cell in his.

It's enough to short-circuit the elevator.

No, seriously.

I stumble forward.

The elevator has just jerked to a … stop.

CHAPTER 7

NATE

A MONARCH BUTTERFLY.

That's how she fluttered into the elevator with me, bathed in a flowy dress of bright oranges, reds, and yellows. Her face flushed, deep bronze skin glowing from her race through the lobby to the elevator. I tried to ignore her, but her fantastic figure couldn't be hidden underneath the soft fabric. In milliseconds, I'd already canvassed her entire body, lingering from the mane of dark brown tresses with golden highlights to her heart-shaped face and long graceful neck to the delectable curves of her chest and hips perfectly balanced around her tiny belted waist.

Her voice was like honey when she spoke.

I didn't bother responding.

Today is not the day to indulge in meaningless banter with a woman, no matter how gorgeous she is. And she is quite the looker.

But not enough to completely distract me. My visit to Williams Tower pushes her into the recesses of my mind. Breaking the news to Dad's attorneys about his condition is the last thing I want to do.

It's a necessity.

Bell Capital can't be left without a CEO. We must enact the business contingency plan before news of Dad's stroke gets out to the media. Issuing our own press release is critical to signal to the market that the temporary loss of King Midas doesn't weaken his kingdom.

And the loss sure as hell better be temporary.

I glance at the illuminated button as the butterfly announces we're headed to the same floor. She beams as if the fact wins us some prize, and it's the highlight of her day. There's a confidence in her small talk, like she's used to forcing even the most resistant of people into a conversation with her … whether they want to or not.

Today, she's met her match.

In my periphery, she smiles at me. I get the feeling that nothing can wipe a smile off her face, no matter how good or bad her day has been. I don't smile back. Staring straight ahead, I ignore her last effort to suck me into her glowing orbit.

My mind shifts back to the unenviable task ahead of me—finding out who Dad wants in charge of Bell Capital if he's unable to perform his duties as CEO.

Seeing everything Dad created handed over to one of his Frick or Frack brothers, even for only a few months, leaves a sour taste in my mouth. No doubt, they'll try to undermine me at every turn. I won't let them damage the company before Dad recovers and gets back at the helm.

If … he recovers.

The thought buries itself deep inside, unwanted but persistent. I force it down, shoving it into the same mental drawer where all my "what-ifs" go to die.

I glance at the elevator's mirrored wall. The butterfly stares into the same surface, but her gaze is firmly planted on me.

I'm no stranger to women checking me out. Growing up the son of a billionaire has afforded me much attention from women over the years. I'm familiar with the predatory gaze of a gold digger sizing me up to be her next meal ticket. I'm equally familiar with the doe-eyed innocent attracted to the brooding jerk she hopes to change into a loving, good guy. And every iteration in between, I've seen more than twice.

But the butterfly isn't giving me any of those looks.

She's assessing me.

Like she's figured me out, but she sees one thing that's a conundrum. Something she wasn't expecting. It's drawing her to me like a moth to a flame. She's so in her head that she doesn't even notice I'm watching her every move as her gaze trails slowly and meticulously up my body.

My heart jumps in my throat.

The steely resolve to ignore her shatters.

I try to tear my gaze away from her lovely face, but it's useless.

I don't budge, not wanting to disturb her scrutiny.

I need her to realize that whatever she thinks she sees in me is a lie. I'm nobody's happily ever after. It's not in my DNA. Bells don't do romantic gestures and definitely don't have the skillset for emotional connections. We have one strength, and that's making money. Anything that distracts from what we do best is a vulnerability to be avoided like the plague.

The butterfly's gaze reaches my face.

Our eyes lock.

My mind goes blank as I stare into hazel eyes, bursting with flecks of green and gold. I can't even think as I lose a grip on reality, falling into her mesmerizing, exotic gaze—

The elevator jolts to a stop.

I stumble forward, reaching a hand out to steady myself.

A loud thud ricochets off the wall, followed by a symphony of clinks, rattles, and metallic pings as the contents of her purse spill out in every direction.

"Oh, you've got to be kidding me!" The butterfly groans. She's on her knees, scooping up pens, lipstick, a dozen combs and small brushes, compact mirrors, small bottles, a curling iron, a flat iron, two candy bars, a bottle of hot sauce, and a fake potted plant—because why not? How on earth does she fit half her life in one bag?

I reach down and grab a stuffed toy resting against my shoe.

A butterfly.

Why am I not surprised?

Turning it over and over in my palm, I hand it to her as she finishes stuffing the contents of her life back into her giant purse and stands back up.

"I think this is yours," I say.

She squeals. "Yes. It's a gift. For my meeting. Well, the person I was supposed to meet with." She pauses to flip her wrist, shaking the bangles down her arm to see the watch hidden underneath. "Fifteen minutes ago for a fifteen-minute meeting. He collects miniature stuffed animals for his little girl. I saw this and thought it was just perfect."

Maybe you're just … perfect. I ignore my wayward thoughts as she gives me a smile that lights up the entire elevator.

"But now, who knows If I'm going to see him. He's so busy," she says, throwing her hands into the air. "Come on, elevator, move!" She looks up at the ceiling like she can will the elevator with the sheer force of her positivity to start moving again. "Are you here for a meeting, too?"

"Something like that," I mutter under my breath.

"You think maybe we should scream for help?" she asks, her gaze flipping between me and the electronic screen, which registers a bright red "E" where the floor numbers had been.

"I think pushing the emergency button is a better option." Turning away from her, I press the red button etched with the outline of a phone. Nothing happens. Not even a buzz.

She raises an eyebrow with a smirk as my suggestion doesn't work. Pushing a lock of her glossy tresses behind her ear, she says, "Well, if you don't think we should scream and pound on the door, we might be stuck here for a bit." She eases onto the floor, then pats her hand to indicate I should do the same.

I roll my eyes.

She says, "Not how I planned on spending my morning, but it could be worse, right?"

"How exactly could this be worse? You have no chance of making it to your meeting, and I'm on my way to get more bad news." I stop myself. What on earth is possessing me to confide in this woman?

"Well, the elevator is stuck. It's not plummeting fifty stories back to the ground to crash and kill us. That's a positive, right?"

"There's still time."

She frowns.

"But unlikely that will happen," I add.

That seems to satisfy her. "And the lights and air conditioning are still working. I'm sure some control room in the building is being alerted at this very moment that the elevator is jammed, and they are working to get us out of here."

"That's one option," I say. As a firefighter, I've had tons of experience with broken elevators and know it's not always that simple.

"How about you not share your thoughts on the other options?" She laughs, a light and effortless sound tickling my ears. For a brief moment, a smile threatens to curve my lips. She reaches into her purse and pulls out a cell phone. Typing frantically on the device, she says, "You should tell whoever you're meeting that we're stuck. That might get things moving."

"They don't know I'm coming," I say, not bothering to tell her that the weak cell signal showing on her phone won't be strong enough to send a text message or make a phone call. Elevators in old buildings like these are notorious for being cell phone dead zones.

"And if they knew you were headed their way?" She asks.

"They'd be in their offices rehearsing how to distract me with patronizing platitudes as they blow my world apart," I say, not sure why I'm explaining this to her. With an edge of tension I can't hide, I add, "If it was up to me, I wouldn't be here at all."

Her hazel eyes grow darker. The gold flecks sparkle. "I see. Maybe you need this pause."

"Why would I need a pause?" I ask, pressing the emergency button again. No response.

"You've already made up your mind about how your surprise meeting will go. But maybe you need time to contemplate what would happen if it doesn't turn out as bad as you think it will," the butterfly says. "Sometimes we prepare ourselves too much for what can go wrong that we're blindsided when something goes right. We don't know how to handle it."

I frown, stifling a groan. "I'll take a hard pass on the optimism. Thanks."

"Suit yourself," she says, shaking her head as several beeps emit from her phone. "My texts didn't go through." She gives the cutest pout, then places it back into her purse. Leaning her head against the wall, she closes her eyes, humming a jaunty little tune.

"That's it. You're giving up on getting out of here?" I ask, annoyed by how quickly she segued from panic to calm.

"I'm recognizing that I can't change this situation. It's better to save my energy and focus on things in my control instead of letting this frustrate me." She opens one eye. "You should try it. Sit."

Sliding down onto the floor, I face her.

She looks pleased, then closes her eyes as she hums again, softly, the same little tune from before. As I memorize the pattern of the annoying melody, the tension leaves my body, and I stop thinking about the millions of things that need to be done now that Dad won't be able to continue as CEO for the foreseeable future. My eyes close, and I allow myself to let go. If only for this one brief moment—

The elevator jerks.

My eyes fling open as it rises. The electronic display is replaced with numbers increasing as it approaches our floor. I stand up and fix my suit in the mirror as the butterfly remains on the floor with her eyes closed. There's no announcement or explanation for the glitch.

As the doors open, I turn back and extend my hand.

The look in her eyes almost makes me forget everything—my father, the company, the future. I exist only in the present moment with her. She's pulling me in like a current I can't fight.

When she places her hand in mine, electricity tingles through my arm, warming every part of my body. I don't bother to analyze why a single touch from this woman has me reacting like a lovestruck teenager. Good thing we'll never see each other again. I can't afford her kind of distraction.

"Thank you," the butterfly says as she stands, still holding my hand. "Good luck with your meeting." She squeezes my hand and then flutters out of the elevator.

I don't bother to wish her luck.

For some reason, I don't think she'll need it.

CHAPTER 8

L EELA

~

The polished floor amplifies every step as I follow the receptionist down the glossy corridor. Each one screams to the folks huddled in cubicles that I'm embarrassingly and disrespectfully late. Floor-to-ceiling windows lining one side of the hallway pass by in a blur, offering a dizzying view of the city below. The skyscraper's interior is all glass and steel, a cavernous space designed to make people feel inferior in the presence of power.

Mr. Sabra exits his office, stops to give last-minute instructions to his assistant, then turns toward me. The faintest frown creases his brow as he catches sight of me.

"Mr. Sabra! I'm so sorry I'm late," I blurt, reaching him. "Traffic was horrendous, and then I got stuck in the elevator with this rude and brooding corporate type who unexpectedly was nice to me once the elevator was fixed and the door opened. He helped me—"

He raises a hand, cutting me off. "Walk with me." Striding toward the bank of elevators at the end of the hall, he says, "Waiting for you is making me late for a meeting with Basel. You have one elevator ride to talk, and then I'm out."

"Of course, I understand." I fall into step beside him, matching his brisk pace.

He pauses mid-stride, his expert eye giving my hair a professional once-over. "May I?"

"You don't even have to ask."

He reaches out, his hands working through my hair, fingers twisting, tossing, and fluffing the strands with the expertise of one who's spent decades in the beauty industry. It's almost clinical, the way he assesses it, though there's a warmth in his expression that's almost … paternal.

"Glossy, healthy, not a split end in sight," he murmurs, more to himself than to me. He brings strands of my hair closer to his face, a specimen studied by his microscopic professional eye. "And so deliciously long. Is this the new product or something special you're working on?"

"It's the new product," I tell him, pride slipping into my tone. "Supposed to be hitting stores in three months."

"Supposed to be?" His brow arches, and his hands pause in my hair.

I exhale sharply. "Hit a snag with production and had to toss the entire shipment. Nothing could be salvaged."

Mr. Sabra whistles, dropping his hands from my hair. "That's an expensive mistake."

"Tell me about it." I press the down button, watching the numbers above the doors slowly climb toward our floor. "Which is why I wanted to talk to you."

"You know I can't." He shakes his head, his expression sympathetic but firm. "Not that you aren't a good investment. If I do it for you, every student in my classes for over a decade trying to launch a business will be hanging outside my office asking for a handout."

The elevator arrives with a soft ding, its doors sliding open.

"I understand," I say quickly, stepping inside with him. "I wasn't here to ask about money. The last time we chatted, you encouraged me to go to the conference held by Bell Capital."

"Yeah, I remember that." He pushes the button for the ground floor, and the elevator descends. "You can learn a lot about ways to take your business to the next level from the people at that company and the speakers they bring. Also, it allows you to get your name out there and network with potential investors."

"It was pricey, but I went anyway." I can't help the grin that spreads across my face. "And I ran into David Bell, the CEO, on my way out. You know me—nothing ventured, nothing gained. I talked his ear off for the entire walk to his car. He was so nice and sweet, listening and even asking me questions. Such a charming man. When we got to his car, he gave me his card and told me to reach out."

"You're joking." He stares at me, eyebrows raised.

"Nope," I say, still grinning. "This disaster with the products in my new Herbal Root Essentials line qualifies as a reason to contact him. His assistant booked a thirty-minute appointment for Mr. Bell and me on Friday. I plan to pitch him for investment dollars, you know, Shark Tank style."

Mr. Sabra's mouth gapes open, and his reflection shows his astonishment from multiple angles. "Did he say he was interested in investing in your company when y'all talked?

"Not exactly. It was more like an offer for coaching or business advice." I swallow, a sudden rush of nerves overtaking my earlier excitement.

"So you're going to blindside the man with a pitch for money instead?"

"I'm so over my head," I admit, watching the floor numbers decrease.

"In over your head is an understatement." He faces me, running a hand over his chin. "Those guys are sharks, and we're minnow fish. He's not going to be happy about an unsolicited pitch."

"But I need the investment." My voice takes on an edge of panic. "I can't replace the inventory without it. I forfeit the deal if I don't meet the deadline for shipping the products to GrabHub. They'll never give me another chance. I'll be sued for the advance they paid me. My business will be dead."

The elevator hums quietly as it carries us downward, and I can't shake the image of everything I've worked for slipping through my fingers. My business, my dreams, my team counting on me—all of it gone if I can't pull this off.

"Desperation is like blood in the water for them," Mr. Sabra warns. "Don't let David Bell's charisma fool you. The man didn't get where he is today by being nice. He's a wolf in sheep's clothing. And I've heard that his son is even worse. The guy doesn't even pretend to be personable. He's a straight wolf seeking companies to devour. A few years back, he and Basel were a thing, and he still didn't lift a finger to help her when we were trying to launch the salons."

"Ouch." I wince.

The edge in his voice fades, replaced with tenderness. "You need to understand who these people are deep inside and not be fooled. Bell Capital is successful because they're myopically focused on what can make them the most money. They don't care about you. They don't care about your business. They only care about the rate of return on their investment. Don't forget that, and don't be fooled into thinking it's anything but that."

I bite my lip, weighing his words. "But what if we can strike a win-win situation for both companies? Isn't that worth it?"

He chuckles, shaking his head. "Trust me, they'll ensure they win way more than you do."

"So, you think it's a bad idea?"

The elevator slows as we reach the ground floor.

He reaches out, squeezing my shoulder gently. "Do the meeting and give it everything you've got. Just don't get your hopes up. It's easier to win the lottery than get Bell Capital to invest in your company."

I nod slowly, absorbing his advice. The elevator doors slide open to the lobby. "Any last-minute tips?"

Mr. Sabra steps out beside me. "They have teams that will analyze every detail of your company. Don't bother trying to sell them on your business acumen. Do what you do best. The same way you got a million followers on social media is the only chance you have to convince him to invest. Make sense?"

"Yeah, it does." I chew my bottom lip as I rummage a hand in my purse. "Before you go, I got something for your daughter." Which I can't seem to find. Dropping my purse on the floor, I dig through the contents, but the stuffed butterfly is nowhere to be found.

"Don't worry about it. She's got enough toys. You focus on the meeting. Call me and let me know how it goes." He gives me a final wave.

Grabbing my purse from the floor, I take a deep breath and reflect on his advice.

The only way I can convince David Bell to invest in my company is to make him believe that my haircare products can improve women's lives.

Well, I've done that before.

Why can't I do it again?

CHAPTER 9

ATE

~

The automatic doors of St. Elizabeth's Hospital slide open with a quiet whoosh. Luke matches my strides as we step into the atrium. Clusters of custom-upholstered couches and chairs are filled with anxious families and friends visiting loved ones. The antiseptic smell hits me immediately, making my stomach churn. Or maybe that's the weight of what I learned from the visit to Dad's attorneys at Williams Tower.

I thought I was the one blindsiding them with my visit. I couldn't have been more wrong. My mind is a jumbled mess trying to sort through it all.

"Glad you're here. I was ten minutes away from driving to Houston and snatching you out of those meetings," Luke says as we take the elevator to the private Bell Wing. I don't doubt my best friend would've done it, too. It was after six in the evening before Susan told me that Luke was trying to reach me. My cell phone had been abandoned as I sat in dozens of meetings to prepare the company for the announcement of Dad's absence.

Stepping off the elevator, I stare straight ahead at three women, preening and posturing inside the waiting area. Dad's ex-wives, like vultures circling, ready to devour a maimed prey.

"You okay?" Luke stops my forward movement and forces me to look at him.

"No," I answer honestly. I never lie to Luke about anything. It's been that way since we met as freshmen on the campus of Southern Methodist University. He was the first friend I ever had who didn't see me as a walking checkbook to be used for any and every little thing they needed. He wasn't impressed with my wealth at all. Still isn't, and that means the world to me. But I'm not ready to bare my soul about the meeting with the lawyers.

I change the subject before he can pry the truth out of me. "Why was Dad moved here?"

A worried expression spreads across Luke's face. "Your mother insisted. She was adamant and made the arrangements."

"My ... mother?" Incredulity drips from my words. Behind Luke, one of the vultures waves at me, seeking an acknowledgment I'll never give.

"Did she say why?" I ask.

"No, but I think your cousin has answers," Luke says. "Willow is in with him now, waiting for you."

I nod. "Can you get rid of them?" I tip my head toward the waiting area.

"I'll do my best," Luke says.

Turning down the hallway, I walk purposefully until I stand outside the door. The nameplate on the outside gleams in brushed nickel: Dr. Nicolas Shelton.

I rap my knuckles against the door and plow inside. The office is cozy, with soft lighting, calm, comforting blue walls, and a minimalist desk that my cousin sits behind.

My sister, Willow, sits in one of the two chairs on the opposite side of the desk. She's beautiful in that way that always catches people off-guard. Her striking sky blue eyes, so like Dad's, are rimmed red from fighting back tears but still hold a familiar steeliness. Her black wavy hair is twisted in a thick braid, cascading over one shoulder. Her crossed leg bounces rapidly as if she's trying to stop herself from drop-kicking every nurse and doctor in this place.

I ease into the seat next to hers. She looks at me like the lifebuoy she needs to stay afloat. But I need her more.

"Where's mom?" I ask my sister.

She responds with an exaggerated eye roll. "Not here. She claims she's done all she can for Dad's situation. If we need help, she thought one of Dad's other ex-wives would be happy to pitch in."

A growl rumbles low in my throat at the thought of relying on any one of those women camped out in the waiting room to help our dad. They're here for only one reason—to try to ingratiate themselves for a payout for their helpfulness.

"Nico wouldn't give me any details until you got here," Willow says.

"What's going on, Nico? Why was Dad brought here?" I demand, cutting to the chase. I don't dispute that it helps to have Dad closer to home, but moving him from the Houston Medical Center to be treated at a teaching hospital in rural central Texas so soon after his stroke feels premature.

"Because I'm Uncle David's doctor," Nico says.

"Since when?" Willow barks.

I'm wondering the same thing. Willow and I have badgered Dad for years about getting annual physicals, which he's dismissed as foolish since he was fit as a horse. Turns out, Dad wasn't as healthy as any of us thought.

Nico clears his throat, glancing between Willow and me. "Since his first stroke two years ago and the second one about six months ago."

The ground shifts beneath me. "What are you talking about? Dad has had two strokes in the past two years?"

"Why didn't you tell us?" Willow bolts forward, her words ricocheting off the walls like bullets at an enemy.

Nico's jaw tightens. "I'm bound by doctor-patient confidentiality. Your father didn't want either of you to know. He didn't want to worry you."

Willow's hand finds mine, and I squeeze it. "What changed?" she asks. "Why are you telling us now?"

"Uncle David's Medical Power Attorney designated your mother as the primary decision maker for him if he were unable to make decisions himself," Nico says, then pauses to allow that bombshell to blow up in our faces.

"But they've been divorced for years," I say, reeling from another unexpected twist in Dad's desires concerning who should control things if he can't.

"It's what your father wanted," Nico continues. "However, given the severity of your father's condition, your mom evoked a clause in the document to allow decisions to be made by your father's closest living relatives."

"So, me and Nate."

"That's right," Nico confirms.

"Okay, so tell us all the details," I force the words out.

Nico lays out Dad's health history in excruciating detail, and it's worse than I'd imagined. For years, Dad has quietly been dealing with high blood pressure, elevated LDL cholesterol, and an irregular heartbeat, all of which put him at serious risk for stroke. He's been on medications to manage it, but Nico's warnings weren't enough to make him change his ways.

Instead of cutting back on work or stress, he doubled down, pushing himself harder, barely sleeping, skipping exercise, and shrugging off Nico's suggestion about lifestyle changes. The pills could only do so much without his cooperation, but Dad didn't listen. It's like he thought he was invincible, as if a handful of prescriptions were enough to keep him going forever. But he was wrong. The first two strokes were mild, and he was released from the hospital without any of us finding out he'd suffered them. But today, everything changed. His bad decisions caught up with him.

Nico glances between Willow and me, his expression steady but serious. "Your dad suffered a moderate ischemic stroke," he says, his voice calm and clinical. "That means a blood clot temporarily blocked blood flow to part of his brain. The good news is that the clot resolved fairly quickly, so there wasn't irreparable damage. With rehabilitation, he can recover most, if not all, of his functioning."

I nod slowly, trying to absorb the information. "What are we looking at, timeline-wise?" The meeting with the lawyers is not far from my thoughts.

Nico takes a breath. "Nine to twelve months for a full recovery, but there are factors we can't fully predict right now—how his body responds to therapy, how committed he is to follow through on the exercises, his overall stamina. If he pushes himself—and knowing your dad, he will—he might be better in as little as six to eight months. But I don't want to set expectations too high."

I let out a breath I didn't realize I was holding. "But he's going to be okay, right? I mean … he's going to be *himself* again?"

"If he fully commits to physical and speech therapy, yes," Nico explains.

"He isn't a very patient man. This will be hard for him," Willow says what we're all thinking.

"To make things easier for you, I've already arranged for top rehab specialists to come to Kimbell and work with your Dad for the next year. He's going to be in excellent hands." Nico rises from his chair. "You ready to see your dad now? I can walk y'all over to his room."

"I need to catch up with Willow first," I say.

Willow gives me a look, a flicker of understanding in her eyes. "We'll be back soon."

CHAPTER 10

Nate

Willow inhales a sharp breath. "Which of our useless uncles is stepping in as interim CEO?"

The words stick in my throat.

Her eyes narrow. "Please, no! Not Uncle Karl."

I grimace, unable to find my voice.

She groans. "It's not one of our uncles, is it?"

I shake my head.

"Did Dad seriously put Aunt Patty in charge?" She shrieks, voice rising. "Unbelievable! As much as I love Nico, his mother is not qualified to step into Dad's seat."

"It's not Aunt Patty, either."

She raises her eyebrows. "You're scaring me, Nate. Just spill it. Who's going to be interim CEO of Bell Capital?"

"Me," I mumble, barely loud enough for her to hear.

Willow leans forward, eyes wide. "What did you say?"

With more confidence than I feel, I say, "You're looking at the interim CEO. When we opened the sealed documents, Dad left ironclad instructions that I should take over if he were unable to perform his duties—"

Willow launches herself at me, wrapping her arms around my neck in a fierce hug that nearly knocks me over. "This is the best news ever! Why aren't you doing cartwheels?"

I pull back as guilt and anger war within me. "Because I'm the reason Dad had a stroke."

Her smile fades, and she studies my face. "Were you listening when Nico laid out all Dad's medical issues? The only person responsible for Dad's stroke is Dad."

"He was in the middle of giving me brutal feedback on my performance when it happened." I swallow, barely able to look at her. "He was livid, screaming at me that I'm a failure in every way imaginable. That's when the stroke happened."

Willow cups my chin in her hands. "Well, you didn't fail when you saved his life. You're not a failure. You're a hero."

I shake my head. "I was just doing my job."

She snorts. "There's the firefighter motto tattooed on your soul."

"His instructions weren't dated." I pause, the words weighing heavily. "He doesn't feel that way anymore. He told me this morning I wasn't ready to lead Bell Capital."

Willow smirks. "Then prove him wrong."

My sister's words have rattled around my brain during my first few days as the interim CEO of Bell Capital. The first day was consumed with fielding investor calls, focusing on not revealing details of Dad's absence while instilling confidence that I could keep the business running smoothly. The following two days have been an avalanche of uncovering the thousands of things Dad does as CEO that I never knew about. How he keeps up this pace at his age is beyond me.

The thought is sobering.

He couldn't keep up the pace.

That's why he had a stroke.

I push the thought away and focus back on the last of Susan's debrief on Dad's open targets for takeover.

"Those last two are top priority," Susan says.

"Anything else?" I ask, refusing to let her see how overwhelmed I am by everything.

"There's a meeting on David's calendar for Friday with the owner of a small business called Sybille Organics—"

"What kind of business is it?"

She hesitates. "I'm not sure. It must be one of the businesses that attended the Capital Connection Conference last week. You know your father. He's always giving out his card and offering to coach up-and-coming business owners."

"Right, the old tough-love, pointing out their flaws and crushing their spirit about ever getting a chance to lure investors like us," I say, knowing full well what Dad does in those meetings.

"He believes it's valuable feedback that will make them better in the long run," Susan says, defending a practice I find pointless and demoralizing. "I can cancel the meeting."

"Has anyone looked into what they do?"

"You can't seriously think one of these companies is worth our time?" Susan balks.

I give her a withering stare that has her squirming in her seat.

If I'm going to do what Willow suggested, I have to find a diamond in the rough. That's how legends are made. It's my ticket to proving to Dad that his confidence in my abilities should be restored. This Sybille Organics company is a good place to start.

Picking up the phone, I call Rick, the Senior Director of the Deal Sourcing Team.

"What can I do for you, boss?" Rick asks, then chuckles. "But I guess you're everybody's boss now, right? Congrats."

I don't have time for the small talk. "I need an extensive work up on a company called Sybille Organics for a meeting in two days. You and the team have three hours to get me everything I need. Understood."

Rick clears his throat. "Yes, sir. I'll have it to you shortly after lunch."

Hanging up the phone, I glare at Susan, who's still sitting in my office for some strange reason. "You can leave now. I'll take it from here."

She looks shocked, then rises from her seat and exits with a huff.

Hours later, I'm eating lunch at my desk while on the most boring conference call when the report on Sybille Organics pops into my email inbox. Ignoring the updates from the various businesses, I devour the details, becoming more excited as I find out more.

The company is on the verge of exploding as one of the top ethnic haircare lines in the country. It's owned by Leela Jamison, a struggling business owner who still lives at home with her parents in an impoverished area of Houston. She built her company out of the garage and grew it on the back of a popular social media profile and one signature line through company website sales.

I skip over the links to her bio and social media videos and skim the team's summary instead:

Despite not having a college degree or MBA, she's grown the company each year and is attracting attention from major consumer product conglomerates as a target for acquisition. The leaked financial statements the team secured show that the business has struggled to break even, but not because the owner mismanaged funds. She barely takes a salary, funneling profits back into the company by hiring the best in the field and managing an in-house production factory.

What's more impressive is how she single-handedly secured a supply of a rare root for her upcoming product line that has the beauty care industry abuzz. And that's on the back of getting a national contract with GrabHub despite being one of the smaller players in the industry.

Leaning back in my chair, I wonder if I could be so lucky to find the diamond in my first foray into the mine. I'm no expert in hair care products for diverse ethnicities, but I know someone who is.

Muting the conference call, I lower the volume to a whisper and then grab my cell phone. Scrolling through the contacts, I find the one I'm looking for and press the call button.

"Javier de los Reyes," a man answers on the second ring.

"It's Nate Bell," I say, then pause.

"The Prince of Private Equity deems me worthy of a discussion?" Javier laughs. "I'm flattered, man. Or should I bow down to you as the new king?"

"This gig is temporary. David Bell isn't going anywhere anytime soon," I say, careful not to give Javier any inside scoop on my father's medical issues.

"Glad to hear it. Just between me and you, there's a lot of angst around the abrupt change. Watch your back," Javier says. "So, why is my former boss calling me? Don't tell me you want to steal me back to take on your old role over Deal Sourcing."

"Would you consider that?"

Javier pauses for a long moment, then says, "No. I'm better off not being in your shadow. Plus, I know that's not why you called."

"You're right. Have you heard of Sybille Organics?"

Javier groans. "Of course I have. One of the top companies in the hottest growing niche in the industry. Our intel says their new line, Herbal Root Essentials, will be groundbreaking. They're the first company to figure out how to unlock the properties of calyxera root in haircare products. A few others have tried but didn't get anywhere. Sybille Organics has nailed it based on the samples they've been sending out. Combine that with the deal with GrabHub, and the company is set up for massive success. Those factors catapult them to the front of the line with consumers and for deals with other retailers."

"Downsides?"

"The owner, Leela Jamison, and her management team are super green. They've done a decent job but lack the business acumen to drive the company to significant growth. The company hasn't turned a profit yet, and it should've by now. That tells you operationally, their processes need a lot of improvement."

A grin spreads across my face. I can always count on Javier to blabber more information than he should, even to a competitor. It was one of the reasons I didn't fight to keep him at Bell Capital. "So y'all aren't interested?"

"Didn't say that. We're definitely interested. Just waiting to see if the launch of the new line lives up to the hype. If it does, we'll position ourselves to make a move."

Drumming my fingers against my desk, I say, "I don't understand why you industry types move so slow."

"The level of approvals needed is daunting. Too many in our C-Suite want evidence of success before moving, even if all the signs indicate there's no way it will fail."

"They run things out of a small in-house factory, right? They could struggle to get the shipment to GrabHub on time," I say, fishing for information.

"Leela Jamison was smart enough to outsource production for the first shipment to a reputable factory while the company works to get their in-house factory up to standards. Surprised you didn't know that," Javier gloats.

I do now.

"Interesting. Just a heads up that it's on our radar," I say, but there won't be a battle if I have anything to do with it.

Javier sighs. "Not surprised. May the best company win."

"Oh, we will."

CHAPTER 11

L EELA

~

FIDGETING WITH THE FABRIC OF MY SILK SCARF, I
rehearse my pitch over and over in my head. Waiting nearly three
hours for the meeting with Mr. Bell wasn't part of my plans. But I can't
leave. I have to shoot my shot and pray he's open to investing in
Sybille Organics.

I keep telling myself that no news from my lawyer is good news.
There's still a chance the third-party factory that botched my first
shipment could be forced to redo the production and help me salvage
the GrabHub deal. In the meantime, I'm languishing in the sprawling
executive conference room of Bell Capital. It's the kind of space
designed to impress and intimidate. A wall of glass overlooks the
sprawling Houston cityscape, while sleek black leather chairs rest
beneath a polished mahogany table. Black and white sketches of iconic

Texas monuments line the walls, adding history and a museum-like quality to the room's commanding and austere atmosphere.

"Apologies for the delay, Ms. Jamison," says Mr. Bell's executive assistant, a demure elderly woman dressed in an impeccably tailored black suit. "He's ready to see you now."

I rise slowly and follow her down a long hallway opposite the sprawling corner office with David Bell's name on the outside above the title, Chief Executive Officer.

The woman pauses at the door. "Go in, he's expecting you."

Before I mutter a word of thanks, she disappears down the hall. I tell myself this is no different from the hundreds of videos and live streams I've done on social media promoting my products. I got this.

I take a deep breath, then enter the room.

My eyes land on the man sitting behind the minimalist glass desk, set against a dark, matte wall with a single striking piece of abstract art behind him. The desk is almost bare—only a Moleskin notebook and Montblanc pen, which he uses to write furiously in the notebook. His head is down, in deep concentration on his notes. But one thing is crystal clear.

This man is not David Bell.

"I'm so sorry. I think I'm in the wrong place," I say, confused. "Or maybe not. Will Mr. Bell be joining us?"

"I am Mr. Bell," He snaps.

"Oh ..." A shiver of apprehension crawls down my spine.

"You were expecting my father," he says, still not meeting my gaze as he scribbles more into the notebook. His words are clipped, monotone, and on autopilot, as if he's had to give this speech thousands of times today. "He's taken a leave of absence. I'm his son, Nate Bell, and the interim CEO until he returns."

I totally don't got this.

"I see ..." the words eke out of me.

So, I've wasted all week preparing for a meeting with David Bell— warm, charismatic, easy to connect with. But his son? I don't know anything about him besides what Mr. Sabra told me, which isn't comforting.

Don't let David Bell's charisma fool you … he's a wolf in sheep's clothing … and I've heard that his son is even worse …

I swallow past the lump in my throat.

This is okay. Sometimes, unexpected changes occur.

I can pivot with the best of them.

Until he looks up.

Dark obsidian eyes lock on to mine.

Yep, now is the time to lose every single nerve I have.

Mr. Tall, Dark, and Rude from the elevator stares back at me.

My knees turn to jelly.

My mouth goes dry.

I can't speak.

I'm not even sure I remember to breathe.

I thought he was handsome before.

But that's nothing compared to how drop-dead gorgeous he is as the heir apparent sitting on his throne. The prince of a kingdom made entirely for him. One he owns and commands with complete confidence and strength.

I study his face for a fraction too long to be sure it's him. Smooth olive skin stretches over sharp cheekbones and a jawline begging to be caressed. He's the kind of man who could easily make anyone's heart skip a beat if he didn't look like he'd rather shatter it.

Those intense, coffee-dark eyes don't soften as they rake over me. It's maddening how someone so cold could look so devastatingly … hot.

I lick my lips slowly, wondering if he remembers me.

Maybe if there's even the slightest flicker of recognition of our shared experience, it would help me break the ice and calm my raging nerves.

But there's nothing but a blank, unimpressed glare as he takes inventory of me standing before him. He frowns as if my bold fashion style isn't just unprofessional but utterly offensive.

I'm regretting my choice of the scarlet red pantsuit that hugs all my voluptuous curves. I felt like Wonder Woman in the outfit this morning, but now I'm wondering what I was thinking. At least I chose a more conservative style for my hair—it's swept back in a loose, elegant bun, with wisps of hair framing my face to add an air of sophistication. At least, I hope.

"Are you going to stand there gawking, Ms. Jamison, or would you like to sit for our discussion?" His tone is ice-cold, every word measured as though I'm wasting his precious time just by existing.

I flash him my best smile and refuse to be ruffled by his brusque tone. I'm here for one reason only—to save my company.

"Not gawking," I say with a light chuckle. "Just taking it all in. After I knock your socks off with my pitch, I'll be spending a lot more time in this office with my future investor." I give him a wink.

His eyes narrow, and he places his pen on the desk. "You're here to pitch … what?" Confusion laced with a hint of annoyance in his tone.

Mr. Sabra was right. Blindsiding the top executive of a private equity firm with a request for investment dollars isn't the most brilliant move, but I can't turn back now.

"An opportunity to become a partner with an ethnic haircare line on the verge of massive growth," I say, with more confidence than I feel.

"I see." He leans back in his chair as if bored but amused by my boldness. "I'm listening."

That's as positive of a reaction as I'm going to get. Without hesitation, I launch into my over-rehearsed pitch. My voice is engaging and entertaining as I unveil the history of Sybille Organics, our humble beginnings, the countless hours of research and dedication to creating products from natural ingredients, and our vision, which is based on the intersection between feeling beautiful and owning inner empowerment.

I weave stories between segments of videos, which he watches on the electronic tablet I hand him. The images vividly display scene after scene of real women touched, moved, and lighting up after a Sybille Organics makeover, almost in tears from their transformed hair. The before-and-after interviews with the women reflect an undeniable transformation of their confidence and belief in themselves.

Each time his gaze lands on me, a jolt of anxiety pulses through my veins. A maddening warmth pools in my stomach. I don't know what he's thinking, and that's both unnerving and … exciting.

After the videos, I highlight operational and financial data, taking him on the journey of our exponential growth. Highlighting our plans for the future with the upcoming Herbal Root Essentials haircare line, I share our first-of-its-kind contract with GrabHub for national placement in their retail stores.

His gaze sweeps over me as I speak, cool and assessing. Heat creeps up my neck. I'm finding it hard to keep my composure under his scrutiny.

Nearing the end of my pitch, I conclude, "For so many in ethnic communities, hair is a critical part of our identity. The styles we choose and the looks we create are symbols of our personalities and unique individualities. Sybille Organics wants every woman to go out into the world, loving their hair and how they see themselves. Bell Capital needs to be on this journey with Sybille Organics, not just helping to make women beautiful, but transforming their lives—no matter her background or budget."

Beaming with pride and relief that it's over, I wait for a response from Nate Bell. I delivered the best pitch I could, and now it's out of my hands.

The silence is deafening.

His face remains a mask of stone, unreadable.

But there's a glimmer in his dark eyes that gives me the teeniest, tiniest hope that maybe he understands how our products transform the lives of our customers.

He rises from his chair and stalks around the desk to stand before me. Sweat rolls down my back, and I resist wiping my damp palms on my slacks.

"Just a few questions," Nate says.

Then, the rapid-fire annihilation begins.

CHAPTER 12

My hands shake as I respond, knowing that our margins are well below targets for hair care products.

A muscle twitches in his jaw, clearly unimpressed. “Your production costs are astronomical. What changes have you made to reduce them without sacrificing quality?”

His dark gaze lands on my face, sending a flush of heat across my skin. I can't tell if it's his exemplary intimidation tactics or the sexiness oozing from his confidence that has my mind drawing a complete blank. Precious and I discuss ways to bring our costs down, yet I can't pull one idea out of my muddled mind to answer his question.

“Well, I'm exploring … options, but nothing's finalized yet.”

The vein in his neck pulses. He lets out a low sigh before launching his next grenade at me. "How do you plan to keep up with demand when inefficiencies mire your production facilities?"

"I'm working on strategies to … um … map that out," I fumble as sweat emerges on my skin. Seriously, how can he expect anyone to think clearly when he looks that … good?

His frown deepens as if listening to my inadequate responses is causing him physical pain.

Come on, Leela. Get your act together.

The questions come faster and harder over the next hour—supply chain issues, customer satisfaction, employee retention, marketing efforts.

I recover from my earlier blunders and do my best to present my business in the best light. Still, his relentless and detailed questions could make anyone doubt how a successful company could exist.

Luckily, he ends with a question about our target demographics, which I'm more than an expert in. These women have been with me for years, and I know everything about them and their haircare needs.

For the first time, his features soften as he leans back against his desk. "What kind of investment are you looking for?"

I pause, trembling with fear, then tell him the amount.

He appears nonplussed by the figure. "We can meet your request with an equity investment. Eighty, twenty."

My mouth gapes open. "You'd give me that much for only twenty percent of my company?"

He levels me with a glare that says 'no wonder your company is in trouble because you're the dumbest business owner to walk in my office in years,' then rattles off the valuation calculation of my wrong assumption.

Nate crosses his arms over his chest. "Do you think your company is worth that much?" A hint of a condescending smile spreads across his lips, and unfortunately, it's overwhelmingly attractive, even if I'm the brunt of his joke.

"No, of course not." I cover my face with my hands, then drop them. I have to remain positive. "Well, at least not yet. But my issue is … you'd have control of my company—"

"Bell Capital is committed to making significant investments in your company that you cannot make. From where I stand, you have considerable challenges in the market, from poor supply chain contracts to production inefficiencies and improper staffing for the growth you're projecting. All areas that we could eliminate in a matter of days. Not weeks," he pauses, seemingly pleased with the awe-struck expression that must be plastered on my face.

Nate continues, "It's impressive that you negotiated a surprisingly favorable contract with a major superstore in the US. But I could get you ten more better than that one … worldwide. That's the power of tapping into our network of facilities and superior operational excellence. Surely, you can see how that is worth eighty percent."

"Well, of course, I can see the value of partnering with Bell Capital. But what you're offering isn't a partnership. It's an acquisition. I want to maintain complete control over the direction of the business I created on my own. Is there any way you could make an exception? This time?" I ask, knowing that it never hurts to ask.

He rattles off an amount quickly. "That's what you get for a twenty percent stake in your business."

"But that's not nearly enough …"

"I know," he says, crossing his arms over his chest. His muscles are barely contained within the tailored suit. "That's why I proposed an offer for an eighty percent interest."

"But I wouldn't control my company anymore. Bell Capital would."

"We're experienced with collaborating with former owners of businesses we acquire for the mutual benefit of the company," Nate responds.

"Collaborating is not the same as owning and making all the decisions. I would never be able to do that again."

"I wouldn't say never," Nate replies. "It's true we're only focused on elevating your company. Once we achieve that, we'll sell to the highest bidder."

"On what planet could I ever be the highest bidder," I mumble.

"It's rare but not impossible. I've witnessed it happening a few times in my career," Nate says, and I believe him.

Still, while I'm proud to be a glass-half-full kind of girl, I can't ignore the glaring warning lights flashing in my head over this deal. My gut tells me that if I give up control of the company to Bell Capital, I won't ever get it back. I'll be an employee of the company I created, a worker on the products birthed from my mind. Something about that doesn't feel right.

"Thank you for your time, Mr. Bell, but I cannot accept this offer." I push the words out quickly before I talk myself out of it. Without this money, I'm putting all my eggs in Olivia Garnet's basket. I hope she'll find terms in my contract with the factory that will force them to make me whole on the production and finish it in time to meet the shipment deadline to GrabHub.

That's a better scenario for me and will likely keep me running my business.

"Ms. Jamison, you should take some time to think about my original offer," Nate suggests, returning to his chair. "It's more than generous. I'll give you until Monday at noon to provide me with your final answer."

"I don't need more time. The answer will still be no."

He raises an eyebrow but looks unconvinced by my response.

"Then it won't hurt to take the weekend and tell me that on Monday, would it?" he counters.

I hesitate, feeling like I've been tricked. I can't think of a good reason to resist his request. Nothing will change my mind. After several seconds of silence, I give in. "Fine. I will call you on Monday to confirm that I'm declining the offer."

A hint of a smile plays on Nate's lips. I swear he's the most gorgeous guy I've ever laid eyes on.

He steeples his fingers. "I look forward to hearing from you, Ms. Jamison."

CHAPTER 13

"SHE TURNED YOU DOWN, AND YOU PRACTICALLY BEGGED her to reconsider?" Willow sits across from me at the small table in the corner of Gwen's Country Café and stares at me as if I've lost my mind.

"I didn't beg," I say, staring back at her. "Just gave a strong suggestion that she delay her final answer."

"Does she know how many companies would kill to get an offer from Bell Capital? Forget that. You do. Why would you give her another shot?"

I can't possibly tell her the truth.

After the call with Javier, I still wasn't convinced that Sybille Organics was the diamond in the rough that would help me prove to Dad that I'm worthy of taking over the company. The Deal Sourcing Team gathered a few more options that were uniquely more appealing

... until Friday morning when the owner of Sybille Organics strutted into my office. A stunning black beauty dressed in a bold red suit, brimming with positivity, confidence, sweetness, and a touch of sass. Leela Jamison believed in herself entirely and the possibility of walking out the door with exactly what she had hoped for. And she won me over instantly. I knew I was going to invest in her company. It's the type of instinctive move that Dad would rip me over, but I couldn't resist … her.

I point to the folder in front of Willow. "Have you looked at the due diligence my team put together? Historical financials? Market data? Projections for the new line?" I shift to language my brainiac sister would understand.

"Of course. The company is on a trajectory to be a big fish in a niche pond. It's impressive but not profitable."

"With the right guidance, it will be, which I can provide," I say, pointing a French toast stick at her face.

She snatches it from my fingers and pops it in her mouth. "But you have no experience in the ethnic haircare industry. It's out of your wheelhouse."

"Which is why it's so perfect. It's the kind of business that Dad would never invest in. I'll get all the credit when I make it a success."

"There's just one snag."

"And that is?"

"Leela Jamison turned you down."

"She'll change her mind, trust me," I say, confident. The woman maintained a professional demeanor throughout our meeting, but there's no doubt she kept losing focus because she was too busy undressing me with her eyes. I didn't mind since I'd taken the luxury of doing the same with her. Nothing wrong with mutual attraction to help me seal this deal.

"I hate to say it, but I believe you. So, why did you want to meet for breakfast? You gloat just as easily over the phone as you do in person," Willow says, her eyes narrowing. "What do you need from me?"

"Intel on calyxera root," I say, getting to the point. "It's a key ingredient to Sybille Organics' new product line, but I'm struggling to get reliable information about it. Thought you might have some."

"Mom will kill me for sharing this with you," Willow says, lowering her voice.

"Is it being used in the pharmaceutical space?" I ask.

As part of the divorce, our parents hammered through detailed provisions outlining the industries in which their respective private equity firms could participate. Mom grabbed pharmaceuticals, environmental, tech, and Willow, as an employee, to Dad's chagrin. But he got everything else and me. Neither of us was guaranteed to take over the companies, but Willow marched up the corporate ladder much faster than Dad let me. One of the key items in the report on Sybille Organics was to make sure an investment in the company didn't violate the divorce terms.

"Not exactly. There's been exploratory research, but nothing that puts it firmly in development for any products. But that doesn't mean we don't hear that it's considered the next wonder cure for the beauty care industry," Willow says.

"Is that so?"

"But it comes with a slew of problems—rarity, hard to harvest, and expensive."

"If I can get my hands on a reliable supply ..."

"You could put Bell Capital's success in your dust."

"But it's the longest of long shots," I say, seeking clarification.

"Yes, but when has that ever stopped you?" Willow swipes the last two French toast sticks from my plate. "I'm headed to Chesterton's Gym for a workout. Happy firefighting!"

Minutes later, I'm walking from the restaurant to the fire station. Pushing through the doors, I give a quick wave to Erin, the receptionist, then take the steps two at a time until I'm a few feet from the break room.

The guys are already in a spirited debate.

"Ronan should be number one on the board. He and Mya got engaged a long time ago," Darren says.

"The idea of the town wagering on which of the Kimbell guys will be next to get married is crazy," Luke says. "People need something better to do."

The only board they could be referring to is the secret Wager Board set up in one of the back rooms at Baker Bros BBQ. The town is notorious for twisting the brothers' arms into letting them use it to place bets on all kinds of crazy town-related gossip. But putting money on who'll get married next is a new one.

"Yeah, says the guy killing the odds as the next one to jump the broom," Wiley snaps. "Why is everyone treating you and Kennedy like you're hashtag relationship goals."

"They're the feel-good story of the year," Ronan chimes in. "Everyone wants Kennedy to find a lasting love, and who better for her to be with than Mr. Goody-Two-Shoes over there."

"Don't hate because we're Kimbell's royal couple." Luke laughs.

I lean against the door jam as sadness washes over me.

I'm going to miss these guys and our random conversations. I'm not looking forward to leaving this place behind. Missing out on the time with them.

"But don't you think everyone on the list should be in a relationship?" Wiley whines. "How does the town think that Nate will get married before Zaire and me? That's ridiculous."

I clamp a hand over my mouth to stop from laughing. Love isn't on my radar. Marriage isn't in my universe. Seriously, look at my role models. A workaholic mother who loved to compete with my Dad more than she loved being with him. A dad who followed up losing the love of his life by marrying and divorcing three other women whose only interest in him was the billions in his bank account. And did I forget to mention, they were all the same age as me or Willow … or younger?

If that doesn't scream avoid romantic entanglements, I don't know what would. The last thing I need in my life is to be distracted by the crazy craziness of love. Every ounce of my energy is focused on proving to Dad that I'm a worthy successor for him at Bell Capital. I can't do that if I'm walking around like some lovesick fool.

"Now that Santos is a new entrant on the Wager Board, I have to make sure the oddsmakers are wrong. Mya's going to murder me if he and Harlow-Rose beat us down the aisle," Ronan says.

An arrow from out of nowhere slices through my heart. I couldn't have heard him right. It's not possible. "What did you just say?" I press forward into the room to join them.

"Hey … Nate," Wiley says, eyes wide with a nervous chuckle. "How long have you been standing there?"

Ignoring him, I stalk over to Ronan, stopping within inches of him. "How could Santos and Harlow-Rose beat you and Mya down the aisle?"

Ronan avoids looking at me, hesitating for a fraction too long.

"Answer me, Ronan," I say, my voice calm and deadly.

"Santos proposed to Harlow-Rose last weekend, and she accepted. They're engaged."

The roar of blood rushing through my ears drowns out the rest of his words. I might have stumbled to the floor if it wasn't for Luke grabbing my shoulder. After everything we've been through … what we meant to each other. I can't believe Harlow-Rose didn't tell me. Warn me. She's moved on. For good.

Luke steers me toward my chair at the table. I crash down onto the seat and stare ahead, looking at nothing.

"Relax. It happened a couple of days before your dad's stroke. You've had a lot to deal with," Luke says, making excuses for my ex. "I'm sure she didn't want to bother you with this news."

"How's it going at Bell Capital?" Darren asks, giving Wiley a surreptitious glance.

None of them care one iota about my other career. They're trying to stop me from blowing my lid over this news.

It's not like I thought there was any chance that Harlow-Rose and I would get back together. No part of me expected that or even wanted it. In fact, I stepped up and helped her keep her relationship with

Santos a secret when he was part of the investigation into the fire at her family's brewery.

Still, the fact that she didn't tell me herself cuts deep. Deeper than I ever expected it would.

"I've got big shoes to fill. I had no clue how much Dad was responsible for or how much he got done in a single day. How much I now have to take care of … that's why—"

"Don't you do it!" Wiley says, pressing his hands on his ears as he walks away from me. "Do not say it."

I glance from Wiley to Darren to Ronan, then settle on Luke. All four of them look like their dog just died.

"It can't be avoided," I admit. "I need to take a leave of absence from the fire station."

"This sucks," Darren says, pushing away from the table. He turns his back on me and busies himself at the counter, looking for some imaginary item he needs.

Ronan drags a hand down his face and sits down at the table. "For how long?"

"Nico said Dad could be out for up to a year."

"A whole year!" Wiley wails. "No, I do not accept this."

Ignoring him, I say, "There's no way I can do the CEO role and take two to three days off each week to fight fires with y'all. I have to give it up."

Luke looks more devastated than I expected. "So, does that mean you're moving to Houston?"

"This from the guy who was about to move and abandon me only a month ago?" I scoff.

"I didn't leave and answer the question," Luke says, a seriousness in his tone.

"No, and I'm not going to helicopter to work every day like Dad. I'll do a couple of days in Houston, then work the rest of the time from the office we own by Lake Lasso," I say, then level him with a sincere stare. "I'll be around. I'm not going anywhere."

My best friend looks relieved.

I turn to Ronan. "How much time will you need to find a replacement for me?"

"There's no replacing you, Nate. Not ever," Ronan says.

If I were a weaker man, I might shed a tear at this point. I never realized I meant as much to these guys as they did to me.

"But if you can give me a week, three more shifts, I promise I'll get a temp by then. Can you make that work?" Ronan asks.

"I'll make it work."

CHAPTER 14

L EELA

~

Why does my bedroom look like it's a housekeeper's secret lair? Shrouded on top of the modern enclave I tried to create in my childhood bedroom are several piles of clean clothes—on my desk, the chair, and one at the edge of the bed.

Mama's passive-aggressive move reminded me that I promised to help her do the laundry after I returned from my meeting at Bell Capital. However, the meeting was a disaster, and I was in no mood to speak to anyone or do anything. Instead, I holed up in my bedroom and watched Working Girl and The Pursuit of Happyness to shake off my hopelessness.

And it kind of worked.

I knew getting an investment deal from Bell Capital was a long shot, so I was stunned when Mr. Tall, Dark, and Rude from the elevator offered a deal so quickly. No chance he remembered our encounter, trapped in the elevator, which likely worked to my advantage. It was the outcome of my dreams. But the terms were the stuff of my worst nightmare.

As much as I wanted to pounce on the deal and the man, but that's a story for another day, I couldn't let myself do it. I spent almost ten years building Sybille Organics into the company it is today. No, it's not perfect. But it's mine. I don't want to be a glorified passive investor. Nate claimed I'd still influence the company and its direction as the Chief Operating Officer. But the reality is everything I'd want to do with the company would have to be approved by Bell Capital. They would run the show. Not me.

The draft contracts his Chief of Staff sent me last night proved that.

I've got to find a better option than selling out to a private equity firm. Like Mr. Sabra said, Bell Capital will do what's best for Bell Capital. That may not be what's best for Sybille Organics or me.

I inhale a deep breath.

It's not over yet.

I still have some options, especially if Olivia finds something in my contract with the factory that will force them to make good on the botched products.

Rolling over, I scoop up the handful of clothes at the end of my bed and sort them into piles before folding them. I swear, my parents have enough clothes for an army. The amount of daily washing and drying done in this house is unimaginable.

A soft knock raps against my door.

"Come in," I call out.

Mama peeks her head in. "Oh good, you're folding those for me. Appreciate that."

As if she gave me any other choice. I smile in response.

"Olivia Garnet just called the house phone. She said she's been trying to reach you, and you're not answering," Mama says, raising an eyebrow. "Are you avoiding her for some reason? I don't want to be in the middle of some business dispute."

"No, Mama. It's nothing like that. I turned my phone off yesterday after the meeting and forgot," I say as my heart hammers. Olivia's been trying to reach me all morning. That means she must have some good news to update me on a Saturday instead of waiting until she's back in the office on Monday.

"Well, call her back. I don't want her tying up my landline. I keep it for emergencies," Mama says with a huff, then shuts the door behind her.

I reach down into my Faux Chanel and grab the phone. The screen lights up with two missed calls and four texts from Olivia. I skim the texts telling me to call her as soon as I get her messages. No other details.

Closing my eyes, I say a silent prayer that this is the answer I've been hoping for, then dial her number.

"This is no time to avoid me, Leela," Olivia says, a hint of annoyance in her voice.

"I know, I'm so sorry. The meeting with Bell Capital didn't go like I wanted, and it put me temporarily in the dumpster emotionally—"

"So what? You spent the evening watching Working Girl and Jerry Maguire with your phone off?" Olivia asks with a know-it-all tone.

"Close. I picked The Pursuit of Happyness over Jerry Maguire this time. But good guesses. I'm impressed," I say, flopping back on the pillows. "Tell me you have good news to keep me in this inspired state."

"Are you sitting down?"

"I'm lying down."

"That's even better," Olivia says as her voice shifts into stern, lawyer mode. "I've gone through your contract with the factory, and there are explicit provisions in which they are required to rectify any mistakes made at their own cost—"

"That's great news!"

"I'm not finished. The terms indicate that if they make a mistake on formulas signed off by the client, that being you, then those provisions are triggered," Olivia says.

I wrack my brain to remember who signed off on the formulas sent to the factory. It could've been me. Or maybe Precious, as our in-house Production Manager. But what if we both forgot? Does that mean we can't enact the provision?

I hold my questions as Olivia continues.

"The factory sent over copies of paperwork where you signed off on the formula on two separate occasions," Olivia explains.

"And it was my signature? Not Precious's."

"It's yours. I recognized it. So, I had to wait for Precious and her team to send over the independent analysis y'all did on the product received. The products you told me did not agree to the formula." There's an accusation in her tone that puts me on edge.

"And it didn't match! We know it doesn't match the formula. Precious quadruple-checked," I say.

"The problem is that the analysis does match the formula you signed off on … twice." Olivia pauses to let the implications wash over me like a tidal wave.

"So, I signed off on the wrong formula, and that's why the product is wrong?"

"That's the factory's position, and it's bolstered by your independent testing of the product," Olivia says. "So, how did they get the wrong formula?"

"No, the question is how I missed it and signed off when it wasn't right." I drop the phone and bury my head in my hands. "How could I have made such a stupid mistake?"

"Look, a lot was going on. You were eager to prove to GrabHub that you could beat their shipment deadline. It's hard to juggle all these things at once. This was new territory for you." Olivia consoles me.

"It doesn't make any sense. Someone had to have hacked into our email and switched out the formula, or maybe they changed it accidentally before they sent it to me."

"That could be true, but none of that matters. Based on the terms of the agreement, they produce based on the approved formulas. You approved the wrong formula. They made the products with the wrong formula, which, again, you approved."

"This is a nightmare, Olivia. What am I going to do?"

"Let's think about this calmly. Your eagerness to impress GrabHub works to your advantage. You still have three months to get the products made and shipped to them. That's a massive amount of time to correct this issue."

"You're forgetting that I maxed out my line of credit and the advance from GrabHub to do the production run," I say as my body shakes uncontrollably. "If I can't figure out how to pay off my line of credit, the bank will seize my factory. I won't have a way to make up the production, not that I could with what we have anyway."

"And GrabHub will want immediate repayment of the advance as soon as you miss the deadline," Olivia says, almost to herself.

"Do you think I need to file for bankruptcy?"

"Too soon for that," Olivia says, shooing away the idea. "Tell me what happened with the Bell Capital pitch. We can learn from that to pitch smaller investors who might be more likely to give you money. I can ask other attorneys here to help us develop a list."

"Well …" I begin, then fill her in on all the details.

When I'm done, Olivia is quiet.

"That's the conundrum."

"Conundrum? That's your answer, Leela! It's better to own twenty percent of a company backed by a respectable behemoth like Bell Capital than one hundred percent of …"

"Don't say trash."

"I was going to say nothing. The trash is where you're headed if you don't take this deal."

"I have a huge favor to ask, then," I say, knowing I'm pushing my luck.

"I'll do it. Send me the draft contract, and I'll review it for you off the clock. If it's as good as Nate Bell thinks, you promise you'll get all my outstanding invoices paid, right?"

"Absolutely!" I say, bolting up from the bed. "And if you could, see if there's a way something could be built in to help me buy back my company from them. I need a lifeline, you know?"

"I'll see what I can do," Olivia says. "When is your deadline to get back to him?"

"Monday at noon."

"Bye, I have work to do." Olivia ends the call.

I forward her the draft contract, then stare at the piles of clothes waiting to be folded. For once, I'm happy for the distraction.

CHAPTER 15

NATE

I CLEARED ALL MY MEETINGS THIS MORNING.

Every single last one of them. The lawyers, the bankers, the investor analysts, and reporters clamoring for details about my plans for the company while Dad is … unavailable.

After finishing my firefighter shift, I was uneasy. Rattled. Off-kilter. Not myself.

I was pissed about everything.

Missing my friends.

Harlow-Rose still not calling me to tell me she's engaged.

The deadline looming for Leela Jamison to get back to me on my offer.

My Dad … alone in the hospital with no one there with him.

Against my better judgment, I took a detour over to St. Elizabeth's to check on him. I hadn't seen him since the night he was admitted there. Partly because it was hard for me to see him looking so … frail. Partly because I understand his expectations of me. Bell Capital had to be put first above all else.

I walked into his hospital room just as he flipped an arm toward the water pitcher, sending it spraying across the orderly who'd come in to help him shower.

Seeing me did nothing to brighten his mood.

The man could barely talk, but he said enough to let me know he didn't appreciate me stopping by to "babysit" him and I should get my butt in gear and head to the office. I'd already wasted too much time playing firefighter. His words, not mine.

The rebuke sent me racing to the door. I stopped home to change into my business suit, then took the corporate helicopter to Houston.

Susan pounced on me the second I walked into my office. I don't know how Dad puts up with her over-eager attentiveness. She's nothing more than a glorified executive assistant. Maybe that's all he asks of her, but I want a lot more out of a Chief of Staff, and she ain't delivering.

The mind-numbing walkthrough of the week's agenda left me seeing stars. I needed a break from Susan's subtle critiques and suggestions about how my father would act or react to each item as if she knew him better than me. If my father wanted someone to mimic him as a CEO, he would've chosen Uncle Karl.

But Susan didn't get that, and I was losing my focus.

My mind drifted to Leela Jamison. I caught myself glancing at the clock one time too many as the hours ticked closer to noon. I didn't doubt she'd change her mind per se, but her willingness to push my deadline annoyed me.

If she did ghost me, the entire deal team would know I failed to close my first deal as CEO. A sign of weakness and incompetence that would spread like wildfire straight to Dad's hospital room.

Worse, my plans to show the world I'm much more than Dad's Muppet would need to be reworked with another target company. And there aren't any on the horizon as unique as Sybille Organics for what

I need to do—prove to Dad that he can trust me to step up and run his company better than he ever did.

I check the clock on my phone.

11:37 AM.

I'm not sure what she's waiting on.

Passing up on a deal like the one I offered her would be a huge mistake. Any investor or lawyer reviewing the contract would attest it's an excellent deal, without most of the questionable clauses we typically put in contracts to benefit us. For some reason, I didn't want to complicate matters with her deal, removing barriers that might scare her away.

Because I want her close.

Not just her company.

Her bold pitch for investment in Sybille Organics saved me from broaching the subject myself. But I wasn't prepared for how poised, deliberate, or convincing she would be.

And no, it had nothing to do with those mesmerizing hazel eyes, the pouty lips, or that banging red business suit that put every single curve of her voluptuous body on full display. She has the kind of unexpected beauty that's full of surprises. It's not the fake, photoshopped version touted in the media by overdone celebrities. And I should know. I've dated more than my fair share of that lot.

But her business savvy was more impressive than her looks. She has that intangible factor lacking in the uninspired deal team I've led for the past two years.

Leela Jamison embodies creative, out-of-the-box, nontraditional business moves. A fearlessness fueled by positivity and endless faith in her abilities and the good in others. I hammered her with the toughest questions I'd ever thrown at anyone, and she kept her cool. Responded effectively to many of the questions and blew me away with her answers to the rest, all while maintaining that glowing smile and sunny disposition.

It was uncanny the power she wielded with an approach so different from my own. Her authenticity resonated like the perfect prescription for everything that ails me. A secret weapon I could leverage against Dad.

But none of that matters if she doesn't contact me before noon. I pushed for the extension, but I won't grovel. She needs to come to me.

A soft rap taps against my door. I jump, fumbling the mouse to close the browser.

"Come in," I say, leaning back in my chair.

Susan pokes her head. "I know you didn't want to be disturbed, but Leela—"

"She's on the line? Put her through," I say, annoyed that Susan didn't already do that.

"No, she's here," Susan says, suspicion in her eyes. "It's unusual. She turned down our offer, so why is she back?"

"Seems like your spies got their intel wrong. Ms. Jamison and I agreed that she'd think more about the offer over the weekend, and we'd reconvene today for her final decision," I say.

Susan looks as if she's been slapped. Her carefully crafted mask of superiority cracks. I'm not surprised she went behind my back to get intel, likely desperate for some nugget to report back to Dad and maintain her position of power at Bell Capital. But I have no plans of letting her have access to my father. She's on thin ice with me. As interim CEO, I can banish her to any menial role I choose, which I plan to do after I've squeezed every drop of info on Dad's current projects and how he's run things in the past from her.

"Send her in," I snap.

CHAPTER 16

Leela Jamison emerges in the doorway, dressed in a pale pink, silk dress and hair falling in loose waves on her shoulders. My jaw clenches hard to stop myself from smiling at her. I prefer her this way. More natural and casual. A better reflection of the effervescent personality she can't hide.

She floats through my door and stops too far away from my desk. Her eyes gleam with excitement as a smile plays at her lips. "I know you were expecting a phone call. Thanks for agreeing to meet with me in person."

"You didn't give me a choice."

She flinches. That lovely smile fades.

I almost regret snapping at her, but she did keep me waiting.

People don't keep me waiting.

She relaxes her shoulders, shaking off my words, and steps boldly forward. Nothing rattles this woman. It's impressive.

"Do you have an answer for me?" I stand and stalk toward her, blocking her path to the chairs before my desk. If she doesn't give me the answer I want, there's no point in her getting comfortable.

"I do."

"Do you have the answer I want?"

She raises an eyebrow. "That depends."

The playfulness in her response catches me off guard.

Interesting.

Is she suggesting a negotiation?

Has she not heard about my reputation?

I'm aggressive and ruthless, causing even the most experienced negotiators to wither from a single encounter with me. It's a game she can't win. At least not when I'm her opponent. Yet, she's convinced herself that she can.

Why am I not surprised?

I clasp my hands behind my back, in no mood to drag out the inevitable. I'm ready to close on the deal and move forward to the next phase of my plans. And, of course, I know exactly how to do that.

"The contract is more than generous," I say, studying her reaction. All I get is that sweet smile and a nod of acknowledgment. "I can only imagine you want to what? Add a buyback clause to give you a chance to regain a controlling interest."

"Yes!" Leela squeals as her passive calmness is replaced with warm glee. Her arms stretch wide, and the next thing I know, she's hugging me.

Like a bear hug, all-encompassing, smothering, and intoxicating. Her body presses against mine, melding with mine. I register every inch of her delicious curves against my taut muscles, sending bolts of electric currents ripping through me.

"Oh ..." She stumbles back, her hands covering her mouth. "I am so sorry. I'm a hugger. It's something I'm known for ... but that was entirely inappropriate. I just can't believe that you knew what I needed without me having to ask for it. I mean, I was literally prepared to beg for it—"

"Were you?" I ask, not opposed to that idea.

She nods her head as her smile fades. "It's important that I get controlling interest back after you and Bell Capital are long gone from Sybille Organics."

Her statement hits my gut like hot rocks.

"This company is everything to me. My legacy. My gift to women all around the world. But more importantly, my gift to myself. Kind of a self-stamped ticket to my financial freedom. I need your help now, but I'm confident I can get back to running things independently in the future," Leela says. "Are you willing to add the buyback clause into the agreement?" She fumbles in her purse and pulls out a crumpled sheet of paper, thrusting it toward me. "I had my lawyer draft up some language, but I'm sure your team of lawyers could come up with something much better."

Something about her tenacity and hopefulness is tearing down my usual instincts to claim and destroy. Still, I can't turn off my responsibility to strike a good deal for Bell Capital. Every move I make with Sybille Organics will be under extreme scrutiny. I can give a little, but not too much.

"We'll draft a gradual buyback option that allows you to buy back small portions of equity over time. The price will be based on a formula that ensures Bell Capital gets our expected rate of return on the investment. That should be sufficient to close this deal."

"Wow, that's better than what my lawyer and I came up with," Leela says, tucking her thick strands of glossy butterscotch-highlighted hair behind her ears. "So, if I'm understanding you correctly. I wouldn't have to come up with a big chunk of cash to buy back your entire interest at once. I could buy back like two or three percent at a time?"

"Correct," I say, implementing a key negotiation tactic—distract the party with an offer better than what they were expecting so they don't realize what they're not getting. "No waiting period. If you get a windfall tomorrow and want to buy back the ownership interest, you could do that."

The way her face lights up from my response is criminal. Seriously, no woman should look that good. She bounces with happiness, and I feel like she's two seconds away from trying to hug me again.

Which I cannot let happen.

I take a step back from her.

"Do we have a deal?" I ask, eager to lock this up.

"Yes," Leela says. "We have a deal."

She extends her hand toward me, but I don't budge.

"A few things will change when you sign that contract. You need to know exactly what you're getting into," I warn.

Her hand slowly falls to her side. "Okay, I was expecting that there would be some operational and maybe leadership changes as part of this. Do you have more details?"

"You will remain the face of Sybille Organics. Our ownership in the company will remain silent unless you receive explicit agreement from me to make it public."

"That works for me," she says with relief.

"But you will no longer be CEO of the company."

"What?"

I say, "You will relinquish that role but continue to run all operations as the Chief Operating Officer, subject to approval by the incoming CEO."

"Subject to approval?"

Ignoring her concerns, I lay out the rest of the details. "The company headquarters will be moved from Houston to Kimbell, Texas. We have an unused office there, and it will be the new base of operations. Any employees who want to continue to be part of the business will need to move or commute." Her expression changes from slight worry to almost panicked. I'm pleased to see she can be rattled. "You'll have two weeks to communicate this and make the necessary arrangements for the move with the assistance of our relocation team."

"I see ..." Leela says, looking blindsided. "I don't have a problem with this, considering everything Bell Capital will be investing in the company. Most of my employees live in North Houston, so the hour or so drive to Kimbell every day won't be too bad. My only question is ... who will I have to work with as the new CEO?"

"You're looking at him."

CHAPTER 17

L EELA

You're looking at him.

My initial reaction to Nate Bell's announcement that he would be the new CEO of Sybille Organics and my boss wasn't as hard to accept as I thought it would be.

Likely because the man standing in front of me in an expensive, tailored, likely Italian suit was devastatingly handsome. All that brooding, power-exuding, hard exterior is the stuff of bad boy dreams ... until you realize that reality has trapped you in a horrible nightmare.

That's how I'd sum up the last two weeks.

My cell phone buzzes back-to-back-to-back, jerking and twisting on the passenger seat as I concentrate on the curving road ahead of me. I don't need to check the device to know it's my micromanaging, overbearing new boss bombarding me with more things to do ahead of our first official day in the new offices in the quaint and picturesque small town of Kimbell, Texas.

I take a deep breath and remind myself that accepting the deal with Bell Capital was the right move. Without it, Sybille Organics would've collapsed under lawsuits and looming debt that was impossible to pay. The fact that my company is still in operation is the bright spot that helped me stay optimistic over the two most brutal weeks of my life.

To his credit, my new boss more than came through for *our* business. Most of the company's problems were solved in a few days. The debt with the bank was paid off, and all accounts with them were closed to move the accounts to Bell Bank, an affiliate of Bell Capital. The supplies for our replacement products were ordered and paid for under more favorable contracts than they'd ever been willing to give to me. Delivery is on track for this week to the new state-of-the-art factory next door to our new offices.

The turnaround will be tight, but our likelihood of meeting the GrabHub deadline is higher than ever. And if we don't, Nate would call GrabHub's CEO and force him to agree to an extension on the spot.

Even the Sybille Organics employees seemed more excited than annoyed about the move ninety miles west to Kimbell, Texas.

So, why am I the only one not on Cloud Nine?

My phone buzzes again.

I stifle a scream. Yes, that's right, because I've endured the absolute most horrible two weeks of my life working with Nate Bell.

Let's start with the fact that my new boss is … difficult, to say the least. Everything I imagined he would be like when we were trapped in that elevator weeks ago couldn't come close to how irritating it is to work with him.

I've put in sixteen-hour workdays to get through the excruciatingly detailed list of tasks he expects of me, and that's on top of my jam-packed calendar of transition meetings. I've made thousands of decisions over those days, most of which Nate had no qualms about overriding and dismissing before changing them. His steely, cold, constructive criticism doled out in front of the other Bell Capital executives, has done nothing to help us forge a collaborative working relationship. He usually follows up the public embarrassment with a more detailed text of feedback and actions I should be taking. I keep a positive attitude, but inside I'm seething. Nothing I do satisfies this man, and I'm getting worn out by trying.

Throwing in the towel and giving up is not in my DNA. But I swear the man must never sleep. I get texts from him at all hours of the morning, afternoon, night, and middle of the night, with whatever random thought bouncing around in his brain.

My irritation would be justified if he wasn't … brilliant.

Meeting after meeting, I've had a front-row seat to see Nate Bell in all his glory. His track record of shepherding companies to the next level and improving their performance, profitability, and enterprise value is stellar. I understand why people put up with his personality and leadership … deficiencies.

Grumpy isn't strong enough to describe him.

He's downright rude, abrasive, exacting, and relentless.

And he doesn't take no for an answer. Ever.

Like this four in the morning text that woke me from exhaustive slumber:

NATE BELL

Arrangements are being made for your
housing. I expect you here tonight.

Housing? Expect me where?

Kimbell

I've decided to commute from Houston. I don't
think the drive will be bad and it's easier than
packing up my whole life to live there.

You're not commuting. You'll be in Kimbell.

You said my employees could commute. Most of us plan to do that.

That's fine for them. Not for you. As the top operational executive, I expect you to be where I am.

Is that necessary?

Yes. Check your email for details.

That's why I'm driving along back country roads from Houston to the undulating juniper and oak tree covered Hill Country. As dusk darkens the sky in the distance, I take in the splendid beauty of this part of Texas. The change isn't so bad. It's not like being forced to move out of my childhood bedroom at my parent's house is inconvenient. Settling into a house being paid for by Bell Capital could be the thing I need to help me focus without the constant chores and errands I have to run for my folks.

Still, the audacity of being issued a command to move doesn't sit well with me. The only solace is Nate treats all his subordinates the same way. I'm no different.

But I am different.

I went from being the head woman in charge to Nate's "yes-woman." It's a tough pill to swallow. But I keep reminding myself that this isn't my end state. I hit a bump in the road and needed to pivot to ensure my company survived. I sacrificed, and in time, I will regain control of Sybille Organics. I'm confident of that. I have to be. I didn't come this far to give up now. It's not in my nature.

Nate will see that soon enough.

And he's controlled too much of my life over the past two weeks. Slowing at the stop light, I reach for my phone and turn it off. Whatever Nate needs can wait until I arrive at the office tomorrow morning.

"Left turn in fifty feet." The disembodied voice of the GPS informs me.

I slow down, wondering where on earth I could possibly turn in fifty feet. There's nothing but dense forest on each side of the road. I crane my neck to the left as a narrow dirt road blocked by an iron gate comes into view. No other cars are on the road at this time of night, so I pull to a stop and check the digital map. It shows a meandering road between the trees heading to the top of a hill.

"Well, this isn't creepy at all," I mutter, then turn left.

CHAPTER 18

L EELA

~

As I approach the gate, it opens slowly, and I drive through. After a quarter of a mile, the dirt road magically expands into a two-lane paved road lined with a cut limestone border. A guard booth looms ahead, and a constable emerges as I bring my car to a stop.

Rolling down my window, I smile. "Good evening, officer. I'm supposed to be staying at a residence up this road. But I'm not sure if I'm in the right place."

He returns my greeting with a friendly smile. "You're in the right place, Ms. Jamison. Welcome to Bell Family Estates. You'll be staying in the Painted Lady Lodge, which is left of the fork in the road about a mile up."

Painted Lady Lodge? Bell Family Estates?

My words sputter from my lips. "I don't understand. I thought I was getting a rental house in Kimbell, Texas."

"This is Kimbell, ma'am. But it's the private lands owned by the Bell Family. You will be residing in one of the guest properties. You've got the best one, gorgeous views of the hill country and more rooms than you'll know what to do with."

A nervous laugh escapes my lips. "This is unreal."

He leans into the window, lowering his voice. "You ain't seen nothing yet. Prepare yourself because you're about to be blown away."

And the officer's words are an understatement.

Minutes later, I stand in the middle of the foyer, mouth agape, unable to fathom the opulence of the sprawling, single-story lodge house. It looks like something straight out of *Architectural Digest* magazine. The floor is polished limestone. A custom chandelier hangs above, crafted from twisted juniper branches dipped in bronze, each arm extending delicately, holding small glass globes that mimic sparkling sunlight. The air smells like jasmine after a fresh rain. Beyond the foyer is a massive living room. The floor-to-ceiling windows offer a panoramic view of the rolling hills, blending indoors and outdoors, making it hard to tell where one ends and the other begins.

A sandy-haired, sixty-something, distinguished-looking man casually dressed in khakis and a polo shirt introduces himself as Peter, the butler. He stands next to me with an expression of awe as if he has never gotten used to the majesty of where he works each day.

"Welcome to Painted Lady Lodge, Ms. Jamison," Peter says, then beckons me to follow him on a house tour. "Nate insisted that you have the best of what we offer at the Bell Estates."

"Nate … wanted me to stay … here?" I ask, unable to believe what I'm hearing.

Peter nods. "This is the most popular of the guest houses. I made several family members angry for rearranging their stays to other houses on the property, but you know Nate. What he wants, he gets."

I nod as if I understand, but I don't. Nate's family has guest houses on their property for friends and family to stay at when they visit? Rich people …

"In addition to myself, you have a dedicated cook, housekeeper, and driver available to you at any time of the day or night. I'll introduce them to you after you get settled in."

"Oh, I won't need all of that," I say, dismissing the idea with a wave.

Peter looks offended but recovers. "We'll be here if you change your mind."

I follow him through the property, weaving past a trio of bedrooms, a private study appointed with cutting-edge electronics and technology, a library with shelf-lined walls filled with hand-bound books on leather-bound spines, a movie room, and an indoor sauna and steam room combination that bridges to the outdoor infinity pool. Each area is decorated with luxuriously upholstered furniture in cashmere, linen, and animal hides that perfectly embody the unassuming, laid-back Texas charm. The vibe is rich yet casual. Decadent but homey.

Entering the master bedroom, I'm treated to another breathtaking panoramic set of windows that provide a one-hundred-eighty-degree view of the hill country. A four-poster king-sized bed dominates the space, with monogrammed slippers with my initials resting on a cashmere rug near the side. As Peter explains the remote hidden in the limestone accent wall that controls everything from the light color, temperature, humidity levels, and the shades on the polarized glass, which can be adjusted to change the amount of sunlight streaming into the room, I feel like I've walked right into an episode of *Lifestyles of the Rich and Famous*.

Taking a deep breath, I peer out the window at a sprawling two-story mansion constructed entirely of limestone in the distance. "Who lives there?"

"Nate," Peter says.

My heart skips a beat as I stare at the house. "The Bell Family lives there?"

"No, just Nate. His sister has a home about two miles east beyond the nature preserve. The patriarch, Mr. David Bell, lives in the main house. It's about ten miles away on the opposite side of the property near the Bell Botanical Gardens," Peter explains, then lowers his voice to a whisper. "The distance between the homes is the only way Nate and his sister could get their mother to visit them here."

"Oh," I say, unsure how to respond to that juicy gossip. I step closer to the window. "He's so … close."

"Nate wanted it that way. Less than a quarter of a mile walk between the two properties," Peter explains. "It will help when y'all are working late nights."

"I see," I say, swallowing my disappointment. Not only will my new boss be able to badger me via email and text, but if I don't respond, he can pop up in person to make his demands face-to-face. Just … great.

The phone rings in the room.

"Speak of the devil," Peter says with more adoration than malice. He answers the phone. The color drains from his face as he hands it to me.

I grab the device just as Peter slips out of the bedroom, closing the door behind him.

"Ignoring my texts is not a wise move. Don't let it happen again," Nate snaps.

"I was driving. Texting and driving is against the law."

"Has that stopped you before?"

"What do you need, Nate?"

"You." He hesitates for a long moment.

My breath catches in my throat as a flash of his sexy face comes to my mind.

His voice breaks through my haze. "In my home office in one hour. We must prep for our morning meeting with the new leadership team. Peter will show you the way."

The line goes dead.

I glance at the mirror and force a smile on my face.

"I can handle you, Nate Bell. I have to."

N ATE

Leela Jamison is forty-eight minutes late ... and counting.

She's supposed to be by my side, presenting a united front to our newly merged team. Is it too much to ask for her to be on time?

I stroll around the conference room table, each seat filled with handpicked Bell Capital team members and the Sybille Organics managers. Not one of them will make eye contact with me. They stare at the notepads in front of them, riveted by the blank pages.

A vein throbs in my temple as I push through the presentation. "I want to assure all of you that a careful assessment of the skills and expertise of all the leaders shepherding us through this transition was performed. I didn't make any of these changes lightly."

The cowards don't have the guts to speak up about which changes cause the most concern. They're too busy worrying, blinded from seeing the brilliance of the diverse leadership structure I rearranged for the major departments. Nervous gazes pass among them, but they stay silent.

"Change can be difficult even when necessary," I continue, annoyed that I have to give them a pep talk to buy into their new roles. "We have a daunting deadline in front of us. Ten weeks to send the largest shipment in the company's history to GrabHub. A major national contract." I launch into the stark realities of what we're facing. The real challenges we must overcome and the long hours ahead of us. "It's going to require all of us to be better than our best," I say as the conference room door swings open.

I continue to talk, the words on auto-pilot, but my entire attention is focused on the woman walking into the room.

Leela has arrived.

A weird feeling blossoms within my chest.

It only takes a nanosecond for me to drink in the sight of her. She's wearing a fitted turquoise top with the sleeves pushed up just enough to feel effortless, paired with a flowy, vibrant skirt in Caribbean hues that hugs her waist with a wide belt, accentuating her hourglass figure. The colors practically glow against her deep brown skin.

She looks good enough to … I stop the thought before it takes root.

It's been hours since I've seen her. But in that time, could she have become more breathtakingly beautiful? I try to stay livid that she's late. That her grand entrance distracts the managers. Instead, all I feel is excitement prickling along my skin.

What is this woman doing to me?

I wrap up the information on the slide, then pause.

As if on cue, her face bursts with the most gorgeous smile I've ever seen.

"Good morning, beautiful people!" Leela says, then approaches the table. She introduces herself to the Bell Capital managers and engages in small talk with them, giving each her full attention. Then, she follows with hugs, greetings, and more banter with her managers.

Disturbed, I watch as the mood in the room shifts.

Drastically.

The same managers who'd avoided looking at me like they'd turn into a pillar of salt if they did were now relaxed, happy, and laughing with Leela.

What kind of spell is she casting on them?

An office clerk waits dutifully by the door, holding a large box in his arms with the Elevation Cupcakes logo in the center.

"Looks like you guys could use a break," Leela announces without checking with me to see if a break was scheduled on the agenda for right now.

"A little birdy told me that Elevation Cupcakes has the most decadent breakfast pastries," she says, motioning for the clerk to enter the room. "Who could use a sugar boost before we get into the next topic?"

The managers clamor with excitement as the clerk arranges the assortment of croissants, muffins, eclairs, and fruit tarts in the center of the table. Leela discreetly grabs four items from the table and approaches her former team. My gaze never leaves her as she hands her marketing manager a lemon muffin, the sales manager a protein shake, the production manager a granola-topped yogurt, and the sales manager a chocolate-glazed donut. They engage in a frenetic conversation as if they do this exact routine to start each workday.

Do they?

Does Leela spoil her staff every day with customized breakfasts? And for what purpose? It's a waste of time and energy for the leader of a company to do an assistant's job.

Seething, I retreat behind the podium as the buzz of conversation grows louder. I glance down at the next item on the agenda—she arrived just in time for the handover to her part of the presentation. If I find out that was on purpose, she'll regret it.

When I glance back up, Leela is walking toward me. I suck in a deep breath as she focuses her glorious rays of sunshine on me. Those gorgeous hazel eyes playfully sparkle, making me feel alert and more alive than ever. She holds one arm behind her back as she approaches the podium where I'm standing.

"Unfortunately, your beloved cocoa puffs and milk don't travel well," Leela winks at me, then pulls her hand from behind her back. "But I thought a chocolate croissant would be a nice substitute."

I've never had a woman look at me like this.

Like she's genuinely excited to do something nice for me and wants more than anything for me to like her surprise.

I curse Peter under my breath, knowing that her intel comes from his inability to shut his stupid mouth.

"You're an hour late." Snatching the croissant from her hand, I toss it into the trash. "That's inexcusable, and I expect you to make a concerted effort not to let it happen again. It's a poor impression for us as executive leaders of the company."

Surprisingly, she doesn't wilt.

"So is abruptly changing the time of our meeting with the leaders without so much as a text or call to give me a heads up," Leela says, her rebuke dripping with sweetness.

"Don't you check your emails first thing in the morning? The updated time and materials are there," I say, then add, "Funny. All the managers got here on time."

"The new slides don't reflect what we agreed to last night. There was no reason to change anything," she says, lowering her voice. "When did you have time to redo what we'd already done? I didn't leave your home office until two this morning."

"Around four, and I don't make changes without a strong reason, which should be clear since you read through the new slides."

"I saw your reasons, but I still don't think we should blindside the new management team with unnecessary responsibility changes when we're already under a tough deadline."

"Unnecessary?" I balk. Did she have the audacity to question my decisions? Openly and to my face? "The entire restructuring guarantees us success in meeting the deadline."

She flips a chunk of her wavy tresses over her shoulder, causing tingles to race along my skin. As she steps closer to me, the scent of her perfume—soft and sweet, like blooming jasmine—sends a jolt of desire straight through me. My mind goes blank as my gaze drops to her lips—full and luscious. A woman with lips like those has to be a fantastic kisser. I'd love to test out my theory.

No way. Get a grip, Nate.

I drag my eyes away from her to get my bearings. I can't lose sight of the ultimate goal of this business deal, which has nothing to do with kissing every drop of the shimmering pink lipstick off her mouth.

"But we agreed that minimizing distractions was the better approach and reassigning responsibilities right now would do more harm than good. Why did you change your mind after I left?"

"Because you were wrong." My gaze snaps back to her as my muscles turn rigid.

"Was I?" She looks over her shoulder, then back at me. "You had to see that you were losing them with all this change. You freaked out your handpicked managers just as much as you mortified mine."

"Strong leaders should be proficient in change agility. If you're right and they can't handle this, I don't want them on my team."

"Your … team." Her smile fades. I'm almost sad to see it go.

"Perhaps the company wouldn't be in this situation if you paid as much attention to their work responsibilities as you do their breakfast orders."

My words hit like a physical blow as her confidence shatters before my eyes. That'll teach her not to question my decisions in the future. "You're up next to go through the process changes. Are you prepared to do that?"

"Of course," Leela says through gritted teeth, then turns on her heels and walks back toward the managers.

I bite my bottom lip to stop my smile from spreading. She obviously didn't read through my changes to that section. But I'll let her figure that out later. Right now, I'll enjoy the view of those hips swaying as she walks away.

CHAPTER 20

NATE

~

The distance between me and the rest of the team is as wide as the Gulf of Mexico. Leela has grabbed breakfast for herself and is conversing with a few more employees brought over from Bell Capital. A glance at my watch confirms my suspicions: We're far off schedule and need to pick up the pace to finish before lunch.

I'm two seconds away from taking over when Leela speaks up. "Before we dive into the processes, I owe y'all an explanation for why I was an hour late to this meeting. And, no, I can't blame it on the long line at Elevation Cupcakes!"

This elicits laughter and smiles from the leadership team. Leela sits on the edge of the conference table, creating a casual connection with the managers. She proceeds to regale them with a heartwarming and funny tale of the craziness of her first morning as a resident of Kimbell, Texas. All calamities that could've been avoided if she'd used the private driver I arranged for her. I listen closely, noting how deftly she tells her story without revealing I'd arranged for her to have the best accommodations in the county as my neighbor. By the time she's done, they're all eating out of her hands, making me physically ill.

She presses her hands in a praying motion and gives a bow. "I hope y'all can forgive me for my tardiness." The clamor of support and understanding comes quickly.

Leela grabs a chair and sits at the table with the managers. "Our first production run for Herbal Root Essentials failed due to insufficient quality controls over the outsourced factory. Now that we're bringing this in-house, we'll need to implement several new checkpoints to ensure that we retain the highest level of quality and integrity to the product formulas. That's where you'll come in."

What is she talking about? The managers aren't needed for any of this. I step forward from the shadows and stop in front of the podium.

Leela says, "I'm relying on each of you to review your parts of the process with your teams after the tour of our new factory tomorrow and determine the most effective controls to add—"

I stalk forward before she can say another wrong thing.

"The new process documents have already been completed, and adequate controls have been established to ensure quality without exponentially increasing our production time or costs," I say, stopping next to Leela's chair. "These documents were delivered to all of you this morning. You should review them, learn them, know them. Make sure your teams follow them without exception so we can hit our deadline."

Leela swivels around in her chair to stare up at me. Those hazel eyes radiate with defiance and anger. It's hot. "Who created these new process documents?"

The air grows still in the room, and none of the managers dare to move an inch as their gazes shift from Leela to me.

"Expert consultants in the haircare industry," I respond.

"And who reviewed them?" She challenges.

I don't regret for one minute not running the process documents by her. The new factory is far from the substandard facility she used to push out products. I'm surprised they met customer demand with the deplorable conditions.

"Expert consultants in the haircare industry," I reiterate.

"You didn't let our experts—" Leela pauses and waves a hand toward the managers at the table, "review the process documents and give feedback? The very people who are responsible for implementing the process had no say in the changes."

"Putting the burden on them to develop new processes would be too much," I say.

Leela's eyes narrow as I use her words against her.

To pour more salt into the wound, I add, "Given the tight deadline, I want them focused on what they do best."

But she doesn't take the hint to back down.

"Part of the reason they made it to this level in the company is because of their ability to turn vision and strategy into tactical and actionable steps," Leela says. "I think they deserve the opportunity to modify the processes as they see fit, as long as it doesn't create delays and ensures we maintain quality."

"Lowering the astronomical production costs is a key component of the new processes. When they review the details, they'll find no modifications are necessary."

Leela bolts up from her chair, closing the distance between us. "Modifications could be necessary if there aren't enough quality checks. Why didn't you talk to me about this?"

These are the kinds of details she should no longer focus on. Hiring the best and delegating are critical for taking Sybille Organics to the next level, even if she doesn't understand that yet.

"Check your emails. It's there." I take a step closer to her, staring into her intoxicating eyes. The fiery passion blazing back at me is titillating. "Right next to the email informing you that this meeting started at 8 am sharp, not a quarter after nine." Sarcasm drips from my words.

It's one thing to challenge me in a one-on-one conversation, but entirely different to do it in front of the managers. While her gutsiness is admirable, I won't tolerate my decisions being questioned. I can leave no room for confusion about who is in charge here.

Turning away from her, I press my palms on the conference room table and glare at the stunned faces of the managers. "Processes have been finalized. There will be no changes. Get your teams up to speed and be ready for the factory tour tomorrow."

I don't look back at Leela as I walk out the door.

CHAPTER 21

In fact, I beat everyone to the facility except for my boss. After the calculated offensive he launched at me yesterday, deploying his criticism like strategic airstrikes, each one finding its target with devastating accuracy, he was the last person I wanted to see.

It was the absolute worst kind of takedown.

I had no defense because facts supported every hit.

I hadn't opened a single email until I was in line at Elevation Cupcakes, already running thirty minutes late. I skimmed what I thought was essential for the day, ignoring the rest. If I'd checked them earlier, I could have discussed the avalanche of changes with Nate before the managers arrived.

But that's all water under the bridge after Nate orchestrated my humiliation with perfection.

I hate him for treating me that way in front of the managers.

I was horrified and embarrassed.

All I wanted was to slam my fist into his smug, sexy face. Punch him until those gorgeous onyx eyes were bloodshot and bruised. Slap the sensual smirk off his lips and drop-kick him in that infuriatingly perfect physique.

I cover my face, confused by my chaotic thoughts.

I'm not a violent person, and hate is too strong of a word.

All I want is a do-over—a way to erase yesterday's misery. I want to present my best self to the new team, which I thought I'd get to do today.

"Good morning, Nate," I say, taking the high road to reach out to him as he glowers at his laptop perched on the podium in the factory auditorium. He's dressed casually—dark slacks, button-down cotton shirt, and hair tousled without the gel. His sleeves are rolled to his elbows, revealing impressive forearm muscles. No matter what look he chooses, he's always breathtakingly handsome.

"You're off the agenda for today," Nate says without looking at me. "I streamlined the itinerary to give the teams more time in the factory. I'll do the opening and closing alone."

The sucker punch felt around the world.

I put on my steely, positive resolve and respond, "Got it. I'll be over there if you need me."

He responds by ignoring me. After a few moments, I retreat into the first row of chairs and wait for the employees to arrive. But I can't stop watching Nate. How cruel is the world that the man I loathe, who was so horrible to me, looks like every corporate power fantasy come to life?

It just isn't fair.

But all the good looks in the world can't overcome his grumpy, ruthless commitment to making me feel like the most incompetent business owner in the world. As the auditorium fills with employees, I greet them, losing my front-row seat. The clock ticks closer to the start of the meeting. I merge with the employees, finding an empty seat on the seventh row close to the door.

Nate looks agitated on stage alone, checking his watch. At the last minute, his gaze searches the crowd of employees until it locks onto my face. I smile. He relaxes before my eyes. His dark eyes shift from stony to molten. My cheeks burn with heat. I cannot, no I will not, let his good looks distract me. He's the same horrible person who tried to obliterate my professional expertise yesterday.

The employees quiet down as Nate stalks across the stage. After a brief, matter-of-fact introduction to the day, he points to a slide projected onto the screen behind him.

His next words are stern and full of dire warnings. "What we need to accomplish in the next two and a half months is nearly impossible. My job is not only to make sure you understand the vision and strategy but also to make sure you have the best equipment and resources to get things done. I've done my part." He pauses for dramatic effect, giving a blistering stare to the scared faces of the employees in the crowd. "Now it's time for you to do yours. Failure isn't an option. The shipment will go out in six weeks. We'll do this by daily monitoring of individual employee key performance indicators. If you fail to meet your KPI target for five days straight, you will be replaced. Many of these targets depend on collaboration. So it's not just looking out for yourself, but your fellow employee too."

Murmurs and anxious chatter build as he explains each one of the indicators.

Clenching my fists in my lap, I resist the urge to scream. This information was definitely not in any of the emails or presentation decks we discussed. It's like he finds perverse pleasure in changing things at the last minute.

"The KPIs will ensure we have the fastest output to meet the shipment for GrabHub and to meet the demand for both product lines in the future," Nate says. "I'll take questions, if there are any, before the factory tour."

A thousand questions rattle in my head, but I hesitate. The last time I challenged Nate publicly didn't turn out well for me. I hate that he's making me doubt myself. No part of me believes ruthless adherence to metrics guarantees success. But I'll broach this with him privately.

"Mr. Bell—" Precious says as all the heads in the room turn toward her.

"Please, call me Nate," he offers with no warmth.

She smiles at him anyway. "Okay. Nate, I don't think I'm alone in feeling that these targets are too high. Many of the products used in Sybille Organics shampoos and conditioners rely on natural ingredients that are more sensitive and require delicate care in production. Trying to meet these production speeds could damage the natural ingredients and degrade product quality. Was this considered when setting the targets?"

I beam with pride as I turn to see Nate's reaction.

He doesn't look fazed at all by the insights.

"You bring up excellent points, and the short answer to your question is yes. We evaluated the nature of the ingredients in establishing the KPI targets," Nate says. "The longer answer is that we made two key modifications to accommodate your concerns—one was improving the quality of the factory equipment to the highest level which can handle natural ingredients without degrading their benefits, and the second was tweaking the formula to replace one of the most delicate ingredients with a synthetic version—"

"You did what?" The words burst from me before I can stop them. Before I know it, I see red, fumbling over the people sitting next to me as I stalk toward the stage. "What do you plan to replace in the formula I painstakingly worked to perfect?"

A sly smile curves his lips. He raises his hands in mock surrender. "There was only one ingredient change. I had it tested secretly without revealing the proprietary formula, and the change to the end product was negligible."

"You don't know the first thing about testing haircare products," I say, my composure dismantling as I grow increasingly hysterical. "It's not as simple as checking the chemical components of two liquids. You have to use it on a sample of hair types to ensure it delivers the desired look and feel. It's so much more complicated than you realize."

"Calyxera root is too expensive and fragile to be part of the formula. It single-handedly makes up twenty-five percent of the production cost and sixty percent of the batch failures. It has to go."

"That ingredient makes the products successful for all hair types. It doesn't work without the calyxera root. No synthetic version can imitate what it does for the hair," I insist, on the verge of tears.

The clamoring from the employees has grown louder. I glance at them, their discomfort practically radiating in the worried glances they exchange. I want to avoid another public showdown between Nate and me, but it can't be avoided. And this one is much worse than yesterday.

"The synthetic version is cheaper and will get close enough to the performance of the real thing. There's no problem with taking the revised formula through your … rigorous testing methodology," Nate counters, an edge in his tone warning me not to take this any further.

I snatch the mic from his hands. "Everyone take a fifteen-minute break while Nate and I confer on this matter. We'll get back to you with our final decision when the break ends." I drop the mic to the floor.

Turning to Nate, I say through clenched teeth. "We need to talk. Now."

CHAPTER 22

L EELA

~

I DON'T STOP WALKING UNTIL I REACH THE OFFICE SUPPLY room. Opening the door, I step inside with Nate close on my heels.

He slams the door behind him. "What was that? Do you think your little tantrum went over well with the employees?"

"My tantrum! This is my livelihood you are monkeying around with. I'm sorry, how many years of experience do you have creating products for ethnic hair?" I demand, staring at him. "Was that ... zero? And you didn't even consult me on whatever experts you've been listening to about the factory and my formulas. Have they even worked on black hair?"

"I'm not an idiot!" Nate fires back. "You think I didn't thoroughly vet every expert to ensure they were qualified in diverse hair types? Contrary to what you think, I don't buy companies to ruin them. I buy them to make them better than they ever dreamed they could be. I can do that for you, too, if you'd stop being so sentimental and embrace change."

"I think I've accepted more than enough of your changes. Now, it's time for you to listen to me and respect my expertise. I built this company from nothing. I created the formula that has hundreds of thousands of women clamoring for Herbal Root Essentials products. Me!" I say, pointing at myself. "I will not allow you to destroy my formula." I push a finger into his chest. "The calyxera root stays." I push him in the chest with both hands. "There will be no synthetic version in *my* products," I scream, closing the distance between us to mere centimeters. "Do I make myself clear?"

Nate's dark gaze studies my face, swirling passion in his dark gaze. His eyes make a trail from my eyes to my lips as my breaths come hard and ragged from my chest. He leans closer to me, and my pulse quickens.

His voice is low and husky as he says, "Crystal." His arms snake around my hips, jerking me against his hard, muscular frame.

I can't think clearly with him pressed against me. "Good," I say, and the next thing I know, I've grabbed his face and pulled him toward me in a blistering kiss. My mouth devours his, doing everything I'd imagined in the fantasies I try to pretend I don't have, but I didn't know it could be this good.

Can you say best kiss of my life?

No, seriously.

Nate's lips are like heaven, and he's giving me back more than I'm taking from him. The kiss intensifies, and I melt into it, ignoring how wrong it is for me to be kissing my boss. I moan as his hands caress up my back and fingers through my tresses. He grips the back of my head, holding me captive as he takes charge of the kiss. Delving and teasing and enthralling me.

And … no, I can't let this continue.

I push away from him, stumbling backward.

My red lipstick stains his swollen lips, and he looks like he's two seconds away from luring me into another kiss.

"I'm sorry," I stammer.

"Best negotiating skills I've ever encountered," Nate quips, slowly wiping the lipstick from his lips. "I'll have the team adjust the process to accommodate your delicate calyxera root."

"You will?" I ask, shocked.

He gives a slow, sexy nod. "Is there anything else you'd like to convince me to do?"

I gasp, covering my mouth with my hands.

The smile he gives me makes my knees buckle. If I thought he was handsome before, it's nothing compared to Nate with a thousand-watt smile on his face. Pure heaven.

"No?" Nate shrugs and opens the door. "I'm holding you solely responsible for motivating the team to meet the shipment deadline with the increased cost and production time this will cause."

He levels me with a steely stare.

Nate, the ruthless CEO, is back. "I meant it when I said failure is not an option."

CHAPTER 23

L EELA

~

"I will admit, I was one of those haters who thought all this hair couldn't possibly be real," Evelyn Jones, the owner of Textured Tresses Salon, says with the cutest giggle. She looks around the same age as my mama but with an effortless, trendy flair. Her soft, cocoa-colored cheeks have a hint of blush, and her wide, almond-shaped eyes seem to twinkle behind her cat-eye glasses. Short, salt-and-pepper curls frame a face that glows with an ageless vitality.

"Shame on you," I respond, closing my eyes as her fingers work magic with the Herbal Root Essentials shampoo in my thick hair.

After getting her cell number from one of the employees, I took a chance to see if she might be willing to see me after hours to fix the hot mess my hair had become. Nate's insistence that the synthetic version of the calyxera root was a suitable substitute had weighed on me enough that I tried a sample of the product that included it.

Big mistake.

Huge!

It made my hair dull, dry, and crunchy. It was worse than I expected, but it was oddly satisfying to know I was right, and he was wrong this time—not that I got a chance to gloat.

He's been noticeably absent from the Sybille Organics offices since our … kiss. A no-show at every single meeting. Forwards my emails to his minions to respond to me. And he hasn't complained that we missed the production targets last week and are on track to miss them again this week. A conundrum that baffles me since I spent several days working on the factory floor with the team to adjust the processes.

However, one message from my boss came across strongly. HR emailed the entire company with the Code of Conduct, explicitly highlighting the rules against personal relationships between supervisors and employees.

Mortified can't describe my feelings when I read through the document. This was Nate's subtle way of telling me not to cross the line again.

Seriously, what was I thinking?

I practically jumped his bones in the supply closet before the factory tour.

It was unprofessional and out of character.

But Nate has been pushing my buttons in unexpected ways from the first moment I met him in the elevator before I knew who he was. Before I knew his check with a whole lot of zeroes would turn around the bad fortunes for my company. And before I started to find every corporate showdown between us to be equally exciting as it is … frustrating.

All I want is a chance to apologize and reassure him that it will never, ever happen again. I crossed a line, and I deeply regret it.

Or do I?

I should not have kissed Nate. So why have I relived those moments over and over again, delighting in every second that his lips were on mine? When I'm dragging myself to bed at Painted Lady Lounge after the long workday, I can't help but stare out the massive windows in my bedroom at Nate's house in the distance. At times, his lights are still on. On other days, the house is dark for hours. Either way, I can't help but wonder if he's been thinking about the kiss, too.

And I may have initiated the intimacy, but he took it to the next level.

Best negotiation skills I've ever encountered.

His words bounce around my brain.

Definitely not a rebuke of my actions.

From the way our kiss took on a life of its own, he absolutely enjoyed it as much as I did.

The fact that he views me as a marginally competent, sentimental, people-pleasing leader destined to make poor decisions that hold my company back from reaching its full potential didn't block his attraction to me.

The fact that he's an arrogant, overconfident, sarcastic executive who thinks he has to mansplain to me where the problems are in my business and presumes that only he can fix them wasn't enough to kill my attraction to him.

"Don't you fall asleep on me," Evelyn chides, breaking through my thoughts.

"Now I see why people love coming to your salon. Those fingers are divine. Your technique is so relaxing," I say, grateful for the interruption of my Nate-obsessed thoughts.

"And this shampoo is amazing. It restored the softness of your hair in one pass. No wonder people are losing their minds online, clamoring for it to come out," Evelyn says, then leans closer to my ear. "I'm going to place a big order, too. I planned to even before I found out you'd moved your headquarters here. How's that going?"

"Well, my company is a part of Bell Capital now. The new factory here came along with the deal," I say, refusing to tell her that Nate has taken control of my company … temporarily.

Evelyn whistles. "Are you working closely with Nate Bell?"

"Yes, I work directly with Nate," I say, keeping the resentment out of my tone. "Is what they say about small towns true? Do you know him, like personally?"

"Yes and no," Evelyn says. "Everyone knows 'of' the Bell Family. They founded the town, for goodness sake. You can't not know who they are."

"What do you mean, they founded the town?"

"Nate's ancestor was Kimberly Bell, the founder and namesake of our town. She's why we're called Kimbell. It's Kim and Bell smushed together," Evelyn explains.

"I didn't realize that. So, his family has been here for all that time."

Evelyn nods. "Most of the Bell clan has moved away and live all over the world. David, Nate's father, stuck around, along with Nate's uncles Karl and Keith and his aunt Patty. They're our version of the Kennedys."

"That's impressive," I say.

"But to answer your question," Evelyn chuckles. "My family and Nate's aren't in the same social circles. Although, my daughter might be headed that way soon."

"Is that your daughter?" I ask, peeking at a photograph of Evelyn standing between a beautiful, curvy woman and a drop-dead gorgeous man.

"That's my baby, Dr. Jasmine Jones, head of emergency medicine at St. Elizabeth's Hospital. And that's my son, Hendrix. He owns an auto repair shop in town. Just expanded it to a bigger location because business is so good." She beams with pride. "And my daughter just got married to a former football superstar. Life is very different for her now, not that she'll admit it."

"That's exciting. And your son? Is he married?" I ask as I stare at the sexy guy in the photo. There must be something in the water in this town.

"He's a playboy. Trust me, he's not ready for a woman of your caliber—"

"Oh, I wasn't asking for me," I say, waving my hands frantically.

"So, is there a special man in your life?" Evelyn asks.

Why on earth does Nate's face flash across my mind? My lips tingle from the memory of his mouth, exploring and delighting my own.

"I'm too busy launching products to focus on a relationship. But I have a few guys that I hang out with casually to keep things interesting." Not a lie if you count the coffee dates I arrange through online dating profiles a couple of times a year.

"Hmmph." Evelyn turns off the faucet and twists my hair in her hands to squeeze water out of the strands.

"What is that for?"

"You remind me of Quan, another stylist in town. She's the same way, going out with a different guy every night because she's too afraid of getting close to one special guy. To your friends, it looks like you're living the life with all those boyfriends, but you're avoiding finding someone special," Evelyn says.

"Ouch. And you figured that out in less than an hour of knowing me," I say, feeling exposed.

"Trust me. It's worth finding that special person, even if you suffer a string of heartbreaks along the way, just like my Uriah. I love him to pieces and can't wait for him to come home," Evelyn says.

"Where's your husband?"

Evelyn goes quiet.

"Evelyn …" I say, then I see her swiping tears from her eyes.

I jump from the salon chair and wrap my arms around her. "Hey, it's okay to miss him. To let yourself feel sad that he's not here. You don't have to keep it bottled up inside."

She lets go and cries on my shoulder for a few minutes, then composes herself. "I'm sorry about that. I spend too many days keeping up a brave front for Jas and Hendrix. Just gets to me sometimes. My husband was convicted of assisted suicide. He stands by what he did, and I support him, but I miss him so much."

"How long is his sentence?"

"Two years, thank goodness. He's done a year and has one more to go. I visit him every week at that awful prison in Huntsville. Trust me,

I am counting the days until my man is home." She takes a deep breath and then leads me toward a back hallway. "Enough of my pesky emotions."

"It's okay," I say, giving her another hug.

Evelyn says, "Come on, let's get you under the dryer."

CHAPTER 24

Nate

THE BREAK ROOM INSIDE THE KIMBELL FIRE STATION FEELS different.

Quieter, as if the building understands the shift happening.

Typically, at this hour, the place would hum with laughter and idle chatter. The television would be on some random sporting event that we'd barely pay attention to as we talked nonstop while waiting to see if there'd be any calls.

But tonight, the silence hangs thick and heavy.

My last shift with the fellas of Kimbell Firefighter Shift A.

I've been trying to act like this is just another shift. But as the hours crawl by, the weight in my chest gets harder to ignore. Sitting here, surrounded by the men who've become my brothers, it feels like I'm about to leave a piece of myself behind.

I glance around the table. Each of us is in our usual seats, but no one looks comfortable. Wiley, whose crazy antics and ridiculous chatter usually fill the room, leans his chair on the back two legs and stares at the ceiling, dead silent. Darren is beside him, his jaw tight as he traces a deep groove in the wooden table with his finger. And my best friend Luke leans forward, eyes fixed somewhere on the floor as though searching for a way to stop the inevitable from happening.

The only one missing is Ronan, who is downstairs finalizing the paperwork for my replacement.

Not that anyone could replace me with these guys.

We've shared hundreds of meals at this table, told thousands of stories, and saved more lives than we can count. We've been through so much together, seeing each other at our best and worst, and forged a bond through danger, adrenaline, and sheer grit. But I can't shake the feeling that once I'm gone, that bond will loosen and slip through my fingers like sand—

The scrape of chair legs against linoleum breaks the silence as Wiley launches across the table. "I'm going to miss you, man!" He crashes into me, arms wrapping tight around my neck as he wrestles me half out of my chair.

"Get off me. Now," I grunt, trying to push him off, but he just squeezes tighter, grinning.

Darren's snickers, the sound breaking through the heavy quiet.

"I was hoping that Ronan wouldn't find a temporary replacement for you," Wiley mutters, his voice muffled against my shoulder.

"I think we all were," Darren says, his earlier amusement fading as he runs a hand through his dark hair, "but I know that's not fair to you. We can see the extra strain on you from taking over the CEO role. You can't keep doing double duty."

I push against Wiley's chest. "Wiley, I'm serious. If you don't get off me."

"Fine." He reluctantly releases me, dropping back into his chair with a thud. "But this place isn't going to be the same without you."

I force a smile, trying to keep my voice steady. "Look, let's not make this out to be a bigger deal than it is. My leave is temporary. I'll be back."

Luke looks away, the gesture speaking volumes. He knows I can't guarantee that's true. This could be my last shift with these guys ... ever. And if it is, the last thing I want is for us to spend it moping around the fire station, feeling sick over it. I want it to be like all the other times we've shared over the past years – filled with the kind of easy camaraderie that made every shift, even the hardest ones, feel like home.

"Did Ronan tell any of y'all who he found to take on the role?" Darren asks, his fingers drumming against the table's surface.

The door creaks open, and Ronan steps in, his expression guarded. "I didn't because I know y'all aren't going to like it."

"I'm surprised it took this long for you to settle on someone," I say, watching him sink into his usual seat at the head of the table, the old chair creaking beneath him.

Ronan sighs, rubbing the back of his neck. "You wouldn't imagine the bureaucratic hoops I had to jump through to secure a budget for the position. You forget we save a lot of money because the two billionaires on shift don't collect a paycheck."

Darren wags a finger at him as he shakes his head. "I'm not a billionaire."

Ronan scowls. "Close enough."

"I could cover the cost of my replacement," I offer immediately, leaning forward. "I never wanted my leaving to strain the station."

Ronan waves me off, looking exasperated but grateful. "Yeah, I figured you'd say that. But you shouldn't have to do that. No other firefighter would be asked to."

"Darren and I aren't the typical firefighters." I catch Darren's nod of agreement from across the table.

"Still," Wiley interjects, his chair legs hitting the floor with a thunk, "you have enough people trying to manipulate money out of you, Nate. I'm glad Ronan took this route."

Surprise flickers across Ronan's face. "Thanks, Wiley."

"Of course." A hint of Wiley's usual mischief returns to his expression. "While you were getting the budget, did you ask for a raise for us lowly firefighters who need the paycheck? You know my dating app still isn't turning a profit."

The sharp sound of flesh meeting flesh echoes as Darren slaps Wiley on the back of the neck. "If you need money, just come to me," Darren says, rolling his eyes.

Wiley jerks away, holding his neck with an exaggerated wince. "Never. And I'm not asking Zaire either, so don't even mention the love of my life."

"There will be no raise for you or Luke. Sorry." Ronan's lips twitch, fighting a smile.

Luke looks up, his curiosity piqued. "Well, don't keep us in suspense. Who's coming on board?"

Ronan tenses like he's bracing for a fight. "A.J. Paul."

"You've got to be joking." Darren's coffee mug hits the table with a sharp clank.

Wiley surges forward, his eyes wide with disbelief. "Ronan! Do you seriously think hiring Austin James Paul to work at this fire station is a good idea after the chaos he unleashed on this town the last time he was here?"

"Did Gwen ask you to do this?" Luke's quiet question cuts through Wiley's outburst.

Ronan nods, the motion heavy with resignation. "Practically begged me to. She thinks he deserves another chance."

I lean back in my chair, the wood rough against my palms as I grip the edges. "Well, I hope for your sake that he does. But my money is on a disaster happening once that punk shows back up in town."

"I know, alright." Ronan spreads his hands on the table, the fluorescent lights shimmering across his red hair. "I'm not too thrilled about it, either. But Gwen means the world to all of us. She takes care of us every morning when we descend on her restaurant like vultures, camping out and being a pain in her neck. Not that she ever complains or asks us for any help. Ever."

"Until now." Luke's voice is gentle. "You did the right thing by hiring her son. If he hasn't gotten his head on straight, maybe being around us will help make that happen."

Wiley looks dubious, crossing his arms. "From your lips …"

Ronan rolls his eyes and claps his hands, breaking the tension. "Alright, enough of this. Darren and Wiley, you're on cleaning duty. Nate, Luke, you've got garage checks to finish."

CHAPTER 25

Nate

⁓

The smell of motor oil and rubber fills the air, familiar and grounding as we enter the dimly lit garage. I flip the light switch, bathing the bay in bright lights.

"How are things going at Bell Capital with your super secret project?" Luke asks as he checks the pressure gauges, his movements precise and practiced.

The metal tools clink as I move methodically. "Better than I expected."

Luke raises an eyebrow. "How so?"

"We have production metrics that I set for the team. Metrics that are physically impossible based on the mechanical limitations of the machines—"

Luke's head snaps up, his brow furrowed. "Why would you do that? It's not like you to set your teams up for failure."

"To push them beyond what they think is possible," I explain, moving to inspect the hoses. "If I put the real numbers out there, we'd never get their best. Just a leadership strategy that's worked for me in the past."

"And is it working this time?" Luke's voice echoes in the cavernous space.

My chest tightens with an emotion I'm not ready to name. "Leela has them blowing the real targets out of the water. I never thought they could be this efficient with the lowest rate of error I've seen in a factory in years. And she did all of this in a week and a half. Do you hear me? Like 10 days. It's absurd."

"Sounds like you got a winner on your hands, but I'm guessing you already knew that." Luke pauses in his work, studying me. "Her company was the right choice to prove to your dad that you can handle taking over Bell Capital."

I grunt, pretending to be absorbed in checking the equipment.

Luke studies me, frowning.

"While I'm used to you being a grump most days, this is the kind of thing that would normally break your pattern." Luke's knowing tone makes me tense. "You bought a great company with an excellent owner and leader. What gives?"

The words feel like they're being dragged out of me. "I need her gone."

"Why?"

I look away, focusing on the far wall where our gear hangs in neat rows.

Luke's eyes are on me, curious. He pulls out his phone, types something, and then glances at the screen. He swipes a few times, then drops the phone to his side with a low whistle.

"Now you see why," I mutter, knowing precisely what he's looking at.

"She's ... pretty." His attempt at neutrality would be amusing if I wasn't so wound up.

"Nobody's asking you to compare her to Kennedy." The words come out sharper than intended. "You can admit that she's smoking hot. That body with all those delicious curves, thick thighs, and eyes that I swear are casting a spell on me every time she looks at me. It's getting out of control."

Luke raises an eyebrow, his tone teasing. "It's normal for you to be attracted to her. Maybe even distracted by her, but it's not like you haven't dated hot women before."

I run a hand through my hair, frustration building. "It's not that simple."

He looks intrigued. "What's complicating it?"

"We kissed."

The wrench Luke is holding clatters against the truck. "Nate! Are you serious? You can't kiss your employee. What if she goes to HR on you? You don't need that kind of scandal."

"Well, since she initiated the kiss, I don't think that's high on her to-do list." I lean against the truck, the cool metal contrasting with the heat rising in my body at the memory.

"That … changes things." Luke recovers the dropped wrench.

"Not really." I flex my hands, remembering the feel of her. "We were arguing, and I grabbed her, pulled her close." I can still feel the heat of that moment—the way her eyes flared, challenging me, her breath quickening as I held her there, just inches away. "I was a second away from kissing her when she beat me to it."

A smirk tugs at the corner of his mouth. "So, the attraction is mutual." He shrugs. "You two are adults, and as the CEO, I'm sure you can make an amendment or something that would allow you to date her."

"Date Leela Jamison? Never." My voice echoes harshly off the concrete walls. Letting things go that far with her makes my stomach twist. It's too dangerous. "I made sure after it happened to send out the code of conduct to the entire company. Had HR highlight the policy paragraph where supervisors dating employees is prohibited."

Luke tilts his head, giving me a knowing look. "Was that for her or you?"

I don't answer immediately, staring at a spot on the floor. "What do you think?" I murmur, my voice tight. "I need something to keep me in line before I do something … disastrous." I push off from the truck, pacing the length of the garage.

Luke crosses his arms, studying me thoughtfully. "Let's look at this rationally. You and Leela aren't in the typical employee-supervisor relationship. She's the head of her company, which is a division of Bell Capital. An autonomous leader—"

"Tell me about it." I spin around, the movement sharp with frustration. "Do you know she had the nerve to challenge me in front of our direct reports not once but twice in one week? No one does that to me. Ever. Not even Dad."

Luke chuckles, clearly amused. "And you respect her for it. I bet that made her even more irresistible to you."

I grit my teeth, the confession sticking in my throat. "You see what a sick weirdo I am. Me and love don't mix."

"Says who?" Luke's voice is quiet, almost gentle, and he leans back, his gaze steady.

I let out a humorless laugh, shaking my head. "Let's look at my dismal experience in the relationship department. Only one serious girlfriend in my life, and she acts like what we had meant nothing."

"First off, ever since SMU, you've gotten a raw deal. Most women see you as a walking bank account, the sugar daddy they're trying to trap. I can't blame you for keeping things casual with those women. None of them could hide their true colors." He hesitates, studying my face. "Second, I get that you're hurt that Harlow Rose didn't tell you about her engagement to Santos. I'm kind of shocked about that, too."

"Do you know she hasn't even called to ask about my dad? See how he's doing. Check on me." The hurt I've been trying to ignore bleeds into my voice. "I'm not as important to her as she is to me. I can promise you one thing, I'm done sticking my neck out to help her."

"Need I remind you that you're no longer in love with Harlow Rose."

"It doesn't matter." My voice sounds flat, dead. I take a breath, staring past him. "When I look back at my life and all the people who've ever been important to me—truly important—she's on my short list. And I don't even make the cut for her long one."

"Maybe this thing with Leela is a way for you to change that. Grow your list."

The suggestion makes my chest tighten. "No … " I close my eyes for a second, conjuring up her face, her bright smile, and how she lights up a room just by walking in. "Leela is sweet, caring, open. She makes everyone around her smile. Happier." I huff, almost laughing at the thought. "She probably has them dancing around the factory singing that stupid purple dinosaur song and still killing the production targets. It's sickening and irritating." I shake my head, forcing myself to look at Luke. "I'm not going to come into her life and destroy all the good in her. The last thing I want is to be the reason that gorgeous sparkle in her eyes dims. We both know I don't do love."

Luke sighs, giving me a look like he's disappointed in me. "You choose not to do love. There's a difference."

"You're wrong." I keep my gaze steady, forcing myself to believe the words as I say them. "Forget about all the women who've been in my life in the past. Even if they were interested in me as a person, we both know I'm not capable of real love. Look at how I was raised. Look at my parents." I spread my hands as if presenting evidence in a court case. "We didn't get the epic love gene in our DNA. We got a double dose of spinning everything we touch into billions. That's what we're good at. Not cultivating relationships to share all of the money with." I glance down, my voice dropping. "I'm not going to have what you found with Kennedy. I'm alright with that."

Luke shakes his head, a stubborn glint in his eyes. "I don't believe you."

"Why should I be upset about the truth?"

"I don't believe you'll never have an epic love in your life. One that lasts." He takes a step closer, his voice firm. "Despite this prickly exterior, there's a good man on the inside. The right woman will see through, and she will get you. Mark my words."

"Your words are trash."

The shrill wail of the alarm pierces the air, sending vibrations through the concrete floor. Red lights flash across the garage walls as heavy footsteps thunder down the stairs. The familiar surge of adrenaline kicks in as Darren, Wiley, and Ronan burst through the door, their faces tight with concern.

Ronan shouts over the alarm. "Carbon monoxide alarm going off at 221 Maple Street!"

The address hits me like a punch to the gut, and I snap my head around to look at Darren. "That's Evelyn's salon."

His fear for his mother-in-law and her place of business is etched on his face. "I know," Darren says as he starts pulling on his turnout gear, his movements swift and precise. "Stop staring at me, and let's get over there."

CHAPTER 26

N ATE

THE SIRENS BLARE INTO THE NIGHT AS WE PULL INTO THE parking lot of Textured Tresses. Light spills from the salon's windows, painting yellow rectangles on the dark lot. The opposite of what we were all hoping for … the salon should be closed now. If it was dark, there would be a lower chance that anyone was inside.

"I don't see any cars," Wiley calls out, already jumping from the truck. "It's not like Evelyn to leave the lights on after she leaves."

I glance at Darren as he pauses, inhaling a deep breath. Worry rolls off him in waves at the thought of his mother-in-law being inside. Taking his wife's mother into the emergency room that she runs is not something any of us want to do. Jasmine doesn't need that kind of surprise.

Checking my gear one final time as a growing knot stiffens in my gut, I follow him out of the truck with Luke close behind me. The sound of our tanks clicking into place echoes in the evening air.

"Carbon monoxide levels are reading critical," Luke reports, eyes on the detector as we rush toward the entrance. "Way above acceptable limits."

Ronan's steady voice cuts through our growing concern. "Wiley, Luke—find that leak and shut it down. Check the water heater, air conditioning, and ventilation systems first. Those are the most likely culprits. Darren and Nate, get inside and clear the place of any people." He pauses and looks at each of us. "Remember your training. This isn't like smoke. You can't see it, can't smell it. Masks on at all times."

We nod, then disperse. I follow Darren as he bursts through the front door. The cheerful bell rings, a jarring sound against the urgency of the situation. The familiar scent of hair products—floral shampoo, chemical processing solutions, and hot metal—mixes with air that feels heavy, oppressive, and too quiet.

"Evelyn!" Darren's yell jolts me. He charges toward his mother-in-law. She's sprawled on a couch near shampoo bowls. He lifts her slowly, cradling her head in his lap. "Wake up, come on. It's Darren. Open your eyes."

I crouch low beside them, extracting the extra oxygen mask from my gear.

Evelyn stirs groggily, eyes flickering open. She looks dazed, expelling in short, shallow breaths. Her hand flutters weakly. "I'm so … tired … what … what are you doing here, Darren?"

"We got an alert from your security monitoring company about a carbon monoxide alarm going off. You didn't respond when they tried to reach you," Darren says. "Come on, let's get you to some fresh air—"

Evelyn points to a back hall. "No, wait … it's not just me … she's back there … the dryer room."

"Somebody else is here with you?" I ask, looking from Evelyn to Darren.

Evelyn nods weakly.

Ice floods my veins.

"I've got her," Darren assures me, lifting Evelyn to her feet. "You go check the back rooms."

Standing, I press the comms button. "Found Evelyn, conscious but disoriented. Darren is evacuating her now. One other woman inside. I'm going to search the rooms."

"Copy that," Ronan responds. "Nate, be quick about it. Get her and get out of that building."

I charge through the salon, which is bigger than I expected. A zigzag of narrow corridors with closed doors at regular intervals. "Fire department! Call out if you can hear me!" I yell as I pass by styling stations and vacant chairs. I open a few of the doors—all empty. Storage room—clear. A break room—deserted.

Walking past a dark bathroom and an empty laundry room, I see an opening with a line of blow dryers against the back wall. My blood runs cold when I see … her.

Leela.

She slumps under one of the hooded dryers, head tilted forward and eyes closed. Her usually vibrant face is slack and unresponsive. Her wild mass of curls cascades around her shoulders. She's still, and for a terrifying moment, it looks too much like she's …

I push the thoughts away and race into the room.

"Leela …" I say, already moving to her. My training kicks in even as fear threatens to overwhelm me. I crouch beside her and press my fingers to her neck—pulse present but weak, her skin cool and clammy. My father's body collapsed on the floor of his office flashes in my mind. Not again. I can't go through this again. "Don't do this to me. Come on, sweetheart."

"Status?" Ronan's voice crackles through my earpiece.

"Adult female. Unconscious but breathing. Pulse is thready," I say, calm and detached. "No external trauma. Extracting from the building now."

"Copy that," Ronan says.

I have no idea how much carbon monoxide she's inhaled. How long has she been back here passed out with the dryer still running, sending waves of heat blasting over her skin?

Slipping one arm under her knees, I scoop her up and use my other arm to support her back. Her body presses against my chest, and I smell the familiar scent of her perfume, an alluring jasmine. Her head lolls against my neck, and a surge of protectiveness rushes through me. She's going to be fine. I'm going to make sure of it.

I carry her toward the rear exit, kicking the door open and racing out under the night sky. I don't stop until I'm a safe fifty feet from the building. Lowering her to the ground, I yank the oxygen mask from my face and cover her mouth and nose. Her chest rises and falls with shallow breaths. The words tumble from my lips in a low whisper. "Come on, Leela. Open those beautiful eyes for me."

Seconds that feel like hours pass before her thick eyelashes flutter. Relief crashes through me. Her eyes open slowly, the flecks of green and gold bold and sparkling. Her gaze is unfocused as she blinks, and confusion clouds her face. I lift the mask.

"Hey … welcome back," I say, caressing her cheek.

"Oh …" She breathes, reaching up to touch my face with trembling fingers, sending a jolt through me. The soft, warmness of her hand sends a tender ache surging through my chest. A faint smile tugs at her lips. "I'm dreaming about you again …" Her voice is thick with confusion.

My heart stutters. "Again?"

The smile curves brighter. "Mmhmm. But this time, you're a firefighter. That's new … and very hot." She laughs softly, the sound sending warmth spreading through my chest. A giddy giggle bubbles from her mouth. "Get it? Hot? Firefighter?"

I temper my excitement. Who does she think I am? The carbon monoxide has clearly left her disoriented, stripped away the carefully maintained boundaries between us. I study her face as she fights for clarity. And damn, if she isn't the most beautiful woman I've ever seen.

"That's a corny joke," I murmur, letting a small smile slip through.

"Don't be Mean Nate to me in my dreams," she whines. "You have to be Nice Nate. Nice, hot, sexy, Nate."

CHAPTER 27

NATE

~

I shouldn't take advantage of this situation, but I can't help myself —not after she's been dominating my thoughts for weeks.

"How often do you dream about me?"

"Too often," she sighs, her head flopping backward against my palm. Her finger traces my jaw, causing a tingling trail in its wake. "Ever since that kiss … you've been driving me crazy."

I can't breathe.

"But you're avoiding me at work, ignoring my emails, canceling our meetings …" Her voice turns wistful. "All I wanted was to apologize for crossing the line with you—"

"You regret … the kiss?"

An incredulous frown appears on her face, and I almost laugh. "No way. That was the best kiss of my life."

I blink, and for a second, all I can think is that the kiss was the same for her as it was for me. That single kiss that's been tearing through my mind for days. The best … ever.

"I don't regret it, but I hate that it pushed you away … that's why I'm dreaming about you again. Making this whole thing up so I can see you and talk to you … that's all I want. To be with you again."

Heat that has nothing to do with firefighting surges through me. Her words hit me like a physical blow—she's been thinking about me, wanting me, while I've been trying desperately to maintain my distance from her for my own sake. Maybe for hers, too. But my resolve to resist this woman has crumbled.

"Is that so?" I brush a stray strand of her hair from her face. She turns her head and leans into my touch like she's craving it. Like feeling it is all she wants.

"Definitely." Her eyes sparkle up at me, still unfocused. "I'm so sorry I made you uncomfortable—"

"You could never make me uncomfortable. I'm not upset with you about the kiss … at all." The admission slips out before I can stop it.

She smiles. "See? Nice dream-Nate. You tell me what I want to hear." She glances down at herself, a flash of vulnerability crossing her face. "You carry me out of a burning building that's not actually on fire. I can't believe you could lift a big girl like me. That definitely wouldn't happen for real."

"You think I can't carry you?" I scoff.

"I'm not one of these skinny twigs you're used to dating."

"No, you're not. Your body is … dazzling, sexy, enough to drive me crazy. Every soft, gorgeous curve. Every inch of you. Trust me, I'd have no problem carrying you a thousand times."

She covers her face with her hands. "Now I know this is a dream …"

"And if it is, how would the dream end?" I ask, pulling her hands away.

Clarity brightens her gaze, and she chews on her bottom lip, sending my pulse racing. "Usually, right before I wake up … dream-Nate kisses me …"

I shouldn't.

God, I know without a shadow of a doubt that I should not do this.

Every logical part of my brain screams that this is wrong.

She's confused, vulnerable, and suffering from the effects of the carbon monoxide.

But those eyes cast a spell on me that I can't resist. The soft want in her hazel orbs scramble my brain. It's like a dam has burst, and everything I've held back crashes over us. I close the distance between us, my lips brushing against her sweet mouth. I inhale her breath as she wraps her arms around my neck.

That single move is my undoing. I deepen the kiss, losing myself in the taste of her. Her lips part, inviting me to explore every part of her mouth. She tastes of everything honest, pure, and good—things I've been missing and wanting without knowing it. She kisses me back like she's been suffocating, and I'm the air she needs to survive. Wanting me as much as I've wanted her—

"Nate!" Ronan's voice shatters the moment. "Status?"

Leela's eyes open wide, sharp with awareness.

She pushes me away, crawling across the grass away from me. One hand flies to her mouth as reality crashes in. "Oh my God. No, this isn't … wait? You're … what is going on?"

"Easy." I raise my hands in front of me. I shift back into professional mode even as my heart aches to touch her again. "You were at Textured Tresses salon and there was a carbon monoxide leak. The exposure caused you to lose consciousness temporarily. I got you out of the building to fresh air."

"Carbon monoxide?" She looks around wildly, the last of the confusion clearing from her eyes. "Evelyn! Is Evelyn okay? She was doing my hair, and I had to sit under the dryer …"

"She's fine. We got her out of the building, too," I reassure her.

"But why are … you … here?" She gestures at my turnout gear. "Why are you dressed like—"

"A firefighter?" I finish for her, shifting away as the heat of our kiss still buzzes in my veins. "Because … I am a firefighter."

"No, you're CEO of Bell Capital." She shakes her head.

A flashlight beam sweeps over us, and Ronan appears behind me. "And he's been a volunteer firefighter with the Kimbell Fire Station for years. One of the best," Ronan says, then turns to me. "She one of your employees?"

"Something like that," I say, not tearing my eyes away from Leela.

She looks at me like I've lost my mind.

Ronan says, "Ambulance is on the way. Luke found the source. It was from the water heater in the utility room. How's she doing?"

Before I can answer, Leela stands up, arms crossed over her chest. "I'm fine." She stares at me like she's never seen me before. "I'm just confused."

Ronan chuckles. "I'll let you handle this." He turns and walks back toward the salon.

When he's out of earshot, I say, "Every three days, I do my firefighter shift. The rest of the week, I'm full-time at Bell Capital."

"All this time?" Leela drags her hands down her face.

"There's a lot you don't know about me," I say, realizing my mistake. I never should've let myself lose control around her. She can never know how much I want to pull her in my arms and tell her that I've been going crazy not seeing her over the past week, too. How it's been torture for me not seeing her every day.

"I see." She touches her lips gently, no doubt remembering the kiss we just shared. The one that shouldn't have happened. "And earlier, when we—"

"Shouldn't have happened. Won't happen again." I force the words out.

Sirens grow louder. The flashing lights of the ambulance dance across the salon. "The ambulance is here," I say gruffly. "You need to get checked out. Carbon monoxide poisoning can have delayed effects." I rattle off the symptoms automatically, clinging to protocol like a lifeline.

She nods slowly, still looking shell-shocked—whether from the CO exposure, the revelations from our conversation, or that searing kiss, I can't tell. As the paramedics approach with a gurney, I force myself to step back.

"Right … I'll go," she says, turning away.

I can't tear my gaze away from her as she walks to the EMTs and allows them to lead her to the ambulance.

I have to forget about Leela's honest admission about wanting me and the kiss.

Lock away the memory of everything I found out tonight.

She deserves much better than what I could ever offer her.

Better than a man who can't love and would only dim that brilliant light inside her.

No matter how badly I want her, I will stay away.

For her sake.

Even if it kills me.

CHAPTER 28

L EELA

~

MY HEART POUNDS AGAINST MY RIBS AS I STAND OUTSIDE the frosted glass office door. The name placard reads, "Nate Bell, Chief Executive Officer." My palms are damp. I wipe them along the sides of my pencil skirt, grateful that I decided to pair my flamingo pink frilly shirt with a black bottom.

The memory of our kiss … our second kiss … replays in my mind like a movie highlight reel. My cheeks flush hot as I gently brush my fingers across my lips.

Even in my loopy state from the carbon monoxide poisoning, there's no denying that the second kiss was infinitely better than the first. Maybe because it was Nate's choice this time. He was there responding to an emergency alert as a volunteer firefighter, which I still can't believe. He had every excuse not to participate in my dazed confusion. Refuse to play along.

But that's not what he did.

He played his part perfectly.

And that's the part I don't understand.

Was he genuinely interested or just humoring me in my altered state? Or worse, taking advantage of the situation to stroke his ego?

I take a deep breath, still not ready to knock on his office door. One thing I know for sure is that kissing Nate can never happen again. I have too much at stake with my business to let myself get tangled up in some workplace crush. A crush that could easily be one-sided, reckless, and foolish for all I know.

And that's probably why Nate summoned me to his office.

Hearing his perspective on our kiss—well, kisses—could humiliate me, but then it would be over. We could put it behind us and move on, working together solely to make Sybille Organics a success. I can do that. I hope I can do that.

No.

I must do that.

No more mixed signals. No more fantasizing. No more getting swept away by his … well, everything. Nate Bell is my boss and nothing more.

I nod in agreement with my decisive thoughts, then step forward and raise my hand to knock on the door.

It swings open before I reach it.

A tall, striking woman with an air of brisk efficiency strides out. She looks about my age, but something about her posture and the incredible way she carries herself screams "executive." Her features are unmistakably similar to Nate's. Her ice-blue eyes land on me, sharp and assessing.

"Leela Jamison." She extends her hand toward me. "I'm surprised it's taken this long for us to meet. I'm Willow Bell, Nate's sister."

I smile brightly as I shake her hand. "Good to meet you, Willow. I didn't realize you were part of Bell Capital, too. Although I guess it makes sense …"

My words trail off as Willow's face morphs into a mask of scornful amusement, one brow arching high while her lips curve into a strange smirk. "I don't work for Dad. I work for our mother's private equity firm, The Kalinskaya Group."

Now, it's my turn to raise an eyebrow. "Your parents own separate private equity firms?"

"It's a long story. You should ask Nate about it someday," Willow says, a sly smile on her face.

"What brings you to our offices?"

"An acquisition, of course. My brother and I struck a deal that I'm pleased with." Her smile transitions from sly to predatory.

After taking over my company, Nate assured me I'd still have significant influence as the COO for Sybille Organics. What could it mean that Willow is here? Did Nate sell his interest in my company to Willow? Just because we kissed? No. He wouldn't dare. Would he?

I swallow, my mind spinning. "I see. Anything I should know about?"

"Nate will fill you in." She moves past me with efficient grace, her presence as direct and no-nonsense as her brother's. The businesslike demeanor must run in the family, though Willow wears it like a perfectly tailored suit, while Nate's version feels more like armor.

"Okay ..." I say as she walks away without a backward glance, her steps echoing down the hallway.

Turning back toward the open door, I step forward and knock lightly.

"Come in," Nate's deep voice resonates with a hint of weariness.

My anxiety shoots through the roof as I walk through the door and close it behind me.

The sight of Nate behind his modern chrome and glass desk steals my breath. His crisp charcoal suit starkly contrasts with the firefighter gear I saw him in a couple of days ago. Both versions radiate the same commanding presence and irresistible sensual appeal. And yes, both versions make my knees feel like jelly. The morning sun streams through the windows, casting a glow on his olive skin, and I swear he's never looked more handsome.

Focus, I scold myself as I sit in the chair across from his desk.

Nate's eyes are unreadable as they meet mine. "Before we start, I trust you haven't told anyone about what happened at the salon."

My fingers twist together in my lap. "No, of course not. I would never tell anyone that we—"

"Good," he cuts in, his voice like a closed door. "No one at Bell Capital besides my dad knows I volunteer as a firefighter. I prefer to keep it that way."

Relief and disappointment war in my chest. "Volunteering as a firefighter, right. No, I haven't told anybody about that."

"Excellent." He opens a drawer, pulling out a slim packet of paper. "Then I assume you'll have no problem signing this nondisclosure agreement."

The casual coldness in his tone stings. I cross my arms, trying not to let him see how much this gets to me. "Wow. I guess my word isn't good enough?"

"It doesn't hurt to have insurance," he replies, sliding the papers across the desk toward me, along with a pen.

The leather of my chair creaks as I shift forward. I scan the document, the words blurring as I realize how foolish I was to think he wanted to discuss our kiss. My signature comes out shakier than I'd like as I berate myself for thinking he cared about my lovestruck ramblings. He must have found the whole scene hilarious—a needy mess of a woman professing things she shouldn't be feeling for her boss. Well, lesson learned.

I shove the signed NDA back toward him. Straightening my spine, I clear my throat. "The doctor told me that carbon monoxide poisoning can have strange impacts on the body, including confusion, disorientation, hallucinations." I clear my throat. "I don't even remember half of what I said to you." A lie I desperately need him to believe. "So if you could just forget about whatever we discussed, I'd also appreciate that."

Something flickers in his dark eyes—shock? Irritation? Anger? But it vanishes quickly. He nods, his mouth set in a hard line. "Already forgotten."

The words are as cold as they come. I can practically feel them freezing the air between us. The ticking of the modern chrome wall clock fills the silence before I ask, "Is that all you wanted to discuss with me?"

"No," he says, leaning back in his chair. "There's also the matter of the company town hall meeting happening in thirty minutes."

"A town hall meeting?" My hand grips the arm of my chair. "Today? Why?"

"You've seen the production numbers for this week." He crosses his arms over his chest. "They've taken a hit from the gains we made last week because of your latest … stunt."

"What stunt?" I ask, brows knitting together.

"The putt-putt golf, ping pong tables, and arcade games crammed into the factory entrance," he replies, his tone dripping with disdain.

I bristle. "It's to improve morale. And it's working."

"It's causing a dip in our weekly production."

I mirror his pose, crossing my arms over my chest. "It significantly reduced the batch errors and improved the quality of products coming off the floor."

He leans forward, steepling his fingers on the desk. "Need I remind you that GrabHub expects a shipment of the Herbal Root Essentials products in two months? Our production rate doesn't come close to fulfilling that order in that time."

The urge to defend myself takes over. "We've improved the production rate over the last two days—"

"Not close enough," he retorts, holding up a sheet of paper. "Which is why I purchased another factory in Lasso County to make up the slack. It will only take a week to convert it to produce hair care products, and it's almost entirely automated."

"So that's why your sister was here?" I ask, putting the pieces of the puzzle together.

"She didn't make it easy. I gave up a lot more than I wanted to,"

Nate says as his eyes soften. "But I had to give us the best shot of making that deadline."

I'm blown away. Bell Capital swooped in to save my fledgling company, and now Nate is throwing more money at our problems to make us successful. I'm beyond grateful and want to tell him, but he keeps talking.

"And on top of that financial setback, we have the engagement survey results to deal with," Nate snaps.

My jaw drops. "You sent an engagement survey to our employees without telling me?"

His eyes narrow, unamused. "You turned our factory into a game room without telling me. I'd say that makes us equal."

I clench my hands in my lap. This was not what I was expecting. He ridicules and belittles all the goodwill and positive vibes my changes generated among the employees. Can't he see the good I'm doing? I'm with these employees every day. I know what they need and what motivates them.

Nate releases the page from his hand, and it plummets toward the desk, coming to a rest near the edge. "The survey results show that we have a team morale problem, but it's not because they need more toys to help them work."

"What does it say are the root causes of the declining morale?" I ask, curious despite my frustration.

"They don't think you," he points at me, "and I," he points at himself, "are aligned on the strategy needed to move this company forward. They think they're getting mixed messages from us, and it's making them uneasy and unfocused."

My stomach churns as I process his words. I may have downplayed parts of his strategy, subtly steering the employees toward my philosophy, which takes a more collaborative approach.

And clearly, they've noticed.

Now they're caught between loyalty to me and loyalty to the paychecks coming from Bell Capital. I exhale, frustrated with myself for putting them in this position.

"So how do we fix this?" I ask.

"The town hall meeting."

"There's no way we can pull together a successful town hall meeting in less than thirty minutes."

"Check your email. You'll find the script for the meeting, which highlights speaking parts for both of us. There will be a teleprompter, so no need to memorize anything," Nate explains.

A protest rises to my lips, but I push it down. He wants me to be a talking head of the company's message without even giving me a chance to have input on what I'm saying. The employees know me. They'll see through it if I'm not genuine. I take a deep breath.

After what Nate did to help meet the shipment deadline, perhaps I should do this ... for him.

I stand quickly and give him a curt nod. "I'll be ready. See you at the town hall."

CHAPTER 29

L EELA

~

THE FLUORESCENT LIGHTS IN THE AUDITORIUM-STYLE meeting room buzz overhead as a sea of anxious employees file in. Their whispered conversations echo off the cream-colored walls. Wary glances bounce between Nate and me as we stand on opposite sides of the stage.

After leaving Nate's office, I rushed to my own and opened the email with the script and engagement survey results. All the data wasn't bad, but Nate was right that employees were concerned about the different messages we presented. I had good intentions, trying to be the bright spot in his dark, rigid ways, but the consequences weren't all positive.

I opened the script with some trepidation but was met with pleasant surprises. The tone was casual, and the content perfectly blended both of our management strategies. I was committed to presenting a united front as Nate requested. I had to if we were going to be successful in the future.

Stepping off the stage, I greet the employees as they enter, hoping to lighten the tension. Nate retreats to the corner, consumed with something on his cell phone. I had to give him credit, though. He arrived at the auditorium without his business coat or tie, giving him a more casual and approachable vibe.

As the auditorium fills up, I internally rehearse my part one last time. It sounds good in my head, but I'm not sure what the employees will think about me doing so much corporate speech. I'm the cheerleader. The bright spot. The one who disseminates information with humor and a dash of sass. That's what they expect from me.

As much as I don't want to let Nate down, I don't want to come off as a puppet of Bell Capital in this town hall. It would ruin all the trust and goodwill I've built with them over the past few weeks. Pacing along the back of the stage, I stare over at Nate. He's still bent over his phone, looking at ease. Lucky him. He doesn't worry about winning hearts. He delegates that to others while he focuses on the numbers.

The meeting organizer approaches me as the auditorium is almost packed. She hands me a microphone and then gives one to Nate. There's no presentation deck running behind us. Just a good old-fashioned conversation between leaders and employees.

Nate kicks off the meeting after glancing at me to see if I'm ready.

"Alright, I appreciate everyone showing up on short notice. I know how much you all love a good surprise meeting," Nate says, then smiles. "In Kimbell, y'all know a meeting called this suddenly usually means someone hit a deer and needs help dragging it to the taxidermist. But don't worry, there's no heavy lifting required today— just listening."

Laughter fills the place. I blink, caught off guard by the way he's *connecting* with them. Who is this man, throwing out jokes and leaning into his small-town roots? And is he borrowing from a style he's watched me employ many times at our leader meetings?

I ignore the strange flutter of pride in my chest. I'd always wanted him to understand this—the power of meeting people where they were, of showing a little bit of himself. Part of me can't help but wonder—is this a one-time act, or is he learning something from me? And if he is ... what else might he be starting to see in a new light?

The laughter dies down, and Nate communicates the engagement survey results, emphasizing that we, as leaders, take the results seriously and commit to improving because of them. He seamlessly reintroduces the vision and our strategy for meeting the GrabHub deadline. He then announces the acquisition of the second production facility.

I scan the room, gauging reactions. The nods and murmurs of approval grow. The energy shifts, bit by bit. Nate isn't a distant "higher-up" anymore. He's becoming part of the team.

"I think I've done enough talking," Nate says with a chuckle, then smiles at me. "I'm not the one y'all want to hear from anyway. Let me turn this over to Leela to share her views. Leela?"

"Thanks, Nate," I say, then walk off the stage to get closer to the employees. "How many of y'all like this more laidback version of our CEO? I mean, well, as laidback as we're going to get."

The clapping is deafening, mingled with hoots and hollers from the crowd.

"I'll start by saying that I wholeheartedly believe in the vision and strategy Nate just covered. I feel so proud and honored to have partnered with Bell Capital and to see that they don't just talk the talk, but they walk the walk, too. A walk that has my biggest dreams for a company I started in my garage ten years ago now within reach," I say, then pause as the clapping gets louder.

Over the next fifteen minutes, I cover all the points in the script in my own way. The shift in the auditorium is undeniable. We're changing their views of us as leaders, which will significantly improve productivity across all departments.

"Okay, so now we'll open it up to Q&A," I say, then turn to Nate and ask him to come down. I hoist myself to sit onto the stage and feel a tingle surge through my entire body when he sits next to me. So close that our arms and legs brush against each other.

I suck in a deep breath, then try not to focus on these pesky, wayward feelings for him I'm trying to banish to the moon. No, the sun … where they will burn up and die for good.

The questions start easy. People are too polite or intimidated to bring up the real concerns. A few softball questions about timelines and training materials, which Nate and I answer smoothly, presenting a united front. For now, at least.

"If we had a mascot, what would it be?" A fun question comes from the middle of the crowd.

"I can answer that," Nate and I say in unison.

"Where is the chivalry? Shouldn't it be ladies first?" I tease.

Nate licks his lips slowly, leveling me with a playful challenge in his eyes. "Only if the lady gives a good answer."

"How about we answer simultaneously and see who's is better?" I say, leaning in closer to him.

"I'm always up for a challenge," Nate says, hinting at something more.

Our eyes meet, and everything around us fades away—it's like we're the only two people in the room.

Someone yells from the crowd, breaking the moment. "On the count of three. One. Two. Three."

Nate and I blurt out our responses, which couldn't be more different.

Laughter erupts.

"Looks like both of you got it wrong," another employee calls out, laughing even louder.

I cover my face in my hands as Nate wraps an arm around my shoulder, pulling me into a half-hug. I lean into his strong arms as memories of our two kisses flash like lightning through my mind.

"Okay, we both missed the mark on that one, but I'm sure we'll nail the next question," Nate says, then his voice dips lower. "Won't we?"

I can only nod in response as heat flames up my neck.

The moderator interjects to inform everyone that there's only time for one last question. A hand rises from the back. A young woman—probably one of the new hires—stands up, her brow furrowed. She glances around nervously but steels herself and speaks up, her voice wavering.

"All the new information shared today is encouraging." She swallows, glancing between us. "But ... with so much focus on super tight deadlines and production metrics, we can't help but feel like cogs in a machine. We're clocking a lot of overtime just to keep up, and the quality control checks are getting so strict that it feels like we're constantly under a microscope," she continues, her voice gaining strength. "I know we're here to make great products, but ... sometimes it feels like there's more focus on numbers than on the people who make those numbers happen. Are we just numbers to you?"

A murmur of agreement ripples through the crowd. My heart sinks. More heads nod and a few others lean forward, clearly emboldened by her words. This isn't just a passing concern. This is a real issue.

Nate stiffens next to me. His jaw tightens, and a flicker of defensiveness crosses his face. Nate is a numbers guy, through and through, and the idea that metrics might make people feel like they weren't valued went against everything he believed about good management.

Before he can respond, I speak into the microphone, determined to ease the tension. My voice is steady and confident as I give my most heartfelt answer. "You are not numbers to us. We value and appreciate each and every one of you. Metrics only tell part of the story." I pause to make eye contact with many of the employees in the auditorium. "I have every confidence that we'll make the deadline, not just because of the new factory but because we're doing this ... together," I say. "We're working as a team that encourages and supports each other."

I remind them of all the efforts implemented in the past few weeks, which show a commitment to caring for and supporting them in their new roles and to meet the deadline. I see heads nodding in agreement and a collective relief settling over the room.

"Our motto at Sybille Organics is 'Rooted in Care,' and that's what we're about—not only caring for our customers with high-quality products but caring for each other as a team." I pause, letting the words sink in. "That commitment will be the driving factor in our success."

I lower the microphone and feel Nate's gaze, sending my body temperature through the roof. The moderator closes the meeting. As the auditorium empties, a few employees pause to shake our hands and offer tentative smiles.

Nate and I exchange polite nods with each person until the last employee leaves, and I'm left wondering if he's going to say something —*anything*—about how he thought the town hall went.

Nate turns to me, a small, almost reluctant smile tugging at his lips. It's subtle but there—just enough to make my heart skip.

"Well," he starts, and I brace myself, leaning in.

But then, as if on cue, his phone buzzes. He looks down, frowns, and sighs. "We'll catch up later, Leela," he says, distracted, before slipping his phone into his pocket and heading toward the door without a backward glance.

I stand alone in the empty room, left with nothing but questions.

CHAPTER 30

N ATE

THE URGENT TEXT FROM THE HEAD NURSE IN CHARGE OF Dad's care has me on edge as I park in front of the sprawling estate, with red-tiled roofs, white stucco walls, and an imposing, centuries-old charm. I don't understand what could've changed. He was fine when I checked on him before work.

Exiting the golf cart, I sprint along the curved stone walkway and barrel through the carved wooden double doors. The house I grew up in is eerily quiet, the air charged with a sense of foreboding and fear.

That can mean only one thing—Alona Kalinskaya is here.

As if on cue, she rounds the corner with a slender arm pointed toward the doors. A blur of powerful sophistication and effortless dominance dressed in Prada.

"Out," she growls as the head nurse and her team rush past, eyes downcast as they pull their luggage behind them.

"Mom …" I tentatively step forward as the door shuts behind me. "What happened?"

She tsks. "That man." She shakes her head. "Broke wrist."

"He can barely move. How in the world did he break his wrist?" A broken wrist is a setback to Dad's limited progress over the past month. He's been a nightmare to the medical team, and this will only make things worse.

"Incompetent! They had no answer," she says, raking her hand through her long dark mane. "They must go."

The door opens, and Willow rushes in, brushing past me and hugging Mom. "You came." Willow gushes.

I should have known Willow would call Mom, even though that's the last thing Dad would want. Not because he doesn't want to see her. But because he wouldn't want her to see him as an invalid.

"Someone had to take charge," Mom responds, wrapping Willow in her arms. She gives Willow the same clipped, brief update she'd given me, then says, "David is reckless and impatient. It's his fault, but they should be more attentive to him and his needs. Russian qualified nurses will arrive tonight."

I'm not surprised that Mom has already rectified the situation, but I need to do something to help. "I'll go talk to him," I say.

"Not you." She stops me with a hand to my chest. "Willow."

My sister's face goes pale. She's had a difficult time dealing with Dad's stroke, making every excuse not to visit him.

"You will talk to him," Mom says. A command, not a request.

Willow reaches for my hand and I give it a gentle squeeze.

"I don't know what to say," Willow says, her gaze finding mine. She's worried Dad will be upset she hasn't checked on him more or been around.

"Start with I love you," Mom says, rolling her eyes. "Then remind him of what's at stake if he doesn't take better care of himself."

"Did you see him?" I ask, unable to hide my curiosity.

A hint of a smile plays on Mom's lips. "Of course. It's time for me and Willow to help shoulder the burden you've been under, my sweet boy." She levels Willow with a stern stare. "Go to your father."

Willow nods and releases my hand. Once she's far down the hallway headed toward the South Wing, Mom turns to me.

"He has a soft spot for her," Mom says. "She will get him to behave."

"He has a soft spot for you, too," I say, stopping short of telling her that Dad has never stopped loving her. All the women and marriages after Mom were his feeble attempts to get over her after she left him to chase professional success. Their love couldn't survive the competition for money and power between them, even if it brought them together in the first place.

I often wonder how much more they could've achieved if they'd found a way to work together than against each other. If they'd recognized and appreciated their differences, understanding that it could have made them a stronger team. Admitted their mutual respect and admiration for each other instead of seeing that as a sign of weakness that could be exploited.

It's impossible to know …

But maybe not for me and … Leela.

Have I been doing the same thing to her that I witnessed between my parents growing up? She's doing a fantastic job, but I don't tell her that. Instead, I raise the bar higher, set more challenging goals, and compete with her for the employees' respect. I can only imagine she feels like a failure when she's outperforming all my expectations. All this because of the dysfunctional role models I've had to look up to my entire life.

Mom expels a contented sigh as if she knows the secret I wanted to spill. "I'm sure seeing me will be some sort of motivation for him. He has long road ahead of him. I won't allow him to sabotage progress to recovery."

"Are you going to stick around Kimbell for a while?" I ask, realizing how much I want her to be close for Dad and me. Stepping into Dad's

CEO role and being the primary decision-maker for the entirety of his medical care has been harder than I've even admitted to myself.

Mom pulls me into her arms. I'm transported back to my childhood with the take-no-prisoners mother who always knew when I needed to be comforted without me saying a word. She pulls back, then gazes at me with dark eyes identical to mine. "Have Peter set me up in the master suite in the North Wing. The one that overlooks the lake."

Emotions clog my throat, and I can't get the words of gratitude out.

"I'll text him now," I say after I'm sure I can speak without showing any signs of weakness.

"Nate," Mom says, grabbing my hands. "I know what you are doing with Sybille Organics, and I approve." She ruffles my hair with her hand. "That is where your focus should be. I will handle your father from now on. Understood?"

"Understood," I say, a more profound truth unfolding in my mind. A chance to break free from my old ways and try something my parents didn't have the courage to do.

"Go make me proud," Mom demands.

I kiss her on the forehead. "Call me if y'all need anything. Day or night."

She dismisses me with a wave and pushes me out the door.

I return to the golf cart, knowing I'm not going home. There's someone I need to see first.

CHAPTER 31

N ATE

Shifting the golf cart into gear, I take off along the backroads toward Painted Lady Lodge. I'm more convinced than ever that my plan is the right thing to do.

There's no doubt things changed between Leela and me today. The Town Hall proved how formidable we are when we borrow from the other's style. Sybille Organics could become the dominant ethnic haircare line if we continue to tap into our collective strength. Working together, there's nothing we can't do.

The only thing that can ruin our progress is if I act on my feelings like I did back at the salon. That was a mistake I won't let happen again. Even she regretted revealing her feelings for me. The moment she passed her admissions off as the delusional ravings of a woman under the influence of carbon monoxide poisoning, I knew she was right to dismiss them. Even if that made me so angry, I wanted to punch my fist through my glass desk.

Nothing good can come of either of us acting on this attraction.

So, it's good we're on the same page about putting the kisses behind us.

But that has nothing to do with me telling her what I think of her professionally or letting her know how convinced I am that we can accomplish so much more if we work together openly and honestly instead of being at odds. To prove this, I'll take the first steps to change my actions toward her and the team.

Fifteen minutes later, I steer the cart toward the pathway to the pool, where hip-hop music blares in the air. Parking along the hedges, I jump out. The sounds of giggling and water splashing as Leela sings along off-key with the lyrics.

For a second, I hesitate.

Did she invite someone over? A date, perhaps? Some guy she misses from Houston who drove over a hundred miles to lift her spirits since she no longer has feelings for me? Has she been yearning for companionship with a man who can make her smile and feel appreciated? Instead of me, who greets her more often with derision and contention than anything else.

I squat low, trying to peer through the hedges to see if she's alone. If another man is hanging out at my pool with her, maybe that's what I need to kill these fantasies of her that haunt me. Seeing her with another man would be the tough wake-up call I need.

Leela can be with anyone she wants to be with … except me.

Our relationship has to stay strictly professional.

Satisfied that I'd set myself straight, I head down the crushed limestone walkway to the pool and let myself inside. Leela sits on the edge of the pool, her legs kicking the water as she dances and waves her arms to the music. Her energy is positively infectious. If I could dance, she'd make me want to join in.

But I didn't come here to look like an idiot.

I scan the pool area. She's most definitely alone. A fruit tray and pitcher of margaritas rest on a nearby table. A glass of the liquid sits next to Leela. Her eyes are shut as she undulates and twerks her body to the sound. I can't take my eyes off her. The urge to be next to her grows with each passing second. I walk forward slowly, careful not to startle her. As I pass by the outdoor bar, she reaches for her glass and catches sight of me.

"Nate …" she says, out of breath. "What are you doing here?" She turns to grab her cell phone, pausing the music as I come closer.

"I told you we'd catch up later," I say, my tone more brusque than I intend.

"And I wasn't there because I gave everybody the day off after the town hall meeting," Leela says, her voice faltering. Her shoulders draw tight, and she absently fidgets, one thumb brushing over the other in a frenetic rhythm. "I would've come to your home office or met you back at the office. You should've texted me. It's no problem."

She's about to move, but I raise my hand and shake my head. She freezes. I pause and take a deep breath, trying not to be mesmerized by how stunning she looks with her hair in a ponytail and face devoid of makeup. "I'm not here to berate you about giving the employees the rest of the day off or to ruin your afternoon."

"You're not?"

"I just wanted to let you know that you were amazing today. I ambushed you with that town hall meeting, and you handled it better than anyone."

Her hazel eyes grow wide as she turns toward me. "Who are you, and what have you done with the real Nate Bell?"

I chuckle and shake my head, not surprised she's doing a double take at the unexpected compliment. I rarely give any, but Leela more than earned it and deserves it for today. "You heard me. You were amazing. Brilliant. Compelling. Dynamic … I'm struggling for an E."

"Extraordinary?"

"Good one. Fantastic. Great." I pause and smile.

Did she just swoon, or is that my mind playing tricks on me?

"Shall I go on?" I ask.

"No," Leela says, grinning as she clasps her hands in front of her. "I think that was a good start." She laughs. "But any future feedback should start with the letter H."

I salute her in response. "That I can do."

She says, "I hoped you thought it went as well as I did. We changed a lot of minds today and boosted morale. The team is going to be more productive than ever. You'll see."

"I agree. Giving them the afternoon off was the right move. An action that speaks a lot louder than words that we don't view them as just numbers. I support your decision to do that."

"We make a great team when we stop treating every decision like some competition we have to win."

"Yeah, we do," I say, not surprised she's come to the same conclusions and a lot faster than I did. "The important thing is that we gave the same message in our own ways. I almost forgot I wrote a script for you."

"I stand behind everything I said at the town hall. I truly believe it. We've always been aligned, even on the cost-cutting. It was just the methods to get there we didn't always agree on."

"But today, you supported my methods, too. Why?"

"Because I realized they complement, not contradict, my own. We can make Sybille Organics one of the premier ethnic hair care lines if we focus less on our differences and more on what we have in common."

"That's what we're going to do," I say, dragging my barefoot through the water. "We own a controlling interest, but it's still your company at its heart."

"Thank you for saying that and the feedback. It means a lot," Leela says, then leans back. "You taking the afternoon off, too?"

"I have to be a good role model for the team, don't you think?"

"It's about time," she says, then points to the pitcher. "Margarita?"

"No, I'm good." I roll up the sleeves of my shirt and undo the top few buttons. "Mind if I hang out with you for a while? I have swim trunks stashed at all the guest houses."

"Not at all."

Minutes later, I return from the changing cabana, ready to relax at the pool with Leela. But I don't trust myself to be close to her. Instead of sitting next to her, I walk past her toward the opposite end of the pool, putting as much distance between us as possible. I ease into the water, enjoying the cool reprieve from the afternoon heat.

Leela smiles as she watches me. "Do you want me to get the cook to make some food for you?"

"So you decided to use the staff now?" I tease.

She scrunches her face in the cutest way. "In a limited capacity and only occasionally. Feels weird to have a team of people at my beck and call."

"But not weird to perform a rap video dance routine at the pool?"

"Okay, I'm officially embarrassed. But that's one of my favorite songs," Leela says.

"Well, I got more feedback for you."

Her eyes narrow as she looks at me. "Give it to me."

"Starting with the letter H. Hideous."

"What?" She balks. "I can dance good, sir! I practice these moves in the mirror and know what I'm doing."

"I'm not talking about your dance moves. I'm talking about what you're wearing. That's the ugliest swimsuit I've ever seen," I say, disappointed she's hiding all those gorgeous curves beneath what looks like a regrettable combination of a ballet leotard with short sleeves and biking shorts. Who wears that to the pool on a blazing hot Texas summer afternoon? Especially someone with a body like hers.

Her laugh tickles my ears. "Come on. I'm not a size 2. Not even a respectable size 8. This is all I want to show, even at a pool on a secluded property owned by my billionaire boss."

"You seriously don't own a proper swimsuit?" I ask, hoping her answer isn't a travesty.

"Nope. Can't swim anyway, so wasn't high on the list of things to buy."

That explains why she's only sitting on the pool's perimeter. I make a mental note to fix her swimsuit deficiency. "What size are you anyway?"

"You're not supposed to ask a woman what size clothes she wears! That's rude!" Her eyes grow wide.

I level her with an intense stare. "Answer me."

She hesitates, likely contemplating whether to respond or not. If she doesn't tell me, I'll get Peter to figure it out.

After a few seconds, she shrugs and says, "Sixteen."

"Isn't that the average size of a woman in the U.S.?"

"Right, and that's what men think of us. We're average, not special or overtly desirable. We're not the symbols of beauty perpetuated across media. Don't get me wrong. I think I'm a cute girl," She pauses to strike a few poses that send my body temperature through the roof. "But no one prefers all of this," she gestures toward her ample chest, "and this," she slaps a hand on her hips and round butt, "to those skinny models."

Her words hit me like a sucker punch. How could she believe this? She doesn't get it—she doesn't know how breathtaking she is, how she commands my attention without even trying. It's maddening, but mostly, it makes me want to prove her wrong.

"If you could see yourself through my eyes, you'd know how wrong that statement is. You'd never make the mistake of saying it again ..."

CHAPTER 32

Nate

THE LOOK SHE GIVES ME SHATTERS EVERY OUNCE OF MY resolve to stay away from her. The vulnerability in her hazel eyes, reflecting unrestrained longing and raw desire, undoes me. Leela's gaze caresses from my face down my chest to my abs. It's the only invitation I need. I plunge into the water and swim the length of the pool to where she's sitting, reemerging next to her.

Resting my hands on her thick thighs, I say, "You are the most beautiful woman I've ever met. Hands down. No contest. Inside and most definitely outside."

"You should stop speaking now … before things get out of hand," Leela says, but she doesn't budge.

"What if I want things to get out of hand?"

She bites her lower lip. "You're my boss. We can't."

"You think I can't change the rules?" I challenge. "You think I wouldn't break the rules for you?"

"Nate ..." her voice is breathy. "We already kissed twice, and all it did was make things weird between us."

I slip my arms around her hips, pulling closer to her, and stare into those bewitching hazel eyes. "Weird because we can't deny how attracted we are to each other, can we?"

"No, we can't." She rests her hands on my bare shoulders. A surge of excitement floods me as she lets her hands slide down my arms, lingering just long enough to drive me insane. "But being attracted to each other and acting on that attraction are two different things. We should not act on it."

My hands move to the sides of her face. "Why not?" I ask, lifting myself out of the water until our faces are inches apart. I'm so close I can feel her breath cooling my wet skin. There's no way I'm not going to kiss this woman right now—

The discordant sounds of two cell phones ringing burst through the air. I frown as Leela's shallow breaths grow more ragged.

"What's the likelihood that both of our phones start going off at the same time?" I ask as the ringing continues. My muscles tense. Annoyance claws at me, but the calls could be important.

"We need to answer ..." Leela says. She doesn't move because my hands still hold her face, ready to kiss the lips I think about before sleeping at night.

I clench my eyes shut and curse under my breath. "Fine. Get yours, and I'll get mine."

Tearing myself away, I get out of the pool, shielding her from the obvious effect she has on me, and stalk over to my phone. Tapping the screen, I answer, "Nate Bell."

"It's Jannik. Production slowed because the product's viscosity running through the machines is off. So, I tested the ingredients one by one. The culprit is the calyxera root."

"What's wrong with it? We just got a shipment in from Brazil," I say.

"It's not calyxera root. A close replica from the same genus family, but not it. That's wrecking the product."

"You mean they sent us fake roots?" I ask.

"Yes, and it had to be on purpose not to lose the contract," Jannik replies. "Like I said, very close to calyxera. But Leela is right. There are unique properties in real calyxera roots that are critical for the formula. Any deviation throws everything out of whack."

"Get me a list of other producers of that root ASAP," I say, then toss the phone onto the table. My mind races with the plethora of next moves I need to make, starting with calling the lawyers to sue the company for breach of contract. I turn around to look at Leela.

Fear clouds her face.

I rush toward her. "What is it?"

Dropping the phone from her ear, she says with a shaky voice, "There was a fire at the company in Brazil where the calyxera root is grown. They lost everything. It'll be years before they can cultivate and grow more. That's it. We're done. There's no way …" her voice chokes with emotion. "No way we can make the deadline now."

"You quitting on me?" I demand, grabbing her hands. "Giving up already?"

"Nate …"

"What happened to all that positivity and can-do spirit you boost the employees with daily?" I ask, knowing that there's no way I'm letting her down. She came to Bell Capital for help to make the shipment deadline. Trusted me to be the one to do that.

"We can't fix this. I'm not sure there's another reliable source of as much calyxera root as we need anywhere. And without it, there's no Herbal Root Essence line. The contract with GrabHub is dead." Her body slumps in defeat.

I refuse to believe we've come this far to fail. This is the worst thing that could've happened to us. I have no clue how to fix this problem. But I'm not giving up and won't let her either.

"Didn't we just agree that together we can do anything?" I'm rattled by the desire to do whatever it takes to keep her happy. Keep a smile on that gorgeous face. Help her to reach the heights she deserves.

She nods her head slowly, chewing on her lower lip.

"Get on the phone with all your contacts." I cup her cheek with one hand, forcing her to meet my gaze. "We're going to find more calyxera root."

CHAPTER 33

L EELA

~

THE WARM GLOW OF THE LAMPS ILLUMINATE NATE'S HOME office as I sit cross-legged on a couch nestled in the corner. Home office is an absolute understatement for the standalone structure that sits in the shadow of Nate's massive mansion. Inside is a replica of Bell Capital's executive floor—Nate's office, the boardroom, two conference rooms, one extra office, and a spa-worthy bathroom suite—all so no one on video calls will know when he's playing hooky from the Houston office to work from Kimbell.

For the past two weeks, we've put in full days at the office, then retreated to this space after hours to continue working, fueled by a rotating arrangement of decadent food brought in at regular intervals by his staff while we search the world for calyxera root. So far, we haven't found a single lead on a supplier who produces enough for our needs.

We gravitated to the boardroom tonight, where our laptops were projected onto two massive televisions, and several conference lines were running simultaneously. After ending my latest disappointing call, I stretch and watch Nate make another lap around the room.

He's barefoot, wearing jogging pants that slouch low on his hips and a plain white t-shirt that costs more than everything I have on combined. His voice is harsh, brutal, and demanding as he rattles off instructions to another team at Bell Capital, culminating in the same request—find another source of calyxera root, or you'll be fired.

But I'm the one who should be fired.

I stumbled upon the email in my sent folder that started this nightmare. Everything we're going through is my fault.

"What are you thinking about over there?"

I look at Nate, surprised I missed when he ended his call. He's leaning against a round globe carved out of limestone with meticulous detail of each continent outlined in gold. His hair has dried into loose curls hanging over his forehead. The dark eyes, usually so intense, carry an unexpected gentleness.

Clearing my throat, I say, "I can't seem to get out of my own way, no matter how hard I try. Just when I get so close to having it all, another obstacle comes up out of nowhere, and I'm in another fight to get past it. One of these days, I'm not sure there will be any fight left in me."

"I don't believe that," Nate says. "If there's one thing I've learned about Leela Jamison, you don't know how to give up on anything. No matter how daunting it seems, you find the silver lining. You believe in yourself and that things will work out, even if you're not sure how. That's one of the best skills an owner and leader can have."

"I've been lucky enough in the past doing that, but maybe my luck is running out," I shrug, looking away. Relying on such a delicate ingredient in the formula for my products was a risk. I knew it when I discovered how rare the root was, yet its effect on hair couldn't be ignored. This was how my products could stand out in a crowded field of ethnic hair care products, and it worked.

"What luck?" Nate asks, scoffing. "Luck hasn't gotten you this far. Your hard work and tenacity have."

"There's a reason no other hair care products use calyxera root. Not only is it a temperamental ingredient, but you can hardly find enough in the world to give any type of security that you'll be able to consistently source products that use it," I say, running my fingers through my hair. My excessively glossy and tangle-free mane due to the cursed calyxera root. "Why did I think that things would be different for me? Sure, I found the company in Brazil and entered into the long-term contract to source the root for years, but there are other risks that I just ignored."

"No one could've predicted a fire in the rainforest. That's one of those business risks that are too low to let drive decision making," Nate counters. "Don't beat yourself up over this."

"They set the fire to burn trash, and it got out of hand! This fire never should've happened. The company was run by people with no experience. Their processes were shoddy at best. If it wasn't this fire, I'm sure there would've been something else that would've gone wrong. I just wanted to give a small, up-and-coming business a chance like I wished others had done for me. I got no help because all I had was a dream, a high school diploma, and a cosmetology license. No one believed in me. So, I had to do everything the hard way," I insist. "But again, I made a bad decision about that stupid calyxera root. My company is suffering because of it. If we can't find more …" I shake my head, my breaths coming quick to the point of hyperventilating.

"What do you mean, 'again'? What other wrong decision did you make?" Nate crosses the room to sit next to me.

I freeze, refusing to look at him. How did I slip up and say that? The secret I haven't told anyone. He's so close I can smell the heady scent of his cologne, luring me into a daze.

"Leela," Nate says, his hand resting on my thigh. "What happened before?"

"Nothing. Forget my crazy ramblings," I say, then force a smile on my face. "This is why I'm the one who listens and gives advice, not the one who spews all her problems." I twist my hair into a top-knot bun, then mumble, "Not that I have any friends to tell anyway."

His gaze makes me uneasy as if he's reading the truth from the canvas of my soul.

"What? Why are you looking at me like that?" I swipe at my mouth, hoping there are no crumbs from the decadent ham and gruyere stuffed croissant I devoured minutes earlier.

"You don't have any friends?" There's no incredulity in his tone, just a desire for … confirmation.

I freeze as a few people come to mind—Olivia, my managers, Mischa, Sade, Precious, and Faye. But those are all work friends. Once we leave for the day, I don't have any contact with them. It's not like we're hanging out and doing what real friends do after hours or on the weekends. I spend that time alone at home while Mama and Daddy watch one of Harold's concerts on television for the hundredth time.

Nate's gaze hasn't left my face.

He wants an answer, so I give him the truth.

"Not … really." I'm embarrassed and saddened to admit it. Growing up, I spent so many days falling over myself to be the friendly, helpful one. Hoping that I'd be accepted and liked and have friends once everyone could see how nice and generous I am. But all I got was used and ridiculed for being the big girl. Nothing I did ever mattered to the girls at school. Graduating was a relief because I could finally stop trying. But I'm not sharing that sad story with Nate.

"Family?"

"Not that I can talk to like that." I shudder thinking of the rebuke I'd receive from Daddy if he knew a fraction of what I deal with at my company. He'd insist I should throw in the towel and work for one of Mr. Sabra's salons.

Nate drags a hand down his face. "I'm not the easiest guy in the world to be around, but I have Willow and a small group of true friends I can talk to about anything. I don't know how anyone can make it without a support system."

"It's possible …" I look away. The last thing I want to see is pity in his eyes.

Nate reaches for a strand of my hair, twisting it between his fingers. "I can be that friend for you."

"Why would you do that?"

"Because you need one."

"But you're my boss."

"Not right now. Anything you tell me won't be used against you in our professional relationship," Nate says, then crosses a heart over his chest. "I kept our kisses out of our work relationship … for the most part. That should show you I can be trusted."

My face flames with heat.

"You're so cute when you blush."

"Black people with my skin tone don't blush. No way you can see that."

The smile that spreads across his lips proves I'm right. He says, "So, I was right. I did make you blush."

"You sneaky …"

"Tell me what mistake you made. It'll be good to get it off your chest," Nate persists. "And if coming clean doesn't make you feel better, then you can ask me for anything, and I'll give it to you."

I bite my bottom lip as I look up at him. "Anything?"

CHAPTER 34

L EELA

~

"W AIT ..." N ATE RAISES A HAND, A SMIRK ON HIS LIPS. "T HIS offer isn't from your boss. Not Nate Bell, the acting CEO of Bell Capital. But from just me, personally, to you, yes."

Chewing on my bottom lip, I wonder if Nate is right. Wonder how good it would feel to unload all my dirty laundry and baggage right at his feet and have him do ... what?

Have him do what I need. Look at it with me and say, yeah, that sucks. But you can do this. I spend so much time encouraging myself because no one else thinks I need it. Yet, Nate is offering me precisely that. And it's what I've wanted for years.

"Okay. But promise me this will not impact any business decision related to Sybille Organics," I say, double-checking.

Nate squeezes my hand. "Promise."

"You already know a lot of this. I negotiated with GrabHub to pay us in advance for the products because I knew we didn't have enough cash flow to produce an order that large."

Nate is quiet, waiting patiently for me to continue.

"But the other issue was that our factory didn't have the capacity to produce at that level. I needed to outsource to a bigger factory. One that cared as much about natural ingredients and quality as we did. I found one, and all the stars aligned for us to do the production run and get the shipment to GrabHub months before the deadline, which I hoped would convince them to extend our contract," I say, then pause as my heart pounds in my chest. I'm reliving the moment all over again as tears prick my eyes. "When we got a sample of the completed shipment, something was wrong. The calyxera root hadn't been added in."

"I heard they botched the production run. How was that your mistake?" Nate asks, his fingers caressing circles on my palm.

"I took the lead with the factory and worked directly with them, providing everything they needed, including our proprietary formulas for the Herbal Root Essence products. But I sent them an outdated formula that didn't include the calyxera root." I bang my fist against the couch. "Then, I made it worse by signing off on the wrong formula … twice. Quick cursory reviews because I never fathomed I'd make a mistake." Clenching my eyes shut, I continue, "When the formula didn't include calyxera root, they figured it was sent as an ingredient by mistake and threw it away. They trusted my sign-offs and produced based on the formula I insisted was correct." I swipe at the tear rolling down my cheek. "Everything was my fault. I couldn't sue them. There was no recourse but to try to raise money and start the production run over again." I glance at Nate, who looks unimpressed with my big reveal.

"You did good," Nate says, squeezing my hand. "I'm sure it was hard on the employees to find out why the products had to be thrown out, but you got them back focused on moving forward."

"I never told them."

"You didn't? Why not?"

"Because they would've stopped trusting me and my decision-making. They rely on me to make sound decisions for their livelihoods. I didn't want to disappoint them. Not until I exhausted every option to make things right."

Nate frowns. "You don't owe anybody perfection, Leela. Not your employees, not your family, and not me. You're allowed to make mistakes and not feel you have to hide them from the world."

"Easy for you to say. No one will think twice about a mistake you make because of the billion-dollar fortune attached to the Bell name. It's different for us regular folks."

"Only if you allow it to be different," Nate says, his words resonating within me. "I'm telling you to stop allowing it. That's within your control."

"Maybe you're right," I say, leaning back on the couch.

"I'm always right," Nate says, smiling. "So how do you feel now?"

"Like I just missed out on asking you for … anything," I admit, my gaze betraying me by dropping to his lips. "I should go now. It's late."

Nate's head tilts to the side as he looks at me with a softness in his eyes. "I know that was hard," he says, his voice gentle and understanding. "But I'm here if you ever want to talk again."

My heart swells with emotion at his words.

"And as a reward for your courage, I'll give you what you would've asked me for."

A hint of a challenge creeps into my voice as I say, "You don't know what I would've asked for."

Nate leans closer to me. His fingers tangle in my hair, sending shivers down my spine. His voice is low and husky as he asks, "Don't I?" Before I can respond, his lips brush against my neck, delighting me with soft kisses that trail a path toward my lips. A soft moan escapes me as his mouth meets mine in a passionate kiss. Warmth consumes my body, and I let all my worries fade away. I focus only on Nate. His lips are insistent, claiming mine as we move in perfect sync. Every inch of my body ignites under his touch, powerless to resist him. My arms find their way around his neck. He responds by deepening the kiss, a move I eagerly welcome. Nate takes his time, exploring and teasing my mouth with slow, deliberate caresses that send sparks flying through my veins. It's as if he doesn't want to rush this moment between us, which is both familiar and intoxicating at the same time.

Too soon, Nate pulls away, leaving me breathless. One look in his eyes, and I know why he stopped our kiss and why we have to be careful.

Nate stands and offers his hand to me. "Come on, I'll walk you back to the lodge."

I take it without hesitation, but I can't help but wonder if we've crossed a line that we won't be able to come back from.

CHAPTER 35

NATE

~

The view from my Houston office window is dominated by gridlocked cars stretching as far as the eye can see. Dozens of fire trucks race along the shoulder to an accident in the distance. The glowing red and white lights pierce the harsh rays of the morning sun.

A perfect metaphor for my life.

I'm the firefighter heading straight toward the wreck in the distance.

Drawn to the disaster as if I can do something to make it right, knowing that when I get there, I'll only make things worse. But not going isn't an option.

Resisting Leela isn't in the cards anymore.

Not after last night.

She opened up to me. Showed me a vulnerability—a sadness and loneliness I never expected her to have. The woman with the vibrant and bold personality, luring people with heart and sass, is the same woman who goes home and deals with all her problems alone. Every move she makes puts the needs of others above her own, hiding truths they can't handle. Protecting herself from their disappointing looks, ridicule, and ire. The strength she has to do that amazes me. But just because she's strong enough doesn't mean she should. The gratitude in her eyes wasn't lost on me when I offered a shoulder to unload her burdens. She needed to vent, and she trusted me to listen. Trusted me with secrets she didn't want anyone else to know.

It made me feel …

I want more with her, even if I shouldn't.

And I wasn't raised to walk away from things I want.

Grabbing my phone, I call Peter.

He answers on the first ring. "Yes, sir?"

"Oh, I'm sir now?" I scoff.

Peter laughs. "What can I do for you, Nate?"

"Tell the staff not to park their crappy cars in front of the lodge. I saw one out front when I walked Leela back last night. We have an employee parking lot for a reason," I say, irritation clawing at me as I try to figure out how to broach the topic of the real reason I'm calling without Peter seeing through me.

"That crappy car is … Leela's."

"That's her car?" I lean back in the chair, scratching my eyebrow. Then I remember the intel from before our deal—her paltry salary, living with her parents to funnel all money back into her business. It all makes sense. Makes me understand and admire her more.

"She asked if she could park it out front. Your explicit instructions were to give the lady any and everything she wanted. Would you like me to encourage her to park it elsewhere?"

"No, don't say anything," I say, then explain why I called. "I need to contact Willow's personal shopper at the Chanel store. I'm going to make a purchase." I hold my breath as I wait for Peter's response.

He's quiet, then says, "That's Tania. I'll arrange for her to be at your office in an hour. Anything else?"

I'm stunned he doesn't grill me for details like he usually would, but I take the small win where I can get it. "No."

I drop my phone on the desk.

Leela is always thinking about others. It's about time she learns what it feels like to have someone thinking of her.

Nine long hours later, I ease into the seat next to Willow and buckle my seatbelt as the helicopter lifts toward the indigo night sky. The city's bright lights drown out any chance of seeing the stars. A view I'll be treated to once we get closer to the hill country.

"Mom was right," Willow says, breaking the silence.

"She usually is," I agree, then add, "he's always in a much better mood after you've stopped by for a visit. But you … aren't."

Willow looks out the window. "It's hard to see him like that. He doesn't even seem like Dad, you know. A shadow of the powerful, boisterous man I always relied on to be there for me. I hate it."

"We all do. But it's just temporary," I say, then reach for her chin, turning her head to face me. "He's going to get better, and you'll wish for this quieter version of him."

"From your lips …" Willow says, then glances down at the bag between my legs. "Shopping at Chanel? For who?"

"None of your business." I reach over and pinch her nose. An action reminiscent of when we were little kids. She shakes free of my grasp, then slaps my hand. Hard.

"Ouch," I mutter, then turn to the window. The houses perched on the hilltops of our property come into view, each sprawling complex illuminated in soft lights as a beacon of home.

I can feel Willow's stare, but I don't turn around.

I'm in no mood to explain myself to her.

That day will come, but it's not today.

Willow leans forward and rests a hand on the pilot's shoulder to get his attention. "Change in plans. We're dropping Nate off first …"

She gives me a sly look, then continues, "At the Painted Lady Lodge. Then you can take me home."

I glance at my sister, but she looks down at her phone, pretending to be busy checking emails, and doesn't give me a second look.

She's giving me a pass that I'll gladly take.

CHAPTER 36

I WALK ACROSS THE GRASSY KNOLL IN THE DARK AS THE breeze from the helicopter whips my clothes and hair into a frenzy. As I approach the front door, I hold onto the black bag with a death grip. Leela's car is parked along the curb under the massive oak tree beside the house. It's almost nine in the evening, but I'm not surprised her lights are still on.

I jog up the steps and stop in front of the door. All the houses on our land are equipped with video surveillance and the most elite facial recognition technology that will unlock any door or window when any of us approach. I don't need to ring the doorbell as the door unlocks, but I do anyway.

As the door swings open, I swear there's no way I could've prepared myself for what I see. Leela stands in the doorway. Her hair is pulled away from her face and tucked into a swirling bun on top of her head. She's wearing a white tank top and coral terry cloth shorts that showcase every God-given curve she was blessed with. I'm careful not to let drool leak from my lips as I drink in the sight of her. Her hazel eyes come alive, the flecks of gold sparkling under the lights as her thick lashes rapidly blink. We stare at each other for a long moment, neither of us speaking.

"Hi …" her voice is higher pitched than usual. "I wasn't expecting you to come by." She pauses, then tugs at the hem of her shorts to pull them lower on her thighs. Realizing the futility of her efforts and what she might reveal if she succeeds, she stops. A slight frown forms between her eyebrows. I resist the urge to kiss it away.

"You look beautiful," I announce, then clear my throat. "Stop frowning and stop messing with your clothes." I stare at her thighs for more seconds than I should before glancing back at her face.

She's trying to fight it, but that stunning smile plays in the corner of her lips. I'm glad I'm the one who put it there.

I lift the bag and thrust it in her face.

"What's this?" She asks, taking it from my hands.

"A real Chanel to replace your fake one," I blurt out, then cringe when I see her reaction. A mixture of shame, embarrassment, and mortification crosses her features.

Not what I intended.

She recovers quickly and laughs too loud. The sound is as fake as her purse and not nearly as delightful as her real one. "You think my Chanel is fake? What do you know about designer bags?"

"I learned a few things from being dragged by my sister to Paris Fashion Week for too many years to count," I say, then cross my arms over my chest. "One of her favorite things to do when we're there is to have them close down the Chanel store so she can shop in peace." I form air quotes as I say the last two words. "Plus, the only reason you'd have a basic black Chanel is because it's harder to tell it's a fake that way. But that color is too dull and mundane for the vibrant woman you are."

Her facade crumbles. She lowers the bag to the ground.

"I didn't do this to embarrass you. I would never do anything to hurt you."

"So why did you?"

"Because I wanted you to know what it feels like for someone to take care of you like you take care of others."

"What are you talking about?" She looks genuinely confused.

"How many business owners bring breakfast to their managers every morning? You remember employees' birthdays and send them hand-written notes with a gift card paid for by you, not the company. You're always showing people how much you appreciate them. This is no different."

"It's very different. Chanel purses cost over ten thousand dollars. All of those things cost me next to nothing—"

"Which you buy from a salary that's a fraction of what you're paying them."

She looks stunned as she realizes I've found out another one of her secrets.

I continue, "And to me, that purse costs ... next to nothing. It's a small way of showing you that you're appreciated."

"So, this is a work gift?"

I scoff, wanting to shake some sense into her. "No. Will you at least look at it? It took me over an hour to pick the perfect one." And judging by what she's wearing, I know without a doubt I got it right.

"You picked this out, yourself?" Her words are slow, and I think she's going into shock.

I jerk the bag open and pull out the large box, resting it in my arms in front of her.

Leela gasps as she runs a hand over the white letters on the black box, then along the white Chanel stamped ribbon tied in a bow. "The box is too gorgeous. I don't need to see what's inside."

"Open it."

She takes a deep breath and removes the bow, looping it around her arm. Lifting the lid, she gasps.

"The purse is in a dust bag!" She lifts it out of the box like a kidney for a transplant, then cradles the purse.

I lower the box.

"No! Do not put that on the ground," she yells.

I laugh and slip it back into the black bag.

She gently pulls the classic quilted Chanel bag from its dust bag, its double C clasp and leather-laced chain strap in a shade I knew immediately was made for her.

"It's coral." she stares at the purse, then down at her shorts, which match perfectly. "My favorite color. How did you know?"

"It tends to pop up more often than not in your clothes. A safe guess. You like it?"

"I love it, Nate. I can't even tell you how much this means to me." She hugs the purse tight to her chest. "No one has ever bought me such a thoughtful and expensive gift." She shakes her head. "I can't accept this."

I cup her face with my hand. "You can and you will. Don't ever turn a gift from me down." My words have a harsh edge that I hate, but she needs to know that refusing my gift would gut me. "Just say thank you."

She relaxes and gives me a beautiful smile. "Thank you, Nate."

I stuff my hands in my pockets and take a few steps back from the door.

"Wait. You're leaving?"

I love the disappointment in her voice, but it's also why I have to distance myself from her.

"I have more work to do," I say, turning my back on her. Then add, "And so do you."

CHAPTER 37

L EELA

~

"WHAT ARE YOU DOING OUT HERE?"

I turn around, startled by the presence of another person on the deserted trail. My eyes land on Nate, and even though I know he's no danger to me, I can't stop the scream that rips from my throat.

He rushes toward me, bare-chested and glistening with sweat.

"Are you okay? Did you see a snake? Did it bite you?" He drops to his knees onto the leaves of the forest floor, checking my legs and ankles. His strong hands grip and caress my skin, sending tingles shooting through every cell of my body.

I close my eyes as I pant and try to calm my racing heart.

The effect this man has on me is criminal.

"No, I'm sorry," I say, reaching down to stop his hands. "You just scared me." My fingers linger on top of his as he gazes up at me with concern in his dark orbs. Slipping his hands in mine, I help him up, ignoring the jolts I feel from his touch. The hands I'd love to wrap around me and lose myself in the feel of his body next to mine.

"I'm fine."

"You're not fine. Where is your hiking guide?"

"I told Peter I didn't need one …"

Nate's frown deepens. "He still should have a guide shadowing you in case you get lost. At a distance so you can still have some space."

"He did mention that, but I told him it wasn't necessary." I reach into my pocket and pull out the small silver disc. "He gave me this tracker instead and told me if I get lost or need help, to push this button, and security would be able to find me in ten minutes or less."

"It only takes a bobcat five minutes to tear you from limb to limb. That tracker is useless," Nate says, reaching for his phone and quickly typing on the device.

"What are you doing?"

"Alerting security of where you are so they can send a few hikers to the area," Nate says without apology. "I'll tell them to be discreet and not to bother you. The preserve is a natural habitat. You shouldn't be out here alone."

"You're out here alone," I challenge.

"Yeah, but I'm packing," he responds.

And I can't help but think he most definitely is …

Nate motions to a small gun clipped to a holster half-hidden beneath the waistband of his shorts. "Tranquilizer gun in case I meet a friend on the path."

"Who knew you had a boy scout in you? Always prepared, right?"

"Not always," he admits, as his gaze lingers on my body.

The way this man looks at me is enough to drive me bonkers. At first, I didn't believe him when he said he thought my plus-size body was attractive. How many people give big girls throw-away comments like that? Too many. But Nate isn't nice enough to lie to me about what he thinks about anything. And the look in his eyes when he sees me tells me he most definitely prefers my thickness over any slim woman.

I push the thoughts away and move to a safer topic: work.

"I may have a lead on a supply of calyxera root," I say. With only six weeks left until the deadline to ship our products to GrabHub, we're running out of time to salvage the deal.

"You serious?" Nate looks hopeful.

"My ex owns an oil sheen business. He tried to use calyxera root in his products but couldn't get it to work. He heard about the root possibly growing in remote parts of Hawaii. So, I'll make calls to some folks I know there."

Nate glares at me. "Your ex gave you this information?"

"Is that all you heard from everything I said?"

"Hawaii. I'll tell the team to get some resources on reaching out to our contacts, too," Nate says, then squats to sit on a rock. "Tell me about this ex."

It's not a request. Dodging his demand for information won't work. I find a bigger rock a few feet away from Nate to sit on. "Things didn't end well between us. He tried to steal one of my formulas. Long story."

"You loved him?" Nate asks abruptly.

I scoff, shaking my head. "No." My lips twitch into a smirk as I add, "Not even close."

Nate looks pleased with my response. "You ever been in love?"

"That's a strange question." I flick a twig out of the way with my shoe, aiming for nonchalant, but his question triggers too many of my own. Why is he asking me this?

"I'm in a strange mood," he says, shrugging. "That's why I came out here—to clear my head."

"Because you're thinking about … love?" I can't help teasing, though my voice softens at the last word. It feels dangerous, like saying it out loud with us alone, together, might summon it here.

He grunts in response, his eyes fixed on the path ahead. "Answer my question."

The chirps of the birds fill the silence as I wrestle with myself.

I know the answer, but I'm not sure I want Nate to know. I don't know what he'll think of me. Then I shake my head. Nate is the one person who, without a doubt, doesn't judge me. No matter what I say, he won't think any better or worse of me. I take a deep breath, the tangy scent of juniper filling my lungs, and say, "No."

He kicks a rock off the trail's edge, watching it tumble into the brush below. "Think you'd know if you did?"

"I hope so," I say quietly. "How about you? How many times have you loved and lost?"

He chuckles, low and almost self-deprecating. "Come on now. With my personality and attitude, I'm surprised you have to ask."

"Trust me," I say, biting back a grin. "Women are known for falling in love with much worse than you. You're not bad—once you get used to the abrupt, snippy, rude way you talk to people." I raise a brow at him, enjoying the rare moment when he doesn't have a comeback ready. "But it's not mean-spirited. You've got a caring heart underneath all that prickliness."

"Surprised you noticed."

"Were you trying to hide it from me?" I shoot back, teasing lightly.

"No." He shakes his head, his voice softening. "But most people don't take the time to see beyond the surface, you know."

"Yes," I say simply. "I do."

He glances over, studying me for a beat longer than feels comfortable. "Is that why you've never fallen in love?" His tone shifts, quieter, more probing. "Dated a bunch of idiot guys who loved your giving and positive nature but weren't smart enough to know they should give the same back to you in return?"

The words hit harder than expected, and I laugh awkwardly to cover it. "Maybe ... That's insightful. Disturbingly so."

Nate chuckles, a knowing look in his eyes. "You're a textbook people pleaser, which isn't bad. There's nothing wrong with being selfless or wanting to help others and make them feel good. But you can't do that at the expense of your happiness."

A hollow ache creeps into my chest. I look away, focusing on the trail ahead, where the path narrows between two large boulders. "It gets exhausting," I admit. "To be the one giving and doing for the other person all the time. Then you second-guess yourself. Does he love me, or does he love that I drop everything to make him happy? If I stopped, would he leave? Would he even care? Or would he move on to the next woman willing to do what I wouldn't?" I shrug, trying to sound breezy, though my words are anything but. Some kind of way, I convinced myself that doing things for people would make them like me. Want to keep me around, but it never actually worked out that way. I never got the close relationships I yearned for, but I didn't let that stop me from being who I am.

"That's why I don't bother with serious relationships anymore. A few nice guys to go out with when I'm bored is all I need," I admit.

"Liar," Nate says, deadpan.

I bolt up from the rock. "I am not lying!" Before I know it, I'm only a foot away from him. He smirks up at me, not buying my protest. I lean against the tree near him, the rough bark scratching my skin. "Okay," I say slowly, "maybe at some point in the future, I'll open myself up to finding love. But I don't have time for that now."

"Because you're too focused on saving your business."

"Exactly." I nod emphatically, relieved he's dropped the subject of my nonexistent love life. "That's the only thing I should be focused on."

"Should be?" His brow lifts. "Like there's some other competition for your attention?"

I shoot him a wry look. "You know, you pay way too much attention to detail."

"I'm a master at nuances," Nate replies, grinning. He should smile more. He's infinitely more handsome when he lets himself do that. "It's what makes me the best at what I do. So, what have you been focused on that you shouldn't have been?"

Kissing you is the answer.

But I can't say that.

Not since we moved past all the weirdness the kisses created between us. As hot as Nate is and as intoxicating as his kisses are, if I had to choose between one more kiss with Nate and one more moment like this, talking to a man who understands me, I'd definitely choose the latter.

But it would be a close race. Super close.

Like 50.01% to 49.99%.

The kind that would require a recount ... by humans and by hand ...

I clear my throat. "I'm not answering any more of your questions until you answer mine."

"I thought I did," Nate says, feigning innocence.

"Liar," I say, then brace myself for the answer I already know and ... hate.

CHAPTER 38

LEELA

~

"I saw the bench swing down the hill near the field of daisies with the carving. A heart. HRR and NB forever in the center," I blurt out before he can say another word. My envy stings like tiny ants attacking my skin.

Nate is quiet for a long moment, his jaw clenched tight.

"Harlow Rose Robinson," he says, his voice low and rough with emotion.

"You loved her?" I ask softly.

"She's the only one. High school sweetheart." Nate plucks a leaf from a nearby tree and studies it. "That kind of thing never lasts."

"It lasted for my parents," I interject. "They started dating in ninth grade and have been together forever since and still so much in love. It's annoying, actually."

Nate huffs out a humorless laugh. "What's annoying is loving someone with your whole heart and finding out she doesn't believe you do. Worse than that, she doesn't even think you're capable of that kind of love."

My heart clenches painfully in my chest. "Please tell me that's not what happened between you and Harlow-Rose. That's awful."

"She broke up with me after graduation to protect her heart because she knew I didn't love her like she loved me. She knew," Nate says bitterly. "The truth is she never knew me at all. Still doesn't."

"Do you still have feelings for her?" I ask, almost afraid to hear his answer.

The look in his eyes is louder than any response he could give. I can't breathe when he looks at me that way. He did it the first time we kissed and the second time. The same look he gave me when he convinced me to let my guard down and tell him about my mistake. And the look he gave when he warned me not to refuse a gift from him ... ever. I won't think about what it means because it can't mean anything. Not while my company is on the brink of disaster.

"For the record, I'm not in love with Harlow-Rose anymore," Nate says firmly. "Haven't been for almost a decade. Still, she's important to me. Still has the power to hurt me."

"You say that like something has happened recently," I note cautiously.

Nate nods, his jaw tight. "She's engaged."

"Oh ..."

"Don't give me that look," Nate grumbles. "I'm happy for her. She's in love with a decent guy who makes her happy, and that's all I've ever wanted for her."

"Let me get this straight. You don't love her. No residual feelings for her anywhere deep inside?"

"That's right," he confirms with a decisive nod.

"You just want her to be happy, and she is."

"Yep." Nate pops the 'p' for emphasis.

I tilt my head, studying him intently. "So what about their engagement hurt you?"

Nate exhales heavily, shoving his hands deeper into his pockets as he gazes into the trees. "I heard about her engagement through a mutual friend. She didn't tell me herself. She hasn't said a single word to me since it happened."

"Maybe she's trying to be considerate," I suggest gently. "You have a lot on your plate, Nate. She might be waiting for things to ease up before talking to you about it. Especially if she's not sure you want to hear how happy she is when you're dealing with so much right now."

Nate shoots me an exasperated look tinged with fondness. "You just can't help yourself, can you? You don't even know Harlow-Rose, and you're already stepping up and trying to put a positive spin on her actions."

I shrug, a small smile playing on my lips. "I'm giving you a different perspective that happens to be glass half full because that's just who I am. Have you thought about reaching out to her?"

"I've been ... distracted ... like you said. A lot of things on my plate right now," Nate admits gruffly.

"Is that the only reason?" I press, sensing there's more he's not saying.

Nate's gaze snaps to mine, his eyes dark and intense. "Are you asking if you make me forget all about Harlow-Rose?"

The air between us shifts, the space too small, too charged. My cheeks flame, and I sputter, "Of course not. I mean, I know we kissed a few times, but we agreed not to do that anymore, and it has nothing to do with her—or with me—or, I mean, I couldn't possibly be a distraction for you ..." I trail off, clamping my mouth shut.

"When I'm around you, you make me forget every woman I've ever dated." His voice is low and steady like he's delivering a simple, undeniable truth. He stands, closing the distance between us, his expression torn between frustration and something softer, something achingly vulnerable. "So it's good," he says quietly, "that you're an employee of Bell Capital and off-limits to me. I can't have more than a professional relationship with you, no matter how much I want to."

I swallow hard, my pulse roaring in my ears. "Or how much I want you to," I whisper.

Nate groans, raking a hand through his hair. "Do not say that to me ever again."

"Right," I say, nodding furiously. "I will keep those thoughts to myself."

"Don't have those thoughts. Not about me." He exhales heavily and takes a step back. "I'll let you get back to your walk."

I don't move. "Nate?"

He pauses, looking back over his shoulder. "Yes?"

"I know we can't get involved with each other, but I like you. Despite your grumpy, moody tendencies."

Nate laughs, the rich, warm sound wrapping around me like a hug. It's a sound I could get used to hearing.

"I'm beyond grateful that we've become friends. Real friends."

Nate's eyes soften, crinkling at the corners as he smiles. "So am I."

With that, he turns and jogs away, disappearing around a bend in the trail. I stand there for a long moment, watching the spot where he vanished, a silly grin on my face.

CHAPTER 39

L EELA

~

THE WHOOSHING OF HELICOPTER BLADES PIERCES MY
sleep, jerking me awake. I glance at the clock—a quarter to six in the
morning and my heart sinks. Reaching for the lamp on the nightstand,
I turn it on and stumble out of bed toward the massive windows. The
helicopter lifts into the sky. I watch it as it becomes smaller and
smaller, taking Nate away from me for the day.

A sobering thought slips into my head.

I miss him.

I should not have these thoughts about Nate.

It's wrong to have these kinds of feelings for my boss. The man
who makes the entire company feel like idiots who can't live up to his
impossible standards. Whose feedback is quick and brutally honest,
leaving bleeding egos and shattered confidences in his wake.

But he's also the caring and generous guy who allowed me to

confide my worst fears without being judged. And the man who recognized there's merit in our different leadership styles. He's the guy I can talk to for hours about everything and nothing, and I never feel uncomfortable or tired of being around him. I'm not even going to remind myself of the off-the-charts physical attraction.

Facts—we agreed to ignore our attraction to each other and keep our interactions professional. But that was before we crossed the line from work colleagues to friends. Real friends.

Yesterday, after hiking for an hour, I finished the trail, which happened to end right at the back of Nate's home. He sat on the veranda with his laptop and a conference call blasting from a set of unseen speakers. The minute he saw me, he beckoned for me to join him. We spent the rest of the day closing deals on distributing my original hair care line to a major retailer in Canada and another in the UK. It was exhilarating to work side-by-side with him, negotiating and strategizing to get more exposure for my products.

But it wasn't all work and no play.

In between, we had too much time to get to know each other better. Shared experiences from our pasts, funny stories, embarrassing moments, dreams of the future. We opened up to each other in ways I think surprised the both of us.

There's so much more to Nate Bell than people realize.

And that's why I'm falling for him.

My cell phone chirps. Groaning, I gaze away from the helicopter and flop onto the bed. Who could be texting me at this hour? I swipe the screen.

NATE BELL

Sorry to wake you. Go back to sleep.

A dreamy sigh escapes my lips as I clutch my phone to my chest. This man …

How do you know I'm not sleep?

Are you sleeptexting me???

LOL! Like sleepwalking??? No!

So, I'm right.

Answer my question.

Saw your bedroom light come on as we took off. Figured the noise woke you.

So you were looking at my bedroom. why?

Nate is typing …

Thinking about you

Wishing I was with you

I jump from the bed and race around the room, dancing happily as I clutch the phone. Glancing back at his texts, I hover my finger over the device, eager to respond but hesitant.

Nate is under tremendous pressure to live up to expectations as the acting CEO while his father is on medical leave. I can only imagine his feelings for me are a connection he craves and a distraction he can't afford. That's why he's hiding behind the corporate fraternization policy to put a wall between us.

But somewhere deep down, he has to know I'd never do anything to hurt him. I want him to be successful—to prove to everyone that he is more than capable of handling the responsibility he was given.

That has to be why he keeps telling me how he feels. To show me what's building between the two of us can't be denied. I've waited so long for a man who makes me feel like Nate. He needs to know he's not alone in this. I feel the same way he does.

I type slowly and press send.

Me too

Is this crazy?

Yes

So we should stop, right?

Nate is typing …
Then, the status disappears.
He doesn't respond.
And that's the only answer I need.
A smile spreads across my face as I reach over and turn the lamp light off.

CHAPTER 40

L EELA

~

NATE'S ADVICE ABOUT NOT HIDING MY MISTAKES HAD BEEN gnawing at me, so I did it—I came clean to the employees about the supply issues with calyxera root. Standing in the middle of our production floor, my voice wavered only once as I explained the uphill battle to meet our shipment deadline had gotten much steeper.

I took a page from Nate's approach and delivered a straightforward and brutally honest assessment without my usual upbeat spunk and pizazz. The employees were riveted as I ended with a somber truth. "I know this isn't the news anyone wants to hear, but I wanted to be transparent with all of you."

What floored me wasn't their response—which was overwhelmingly supportive—but my resolve to accept the consequences either way. Despite the bad news, I didn't trip over myself trying to find ways to make them still like me.

Heads nodded, ideas flew back and forth, and they all seemed confident that Nate and I would figure it out. That kind of blind faith in us was terrifying but also oddly exhilarating.

Still, the emotional cost of that confession left me drained. I wanted to rush into Nate's office and talk to him about it, but he was at the Houston office. So, instead, I took a drive into Kimbell to grab lunch.

Downtown Kimbell is quaint in the way only small towns can be. Parking my car in an open space along the main boulevard, I step out and inhale deeply. The air smells of fresh-cut grass and something faintly sweet—honeysuckle, maybe? A handful of people sit at wrought-iron tables on the sidewalk patio of Brewed Awakening Coffeehouse, sipping iced coffees and chatting under the shade of striped umbrellas. A chalkboard easel in front of the entrance lists the day's specials and a promise of the best pecan pie in Texas, but I barely glance at it.

Instead, my attention drifts toward the sprawling park in the distance. It's immaculate, with emerald-green grass that stretches out in all directions and is dotted with towering oak and juniper trees. A majestic carved limestone sign on the corner proudly declares it Bell Park. Beneath the letters, the fine print reads, "Established 1888— Donated by the Bell Family."

Nate's family.

His family name seems to be etched into every corner of this town, from the stately courthouse perched on a hill overlooking the town to the clock tower, street signs, and antique plaques on historic buildings. Their influence is undeniable. A sense of history and tradition that permeates every corner of Kimbell.

I can almost picture Nate shrugging off his family's influence like it's no big deal when it is an enormously big one. Intrigued to find out more, I cross the street toward the park and the sounds of children laughing. The air feels cooler here, shaded by the canopy of trees. A gazebo looms ahead, painted in pristine white, its string lights draped like delicate lace. I can imagine it glowing after sunset, a slice of magic tucked into this unassuming corner of the world.

I pause at the edge of the grass, dodging a soccer ball that rolls perilously close to my ankle, and dig my phone out of my pocket. Framing the gazebo just so, I snap a few photos.

"Beautiful shot," a woman's voice floats from behind me. "Too bad it's cursed …"

I frown and turn to look at her. "The gazebo is cursed?"

She laughs, tucking a strand of fire-red hair behind her ears. "This gazebo has been the spot for bad luck lately."

"The last thing I need is any bad luck. Were crimes committed here?" I ask, intrigued.

"Crimes?" She scoffs, then laughs. "Only of the heart. Folks around town have started to call it the 'Oh no gazebo.' If your mate asks you to meet up there, it's not good for the relationship's future."

"This place is too beautiful to be used for that!" I say, shaking my head. "What a shame."

"I know. But it would only take one marriage proposal or first kiss to turn things around," she says with a smile. "I'm sorry, where are my manners? I'm Mrs. Wilkerson, the Community Event Planner for Kimbell, Texas." She extends her hand toward me.

"I'm Leela Jamison. Not sure if you've heard about—"

"Sybille Organics move here? Well, of course, I have. And you have been at the top of my list as a person to meet for weeks," she says, looking proud of herself. "You know our great town is built on the legacy of strong women entrepreneurs. Our founding mother, Kimberly Bell, had several businesses, including a hair salon, before she settled into banking."

"Is that so?"

"And that's why I was delighted to hear about Bell Capital investing in your business and bringing it to town. We are so excited that you and your employees are here."

"Everyone has been lovely and welcoming to all of us. The town is charming, and I've enjoyed exploring on those rare days when I force myself to take a break from work."

"And I'm sure your employees need a break, too. With the uptick in visitors to our town, I've been working on a fun activity that will help tourists get to know our town better—a scavenger hunt," Mrs. Wilkerson says. "It's nearly complete, and it just dawned on me that it would make a great team-building exercise for a company like yours. One that has a lot of employees that aren't familiar with the new town they work in."

"That sounds like a great idea. I'm a big proponent of team-building activities. I recently had games added to our factory for that very purpose," I say, loving her idea and energy.

"Great, so I'll send you some dates and an invoice," Mrs. Wilkerson beams. "This is going to be so fun. I know you and your company will enjoy it."

"Well … I'm not sure we're ready to commit just yet—"

"No worries, I'll get it scheduled for a day after the big shipment deadline I've heard you have," she adds, face full of understanding. "I'll throw in some celebratory giveaways from some of the businesses in town as an added perk. How does that sound?"

"Good … I guess." That's all I can muster, feeling railroaded as Mrs. Wilkerson writes quickly on her notepad.

"I'll send over all the documents early next week," Mrs. Wilkerson says. "So good to meet you, Ms. Jamison."

"Yeah, you too …" I say, dragging a hand down my face as she walks away.

"Don't feel bad," a familiar voice calls behind me, deep and smooth as honey.

I whirl around, nearly dropping my phone. Nate stops in front of me. His business jacket is open and tie loose, looking like he walked off the cover of GQ magazine.

A half-smirk plays at his lips as he gives me a sympathetic wink. "Mrs. Wilkerson doesn't take no for an answer. Whatever she's roped you into, we'll cover it."

"Well, that makes me feel better … temporarily," I say, unable to hide the dread snaking through me at his unexpected presence in the park. "Please tell me you're not here to give me bad news."

"I'm not here to give you bad news."

"What happened?"

"That lead you got on Hawaii paid off."

"You found a supplier of calyxera root in Hawaii?"

"I found a family that owns land where calyxera root is growing." He steps closer to me. "Now it's up to us to convince them to sell it."

"And if we do, we can farm the root ourselves," I say, following his thought process. "You know what this means, don't you?"

He replies with the sexiest grin. "It doesn't mean anything if we don't leave right now."

"Leave? Where are we going?"

"To Hawaii … well, Kauai, to be exact," Nate says. "Peter packed bags for both of us and sent them to my plane."

"Your airplane …"

"I don't fly commercial." Nate looks at me as if I'm daft. "Take off is in an hour. My driver is waiting to take us to the airport."

"What about my car? I need to take it back to the lodge."

"There's no time. Leave your keys with my driver, and he'll take care of that."

My mind struggles to comprehend what's happening. I'm about to fly to the Hawaiian islands on a private plane with the man who is driving me wild, hoping to get a root that will make millions for my business.

Is this really my life?

"Leela," Nate says, his tone terse. "We need to go. Now."

He slips his hand in mine as if it's the most natural thing in the world. A flurry of butterflies scurry through my body. It takes every ounce of my willpower not to squeal as he leads me to the Rolls Royce, waiting to whisk us away.

CHAPTER 41

L EELA

～

THE PLANE CREW STANDS ALONG A VELVET BLACK CARPET that leads to a gleaming silver plane. Nate greets each crew member by name as they smile warmly. His hand brushes against the small of my back as we walk up the jetway stairs. A casual gesture that feels intimate. Not like two colleagues heading on a business trip.

I turn toward Nate and ignore the butterflies going berserk inside of me. "So, this is the company jet. Can't say I ever thought I'd be on one. It's surreal."

Nate shakes his head. "The company jet is much better than this. It's a 787 Dreamliner. My jet is just a 747, but it's comfortable enough."

"Just a 747?" I say, glancing around the space that looks more than comfortable. This is nothing like flying coach, with the smell of antiseptic wipes and where overhead bins loom and elbows battle for armrests. It's like entering a penthouse suite.

He laughs. "Don't judge. I'm still just a country boy at heart."

"A country billionaire boy," I clarify, arching a brow at him.

He holds the crook of his arm toward me. I slide my arm in his as he leads me through the forward lounge, galley kitchen, and aft lounge, all luxurious beyond anything I've ever seen.

"Now to the sleeping quarters," Nate announces.

"Wait, there are bedrooms on the plane?"

"Two. I'll take the guest bedroom." He opens the door and lets me peer inside. "And you'll have the master suite."

"No, I couldn't possibly—"

"I insist," Nate says, a warning in his tone that stops me from protesting further. He pushes through the double doors.

The view beyond steals what's left of my breath. A king bed rests in the middle, flanked by nightstands, a crystal lamp sitting on each one. A wardrobe closet and dresser line one side of the room, their dark wood surfaces gleaming. The bathroom is through a door to the right. Inside, a standup shower glistens behind glass doors. Towels rolled into perfect cylinders, their edges embroidered with a tiny silver crest, rest on the counter nearby.

"This is not normal." I shake my head in disbelief.

"It is to me." He falls back onto the king-size bed. "I've never had a normal life, no matter how much I tried or how I wished for it. At some point, you just have to accept the life you've been given, especially when you realize that so many people would love to have the things I have. It feels ungrateful to resent it."

"You resent … this life?" I ask softly, my heart clenching at the wistfulness in his tone as he stares at the ceiling.

"Only when it stops me from having what other people seem to have so easily," Nate says. "You've never had to question people's motives for getting to know you. If they like you for you or your bank account."

"Must have been hard growing up like that," I admit, my heart breaking for him. I flop back onto the bed next to him, gazing up at the silver and crystal chandelier over the bed.

"Not so hard as a kid. Hard as hell as an adult when you can see through people more easily," Nate says.

"Despite the reason for us being in each other's lives, I hope you can tell I know there's so much more to you than your bank account."

"Yep," Nate says, then reaches for a strand of my hair, twirling it around his finger. "I don't have any doubts with you. I can be myself around you. It's comfortable. Nice. Even if I'm not so nice to you all the time."

"That's an understatement!" I laugh. "You are a complex and unpredictable man, but I like it. I like getting to know all the parts of you. I appreciate how you've mentored me since investing in my company. And I appreciate your friendship. Can't say I've had one like this ever." I stop myself before I reveal more.

"You didn't have it easy growing up either, did you?"

I shake my head. "The awkward and chubby kid with wild hair spent a lot of time just me, myself and I. Unlike the movies, the outsider doesn't always find a group of outcasts to be friends with. At least I didn't."

"And the ugly duckling doesn't always become the beautiful swan. Sometimes she transforms into a colorful butterfly," Nate says.

His words pierce my heart. I said them in one of the first videos I posted on social media, pouring out my soul. The one that got so many views and likes. Comments from girls across the country that felt like I did. Comments that saved me and made me feel less alone.

I flip over on my side to gawk at Nate. "You watched that video?"

"I did."

"It has to be almost ten years old. How did you even find it?"

"I might have spent way too many hours poring over your content. For research purposes, of course." His lips curve into a smile. "There's so much to admire about you." His dark eyes smolder with passion as he brushes strands of my hair from my face. His touch lingers, like he's reluctant to let go. The magnetic attraction pulls us closer to each other. His lips press against my neck in a gentle kiss. The heat melts into my skin, and a shiver rolls through me, leaving me helpless.

"Your frustratingly willful positivity." His thumb grazes my jaw tenderly. "Your compassionate strength." His hand rests lightly on my waist, his fingers ghosting over my hip with enough pressure to make me want more. "Your selfless generosity." His kisses move to my collarbone. His breath skates across my skin. I feel like I'm standing too close to an open flame. "You're ... perfect."

I'm breathless as his kisses turn me into putty in his hands. I reach for his face, pulling him to mine. We stare at each other, knowing we're dangerously close to a line we shouldn't cross.

But I don't care.

"Nate—"

He clears his throat. "We need to start prepping for the landowner meeting."

"Right ... now?" I'm stunned, jolted by the abrupt change.

"Yes," he says, slowly removing my hands from his face. "We can't do ... anything ... that would jeopardize securing the calyxera root for the formula."

He's off the bed in seconds, increasing the distance between us.

"Meet me in the forward lounge after you get settled."

CHAPTER 42

N_{ATE}

"WE DID IT!" LEELA SQUEALS, TURNING TOWARD ME WITH A smile that would light up the darkest of worlds. Before I can respond, her arms are wrapped around my neck, hugging me tight. I slip my arms around her waist, pulling her close.

There's only one thought in my head.

She belongs right here … with me.

Forever.

I squeeze my eyes shut, disturbed by the feelings that have haunted me from the first moment I met this woman. Ones that have become impossible to ignore. I lift and spin her around as she giggles with glee, then lower her back to the ground.

"We?" I scoff, remembering how passionately Leela explained her company and the importance of the calyxera root to furthering her mission to bring beauty and confidence to women all around the world. It was serendipity that the owners' daughter uses Sybille Organic's Botanical Essentials products and loves how shiny it makes her hair.

From that moment on, Leela wowed them with her sassiness, and I got more out of the deal than I had ever imagined. She's the best good luck charm I could ever have. The extra land fits perfectly within my plans to prove to everyone that I inherited the Midas touch from my dad. I might even convince the old man himself.

"You did it," I say, inhaling the sweet scent of her hair. "All I did was bring the checkbook."

"Don't do that. Do not downplay your role in this." Leela pulls back. "You were brilliant. I almost fainted when they gave you the amount they wanted for the land. I didn't think you'd go for it."

"I didn't have a choice. If I balked at the price, they might have thought twice about how much land you'd convinced them to part with and pull back on that. The number was high but still within the range of what our models indicated was acceptable to pay."

She looks at me thoughtfully, and I want nothing more than to kiss her. But there will be time for that later.

"If we'd had more time, would you have tried to negotiate a lower price?" she asks.

"The calyxera root is too important to your formula. Drawn-out negotiations increase the likelihood that they could've discovered this."

"And then played hardball to push the cost even higher. Makes sense," she says, walking down the path toward our waiting car. Her thick hair blows in the wind. "I'm still not sure this gives us enough time to meet the shipment deadline. It's only six weeks away."

Her concerns are valid, but failure isn't an option for either of us. "It'll take two weeks to get processes in place to harvest the root from the land. That leaves four weeks to make the products and ship," I say, almost to myself. "With our primary factory working multiple shifts and the automated factory we bought from Willow working round the clock, we'll make the deadline easily."

"I can't wait to get back and give everybody the good news." She tugs at my hands, but I stand firm.

"You'll have to wait," I say, injecting a brusqueness into my tone. I try to keep a straight face, which is getting much harder around Leela.

"Oh, right. The lawyers have to get the paperwork to them and do the official sign-off. How long do you think that will take?"

"That'll be done in the next few hours," I say, having already made the calls to ensure it happens quickly. "You'll have to wait to break the news because we're not flying home tonight."

She stops and turns toward me. Her lips are pressed together as she tries to hide a smile. "Are we staying here? We can't be gone long, but exploring Hawaii would be amazing for a day or two! This is my first time here." She claps her hands. "Please, please say yes."

"After the deal you just pulled off, you more than deserve a mini-vacation to Honolulu."

Leela squeals and jumps with excitement.

"We'll stay at a suite at the Kahala Resort for two nights, hike Diamond Head, have the luau lunch at the Polynesian Culture Center, and get a paddle boarding lesson on the famous Banzai Pipeline on the North Shore," I say, loving the kid-like excitement spreading across her face. "If you knew how to swim, we could've gotten surfing lessons. But I went with the safer option."

"I can't believe you did this for me." She steps closer, eliminating the distance between us.

I trail my finger down her face. "This is just the beginning."

CHAPTER 43

L EELA

~

"You've barely touched your food," Nate says.

He reaches over, scoops up a bite of the poi with his spoon, and then takes a bite. I inhale sharply. Even the sight of him chewing is sexy, especially when his magnificent muscular body is still clad in the skintight wetsuit from our paddle boarding lesson.

"Not a fan of purple mashed potatoes?" Nate chuckles, resting his elbows on the picnic table of the roadside food truck. He levels me with an intense stare that seems to see through to my soul.

"It's ... different. An acquired taste."

"Kind of like me?" Nate asks, grabbing the bowl to finish off the poi.

I smile, then reach for his hand. "I acquired a taste for you from that first kiss in the supply closet. Every moment we're together, it just gets better and better."

"So why do you look so sad?"

"Because this fabulous vacation is almost over." I brush damp, wayward strands of my hair back into the hair tie. "Seriously, I never imagined getting to do any of the things we did today. Hiking Diamond Head before sunrise all by ourselves."

"Kissing you as the sun rose behind you. I'll never forget that picture," Nate says. "Seared into my memory."

"Mine too. Breakfast was amazing, then being whisked off to watch fire knife dancers, dressing up like ancient Polynesian royalty and eating the best Kahlua pig ever."

"And kissing you next to the waterfall as droplets sprayed our skin. I'm loving how you vacation, Leela." Nate says.

"Stop it. I'm trying to be serious here."

"You love kissing me. Admit it."

"So what if I do," I say, then point a finger at him. "I did not initiate any kisses during our paddle boarding lessons. I kept my lips to myself."

"Yeah, I'm kinda ticked off about that. But you'll make up for it later," Nate teases.

"What happens to this when we get back to Kimbell?" I tug at my wetsuit, still damp from frolicking in the Pacific. "As much as I like to see the bright side of every situation—"

"Don't remind me."

"I'm struggling with … this," I say, pointing back and forth between us. "If it were just physical attraction, that would be one thing."

"You can't keep your hands off me—"

"Nate! That is not true," I say, although I did give myself the freedom just this once to be extra affectionate with him as we traipsed across Honolulu.

He frowns and scoffs. "It is true, and I don't mind one bit. But honestly, every morning, I wake up with a conversation in my head that I want to have … with you. It's odd and disturbing."

"And sweet."

"I'm not sweet."

"Prickly pear sweet?"

"Maybe."

"Nate, you've become one of my favorite people in the entire world. I enjoy everything about you—the surly, abrupt, and brutally honest parts and the ooey gooey soft side you only let out once every blue moon."

"I'm waiting for you to tell me the problem," Nate cuts in. "Cause I'm not hearing one."

"You're my boss. We have violated company policy by engaging in this …"

"Relationship," Nate says. "That's the word you're looking for."

"That's what I want for us. But is it what you want?" I'm almost afraid to hear his response, but keeping my thoughts from Nate feels wrong. It's not how we are with each other. If we're not on the same page, he won't pretend. Nate will rip the bandage off quickly and without any remorse. That's what I need. A definitive and clear answer, even if it may not be the one I want.

He looks away toward the crashing waves.

"I know this is complicated. I think this is why we both feel freer to express our feelings here than we ever would back in Kimbell," I say, wanting him to know that I understand the situation, especially how it impacts him as the acting CEO of Bell Capital. "We're two people who against all the odds of how different we are, and man, are we totally different from each other, but we've found this weird common ground and connection that just works for us. And it feels so good and right and natural and like … it's something we shouldn't ignore. But we also can't ignore our professional responsibilities and the code of conduct we must adhere to."

"You think I can't remove every single obstacle to us being a couple?" Nate asks, a demand in his low words. "That I wouldn't do that for you?"

"I … well, I hadn't thought that …" I fumble.

"Open your email."

"My email?"

"Check your work email now," Nate commands.

I reach for my cell phone, remove it from the waterproof bag, and access the app. The first email in my inbox is from Human Resources, with the subject line "Amended Employment Agreement."

"Nate, what have you done?"

"Removed the external obstacles. Permanently," Nate explains. "I had a conference call with HR and the compensation committee of our board of directors this morning before the hike. I'm stepping down as CEO of Sybille Organics."

"What? Why would you do that?"

"Because you've proven that you can excel at every challenge thrown at you without my oversight. I'm putting you back in charge of your company as the CEO."

"You're giving control back to me?"

"Technically, Bell Capital still owns the controlling interest of Sybille Organics. But for day-to-day operations and executive decisions, these will no longer need to be run through a Bell Capital executive. You can run things how you see fit without my involvement."

"But I liked your involvement. We make a great team," I say, fighting the disappointment welling within me.

"The documents outline your new compensation package based solely on the company's results." Nate leans back and crosses his arms over his chest. His voice dips lower, his tone unmistakably intimate, as he says, "Leela, I am no longer your boss."

His words are like a phoenix rising from the ashes inside of me as I understand what he's done and why.

"But that only removes one obstacle to us becoming a couple." Nate drags a hand down his face.

"Like the obstacle of you being a billionaire and me being broke."

He scoffs. "Trust me, you'll get used to having access to my funds quickly. That's not a concern for me."

"I don't need access to your money."

"It's not about what you need, Leela. It's about what I want to give to you," Nate clarifies in a way that brooks no allowed arguments. "You need to understand why I only do casual relationships."

"And I'm guessing it's much deeper than trying to avoid the numerous gold diggers who try to trap you."

"Those are easy to avoid. My issues are deeper than that."

"Nate, you're no different than thousands of people who struggle to be close to others. It's an avoidant attachment style, and we can overcome that together."

"Does it look like I'm trying to avoid you?"

"Well, no …"

"I'm a Bell. We are notorious for putting love and relationships on the back burner to pursue professional success, money, and power. Those are facts," Nate says as if he's reciting a mantra that's been indoctrinated in him. "Most of the relationships that have lasted in my family are because the other person finds a way to be content with being ignored when our ruthless drive takes over and consumes our lives."

"That doesn't sound like the Nate Bell I've gotten to know."

"You haven't seen all the parts of me. And I don't think you're the type of woman who would put up with me for very long once you do."

For the first time, I detect a hint of worry in his dark gaze.

"You need to think long and hard before you agree to this."

"I'm not afraid of a challenge, and I think you're worth it. But what do you think?"

"I think you should run away as fast as you can," Nate says. "Because when I get what I want, I have a hard time letting it go. And I want you, Leela."

"But you think over time that I will see a side of you that will make me leave you?"

"Yes."

"And even believing that, are you willing to try this?"

"Yes."

I study his face as thoughts swirl in my head. He's clearly

convinced himself of a story entirely out of alignment with the man I know him to be. The one who wouldn't hesitate to sacrifice anything for his best friends. Who juggled a side job as a firefighter for years, refusing to let go of the commitment to give back to his community. Those are not the actions of a man who will mishandle and ignore his relationships.

But he can't see that in himself. Not yet. But maybe, just maybe … I can help him and not lose him at the same time.

"So, if I'm comfortable taking this risk, we could be a couple?"

A hint of a smile plays on his lips. "It's your call. But I need your answer before we fly back to Kimbell."

"You love to issue extreme deadlines, don't you?" I say, taking a deep breath. I'm gambling with my heart but can't help but think positively. Maybe Nate and I met at the right time to prove to each other that we could have what we thought was out of our reach. "I'm in."

"Wait." He takes a deep breath. "I have one non-negotiable rule before I accept your answer."

"Lay it on me."

"Do not fall in love with me," he says, a seriousness in his tone that sobers me instantly.

I respond the only way I know how.

I give him an exaggerated eye roll, then laugh. "With all the disclaimers and warnings you've given me in this conversation, I don't see how that can happen." I giggle nervously, hoping I'm not already in love with this man. "So, I agree. No falling in love."

Nate looks satisfied with my response.

"Shall we shake on our new deal?" I ask.

He rises from the table, "Let's kiss on it instead."

Kneeling next to me, he leans his forehead against mine. I laugh as our lips crash into each other, and I'm treated to another one of his decadent and delicious kisses.

CHAPTER 44

L EELA

~

NATE WAS RIGHT ABOUT GETTING USED TO HIS BILLIONAIRE lifestyle. Basking in a Vichy shower in a bathroom fit for a queen after a long day is the stuff dreams are made of. Tugging my robe tight around my waist, I skip and frolic through the three-bedroom penthouse suite of the Kahala Resort. Despite my better judgment, I looked up the cost online only to get sticker shock—fifteen thousand a night. I quickly closed the app and pushed the thoughts away. If I'm going to date a billionaire, the last thing I need is a neurotic habit of looking up how much he's spending on me.

Before I jumped in the shower, Nate left to take care of a few conference calls before the surprise he has planned for the evening. I walked into my bedroom of the suite to find thirty dresses lined on a rack for me to choose from—each one couture and expensive. Wherever he's taking me, it must be fancy and luxurious.

I chose a red dress with a high bodice that hugs my hips in all the right ways without showing my cellulite. Nate loves to see me in warm colors, which are my favorite, too. As a haircare maven, I brought plenty of products to do my hair and dazzle him with how good I can look.

Two hours later, I'm glammed up and twiddling my thumbs, bored as the sun sets beneath the sapphire blue waters. I've wrapped up all the pressing work matters in my inbox from earlier and am left with a buzz of excitement, waiting for Nate to come back.

I wonder what it would be like if this became our life together.

The overwhelming joy of seeing him come home to me—

"You chose the dress I wanted you to pick." Nate's words float across the room. I look toward the door as he closes it. He's dressed in a classic black tuxedo that looks custom-made for his impeccable physique.

"If you knew what you wanted me to wear, why did you give me twenty-nine other options?" I ask, sauntering toward him like a model on a runway and feeling like a modern-day Cinderella. "Those weren't good odds that you'd get what you want."

"Knowing you, I was pretty sure you'd make your decision based on what you thought I'd want to see on that amazing body of yours." He steps back and whistles. "Boy, did you get it right."

"You would have said that no matter what dress I picked," I say, heat blazing in my cheeks as I do a slow turn to give him the full view.

"Not true," he says with a mischievous grin, pulling me into his arms.

"So, where are we off to on our last night in Hawaii, Mr. Bell."

"Don't call me that." Nate's jaw tenses, and he almost pulls away from me, but I stop him. The dynamic between him and his father is complicated and one I haven't figured out.

"What's going on?" I ask, holding onto him.

He says, "Dad's communication skills are much clearer these days. That means he's back meddling in Bell Capital affairs. Checking up on my decisions and demanding details. That's why I was gone for so long."

"Sounds like you need to relax," I say, slipping my hands around his neck.

"Yeah, I'm so tense," Nate claims, frowning exaggeratedly. "My neck is so tight."

"Really? Let me see what I can do about that." His skin is warm against my lips as I trail kisses across his neck, up his jaw, and then land on his mouth. He pulls me in tight, the pounding of his heart unmistakable as he deepens the kiss, taking over from what I started.

We're like this for glorious minutes before he pulls back, checking his watch.

"Come on, we're late," Nate announces.

"You still haven't told me where we're going," I remind him, grabbing the ruby studded clutch purse that matches my dress.

"There's a phenomenal pianist, a prodigy, so they say, who is performing at the Hawaii Theater tonight."

"Is he here? My brother is performing in Honolulu tonight?"

"He is. I thought that would be a great way to wrap up our last night."

Dabbing at the tears pricking my eyes, I respond, "The most perfect way. Does he know that we're coming?"

Nate shakes his head. "No, it'll be a surprise for him unless you want to text him and let him know?"

I shake my head. "Let's surprise him." My parents and I have never seen him perform live as a professional. Mostly, we rely on social media clips and the occasional recording broadcast on public television to see his shows. He's so in demand that he hasn't been home in years. Despite living in his shadow for most of my life, I still can't wait to see him in person.

"Good thing I got VIP backstage access so the two of you can catch up after the show."

"You are the best, you know that, right?"

"Of course I am." Nate winks at me as we leave the hotel room.

Hours later, I'm dabbing at the tears streaming down my face from listening to my brother's concert. Seeing him perform live amplifies his gift.

As the curtain closes, Nate leans over to me. "Time to go surprise your brother."

A group of security guards escort us backstage. Harold's voice booms as he regales his team with praise and gratitude over the night's performance. I stand back, watching him in awe, realizing he and I aren't as different as I thought growing up. Our styles of leading and motivating our teams are so similar that I wonder if I was more influential on him than I realized. Maybe he picked up a few skills from his big sister after all.

I turn to check on Nate, who looks intense as he sits in a chair near the corner, typing frantically on his cell phone. A CEO's work is never done, but I appreciate the effort he's gone through to show me how important I'm becoming to him. Just another sign that he's nothing like the typical Bell he proclaims to be.

One of the musicians brushes past me, and I mumble an apology. At the exact moment, Harold's eyes land on mine. Confusion flitters in his gaze as he stares at me. I raise a hand and wave enthusiastically.

But he doesn't wave back.

Instead, he nods at one of the bodyguards and follows him through one of the side doors. I feel like I did as a kid—not important enough to be noticed, acknowledged, or … loved. All the attention and praise were Harold's and his alone. That's how he was raised, how he wants it always to be. As excited as I am to see him, he doesn't care to see me at all.

I take a deep breath and push away the disappointment.

Harold's behavior doesn't diminish the fantastic gift Nate gave to me. I won't pout and be upset about not getting to talk to my brother. I'm sure he had some other obligation and couldn't come over to say hi.

"Where is he going?" Nate demands from behind me.

"Oh, I think he must have another obligation. It's no big deal. I'll catch up with him later," I say, turning around to give Nate a big smile. "Should we go to dinner now?"

Nate looks past me at the door Harold left through. "Just a sec." He stalks away from me, pressing his phone to his ear. I recognize the tone of his voice all too well—the unmistakable get this done or else command. When he finishes the call, Nate says, "I'm going to grab us some champagne. Wait here for me, okay?"

"Oh … sure, yes, okay," I say, then make my way over to the velvet tufted couch in the lounge. Ten minutes later, the door swings open. "Did you have to fly to France for the champagne?" I ask, teasing, but my words fall away as my brother stands in the doorway.

"Good to see you, Leela," Harold says, walking toward me.

"Is it?" I ask. There's no doubt in my mind that Nate is behind Harold's return.

"Yeah, when I saw you at first, I didn't believe it was you. Thought it was just someone who kind of looked like my sister," he says, then brushes a finger across the arm of my expensive dress. "Never saw you all dolled up like this."

"First time for everything," I say, relaxing. I was being too hard on Harold. Of course, he didn't think it was me standing in the VIP lounge backstage after his concert. Our parents didn't know I'd jetted away on a business trip, and I didn't text him to let him know I was coming.

"You look good," Harold says with a tight smile. "Mom and Dad told me Bell Capital took over your company. I didn't realize that you and Nate Bell were so … close."

"Technically, they invested temporarily in Sybille Organics. I have a buyback clause that allows me to regain controlling interest, which I plan to do after the new line launches. I have a few banks willing to loan me the funds once the revenue numbers come in from it," I clarify, then ask, "How do you know Nate?"

"I don't. Bell Capital is one of the major donors to the not-for-profit organization that promotes my concert series. Without their donations, I wouldn't have the career I have now," Harold says, then glances back.

I follow his gaze and see Nate standing in the doorway. He walks over and hands us the glasses of champagne.

"Congrats on another amazing concert," Nate says to Harold.

My brother jumps to his feet and shakes Nate's hand vigorously. "Thank you! None of this would be possible without you. I appreciate your family's generosity."

"We have a long history of supporting the arts, especially those that aren't as mainstream as others," Nate says, then glances at me. "You good?"

"I'm perfect. Thank you," I say, then turn back to Harold. "Now tell me what's been going on in your life. I only get snippets from Mom and Dad."

Harold relaxes as he gives me the play-by-play of his most recent travels, concerts, and famous people he's had the opportunity to meet. My heart swells with pride as I listen, grateful that Nate is the one who made all this happen.

CHAPTER 45

I TURN THE PRISTINE WHITE LAMBORGHINI SUV INTO THE
parking spot where Leela parked her car this morning. The tow truck
driver is hauling it away. Destination—the closest junkyard.

She's not expecting me to be here—on the day of the company-
wide celebration for meeting the GrabHub shipment deadline. For the
past month, Leela worked nonstop to ensure nothing would stop the
company from delivering the Herbal Root Essentials products to the
big box retailer. She shepherded the company to this significant
milestone all on her own.

I couldn't be prouder of her.

That's why I strategically declined to participate since I'm no longer
the CEO of Sybille Organics. Leela deserves to bask in this success
alone. And she deserves a jaw-dropping congratulations gift from her
man to celebrate her achievement.

The parking lot is almost empty. No doubt, Leela gave everyone the rest of the afternoon off. After tying the gaudy red bow the car salesman forced on me across the hood, I go through the empty halls to her office, stopping outside her door. She's on a phone call.

"He's not?" Leela asks, a hint of worry in her tone. "And he hasn't been there all day?" She pauses, twisting a strand of hair around her finger. "I see. No, no, Susan. It's not an emergency or anything. I'll catch up with him later."

I sneak a glance through the open door. The cutest frown emerges on her face as she grabs her cell phone. Seconds later, I feel my cell buzzing in my pocket.

Leela waits until my voicemail picks up. "Hey, it's me. I was hoping to lure you to play hooky with me this afternoon. But I can't find you. Hope everything is ok. Call me." She gives her phone a death stare, then slams it onto her desk.

I can't stop the smile that spreads on my face. It's time to put this beautiful lady out of her misery. Walking through her door, I ask, "What did you have in mind for our afternoon of playing hooky?"

Leela bolts from her chair and rushes toward me, enveloping me in an intimate embrace. "I'm so glad to see you."

"Not as glad as I am to see you," I say, kissing her. "Now answer my question."

"You're always talking about your boat," Leela says, twisting the ends of the scarf. "So, if it's not too much trouble, I was hoping we could take it out on Lake Lasso. The weather is stunning today. We can lay out in the sunshine and do nothing." Leela grabs my hands and pulls them around her. "Doesn't that sound amazing?"

It's not lost on me that she probably had an internal tug-of-war about whether to ask for this. Leela still isn't comfortable with the canyon-sized gap in our financial statuses. She likely talked herself out of it several times before trusting in our relationship.

I scrunch my face and groan. "The eighty-footer is still in Lake Charles. We'll have to take the thirty-footer out instead. Not as nice, but I guess it will do."

"Oh goodness, you are so spoiled," Leela teases. "My mind is blown by a thirty-foot yacht—"

"More like a cabin cruiser. Can't say it qualifies as a yacht," I interject.

"Fine. Whatever! All I'm saying is that the cabin cruiser would be perfect."

"Not as perfect as my yacht, but it'll do," I say, unable to stop myself from sulking. If I'd had any idea that she was interested in boating, I would've had the yacht brought over weeks ago. I whip out my phone and type feverishly, giving Peter instructions and a ridiculously short time frame to complete them.

"Who are you texting?" Leela asks.

"Peter. To get the boat ready for us." I send Peter another text to have the yacht brought over from Lake Charles. It'll take a couple of weeks, but I want to be ready the next time Leela gets the courage to ask me for a date on the lake.

"How long will that take?"

"It'll be stocked with everything we need by the time we drive over there. Or else," I say, then pause, shifting to my surprise. "But I need you to drive us. My driver dropped me off."

Leela balks. "That's a terrible idea."

"It's fine." I keep a straight face with a lot of effort.

"No, it is not." Leela glares at me. "You don't want to be caught dead riding in my raggedy old car. The same car you make vomit motions at whenever you visit me at the lodge. Don't think I didn't notice."

"I wasn't trying to hide it."

"I know you think I need a new car, and you're right. I plan to research and buy something by the end of the year. In the meantime, just call your driver and ask him to get us."

"He's not available," I say, caressing my hands down her arms. "It's not that long of a drive to where the boat is docked. Only thirty minutes or so, plus I'll have a beautiful woman to distract me."

Her jaw clenches, but she knows she has no option but to go along.

As we walk out of the building, we fall into an easy conversation about a myriad of topics, none related to work. She leads me to the parking spot where she'd left her car.

"That is not my car," Leela announces, then looks at me. Her hands press against those delicious curvy hips as she tries her best to give me a stern look. "What have you done?"

"Took something off your to-do list?" I joke.

"We talked about this. You are not supposed to buy me any more gifts. Don't you remember?"

After Hawaii, I showered her with more expensive gifts. By the time I'd replaced her entire shoe collection with Louboutins, Jimmy Choos, and Pradas, she put her designer-clad foot down with some rules of her own.

"Kind of," I say.

"Your rule is that I can't turn down gifts from you. My corresponding rule is you can't buy me random gifts out of the blue. Don't pretend like you forgot. Gift giving is only for major holidays and relationship milestones," Leela says. She stomps her feet like a cute child. "Come on, Nate. You promised. No more gifts. Especially not vehicles that cost a few hundred thousand dollars. Goodness gracious!"

"As your man, I reserve the right to treat you to something special when you have a major professional accomplishment. There's no way I was letting this pass by without giving you a celebratory gift."

"I don't need gifts, Nate. I just want to spend the afternoon with you."

"And you will. Driving your brand new Lamborghini SUV to the lake," I say. "Best of both worlds, right?"

"I don't want you to think you have to buy me things to make me happy." Leela rests her hands on her face. "I know all about your other relationships. How women always had some angle to get gifts or money out of you—"

"It never worked." I balk. "All of them combined don't come close to being as special to me as you are."

"You're special to me, too." Leela strokes my cheek. "But we're supposed to keep things light and easy and casual. This." She turns to wave a hand toward the SUV. "Does not qualify as casual."

"Do we feel casual to you?" I demand.

Her eyes widen giving me a full view of the gold flecks in her hazel eyes. Her lashes flutter as she seems stunned by my question. The silence stretches between us. She knows I'll wait hours for her response. Finally, she says, "Well … no."

"I gave you a chance to run from this, and you didn't."

"I know."

"And your love language is gift giving …"

"Is that what you want?" Leela drops her hands from my face, then wrings them as she paces away from me. "Do you want me to feel … loved, Nate?"

"Are you asking me if I'm in love with you, Leela?"

"I don't know." Leela almost leaps away from me, but I grab her arm to keep her close. The last thing I want is any distance between us. She continues, "When we were in Hawaii, you had one definitive rule for this relationship. We could not fall in love with each other."

"No." I wag my finger at her. "The rule was *you* could not fall in love with *me*. That hasn't changed. I had no rules about my feelings for you. So, do you want me to answer your question or not?"

Leela looks conflicted as she stares at me. She takes a deep breath, then says, "No."

I'm not surprised or disappointed by her answer. "You ready to drive us to the lake?"

"This car is really mine?"

"It's in your name. Fully paid for, including insurance. It's yours."

Leela does that cute squeal that I adore.

I place the keys in her palm, then say, "Let's go."

CHAPTER 46

 EELA

~

NATE BELL IS IN LOVE WITH ME.

Like truly, madly, deeply in love with me.

He doesn't need to say the words for me to know it's true.

Our date on the lake a few days ago was magical. I want a future with him. One where we'd both be blissfully happy.

There's just one problem.

I told Nate I wouldn't fall in love with him …

And I lied.

How could I not fall in love with this man?

I was already on this road before we left for Hawaii. So when I made the deal with Nate, I knew I was agreeing to a term I'd never be able to keep. My only chance is to convince him to remove his stupid rule so we can admit how we feel about each other.

In the meantime, I figured it was time to tell my parents about the new man in my life. The last thing I need is for them to be blindsided by my relationship with a Texas billionaire when they ask why I haven't been making many trips back home. They are the kind of people who need to be eased into something this jarring.

An hour later, I realize it is easier said than done.

"Why would you waste money on something like this?" My mom asks, tears welling as she stumbles back from my Lambo like it's demon-possessed.

"Haven't I taught you it's better to have a sensible car like your old one?" my dad says, adding, "Low cost and low cost of ownership."

"Babe, can you imagine what the car note is like on this thing?" Mom shakes her head as if the thought is vile.

"More than enough to cover rent on a decent apartment so she can move out of our house," Dad huffs. "But you weren't thinking about that, were you?"

"Did you get some kind of bonus at your job?" Mom asks.

"I own my company, Mom, remember? It's not a job that someone else dictates what I make. I'm the decision maker," I say, trying to keep my voice even. Thanks to Nate, I'm being paid like a CEO and not an entry-level factory worker anymore. But in my defense, I wanted to funnel as much money back into the business to make it successful. I don't regret one minute of my sacrifices, even if it annoyed my dad that I was still living at home.

"Sounds to me like you took a bunch of money out of that company just to waste it on some foolish status symbol," Dad says, shaking his head. "Bet you didn't think about how expensive cars like that are to fix."

"Will y'all just calm down? I didn't buy this car—"

"Oh, thank goodness. It's a rental, babe. She just rented it to try to impress us, I guess?" Mom looks at my Dad as if trying to make sense of my crazy behavior.

"So she wasted a month's rent on a day of joyriding." He shakes his head. "Tell us what prompted this. What happened at your company?"

I suck in a deep breath and blink away the tears. "I called y'all earlier this week and told you the good news. We met the shipment deadline. My products will be in GrabHub stores next month."

"So nothing else happened?" Mom asks.

"That's the biggest contract my company has ever gotten. My products will be in stores all across the US now."

"I guess that's good for whoever buys your shampoo," Mom says.

"That's great. We're happy for you," Dad says, then walks back toward the front door.

"And I have deals with major retailers in Canada and the UK to get my products in their stores before the end of the year," I say, gushing and hoping for even the tiniest glimmer of excitement from them.

"You know Harold's show got extended to more cities in the US, too. He'll be doing one in Dallas in a few weeks," Mom says, beckoning for me to follow them inside. "I asked if he could get us some tickets. He's checking to see if that's possible."

Checking to see if that's possible?

Harold gets free tickets to all his shows to distribute however he wants. I know because Nate told me. It's part of his contract. I don't understand him.

And I don't understand my parents, either.

I have the biggest news of my life. My company is thriving, and they act like I'm selling lemonade in the neighborhood. Nothing I do is ever as grand as what Harold does. A fact of my life that I should be used to. But somehow, the sting of this one is sharper than ever.

Mom heads straight to the kitchen, already pulling out the kettle for tea, and Dad settles into his recliner in front of the television. Harold's piano recital video is still paused on the screen. Of course, it is. They must've been watching it for the hundredth time when I pulled up. It's the concert he performed in Honolulu. The one Nate surprised me with tickets to, then twisted Harold's arm to spend some time with me after it was over.

Mom clasps her hands together, her eyes brightening. "Oh, and did you hear the news about your brother's latest concert? He sold out the

Chicago Symphony Center! The Chicago Tribune even called him a 'virtuoso of unparalleled skill.' Isn't that incredible?"

Something inside me snaps. The hurt and frustration I've swallowed for years surges up my throat, demanding release. I fix my gaze on my mother, my voice trembling but resolute.

"You know," I start, trying to keep my voice steady, "I didn't drive here to talk about Harold."

Dad grunts. "Nobody said you did."

"No," Mom says, setting the kettle on the stove and turning to me. "But why would you drive a gas-guzzling monster all the way here? Your car gets better mileage coming from Kimbell."

"Because I don't have my old car anymore," I snap. "That's kind of the point. The Lamborghini isn't just about the car. It's about what it represents. I've worked hard. I've built something that's successful. And I'm proud of myself." My voice rises, my hands tightening around the strap of my purse. "And I was hoping you would be proud of me too."

Dad doesn't even glance up from the screen as Harold's grand finale floats in the air. "We are proud of you. It's just not—"

"Not as special as Harold's accomplishments, I know," I cut him off, a bitter laugh escaping. "Because Harold's a once-in-a-lifetime prodigy, and I'm just … what? The family workhorse?"

Mom flinches like I've slapped her. "We never said that."

Dad's brow furrows as he interjects, "Now, don't be oversensitive. You know we're proud of you, but classical music is just more prestigious than … shampoo."

"A million women in this country use my shampoo, Dad. Harold hasn't had anywhere close to that many people buy tickets to his concerts." I take a deep breath, squaring my shoulders.

"Leela! You shouldn't be jealous of your brother," Mama admonishes.

"I don't see why not." The words spill out of me, unchecked, and I can't help but think that Nate would be so proud of me. "You forced a life of doting on Harold on me for so long. You made me the family chauffeur. The errand-runner. The tutor. The one who picked up the slack whenever Harold needed to practice for hours or fly across the country for a competition. And I did it all because that was the only way I got attention from y'all when I was helpful to Harold. Making his life easier so he could achieve his dreams. I was so desperate for any crumb of appreciation that I always agreed to help, even if that meant putting my dreams on the back burner. Because I thought that would make you proud of me, too. But guess what? I'm done with that."

"You're being too sensitive," Dad says, pausing the television again. He levels me with a stern stare. "Just because we don't agree with you wasting money on renting a fancy car to celebrate your big shampoo victory when you should be saving to get an apartment doesn't mean we're not proud of you."

"I didn't waste any money on the Lambo," I scream, throwing my hands in the air. "It was a gift from someone who believes in me, supports me, and is proud of my accomplishments."

"A gift?" Mom says with shock, clutching the fake pearls around her neck. "From who? Who do you know who can afford something that extravagant?"

"I'd like to know the answer to that myself," Dad scoffs. "And what you had to do to earn it."

"Oh my goodness." I shake my head. "My boyfriend, Nate, bought it for me. And believe it or not, he thinks the person that I am and everything I've done with Sybille Organics is pretty amazing. I'm not living in anyone's shadow with him."

"Nate … Bell?" Dad asks, an accusation in his tone.

"I was hoping Harold was wrong about it …" Mom says, easing down into one of the chairs at the kitchen table.

"Wrong about what?" I ask, anger blazing through my veins. "What could Harold have possibly told you about me and Nate?"

"He told us you showed up at one of his concerts in Hawaii, and you were throwing yourself at some guy named Nate Bell. Harold heard your company was in deep trouble, and this billionaire bailed you out. Your shampoo business is on the right track because this Nate Bell character took it over. But he was worried that you got on the guy's radar for all the wrong reasons."

"Wrong reasons?"

"Men like that aren't investing in tiny black-owned businesses unless they want something else entirely. Harold says this guy is known for going through women like tissues, and you were the guy's latest arm candy. Looks like he was right," Dad says, shaking his head. He points a finger at me. "I hope you know what you're getting into. He may be into you now, but it's just temporary. When the next exotic lady crosses his path, he will move on. That's what rich folks do. We'll see if you or your business survives when he's long gone."

"Please be careful, Leela," Mom pleads.

Anger radiates from me, flushing my body with heat. Every instinct within me wants to defend Nate and our relationship. But it's pointless. My parents are only going to believe the story told to them by their precious Harold.

Silence stretches between us, broken only by the kettle's sharp whistle. Mom moves to take it off the burner, then grabs three cups from the pantry. "No, don't bother. I'm not staying."

Mom calls after me as I head for the door. "Wait, don't leave like this—"

But I'm halfway to the Lamborghini, my heels clicking purposefully on the driveway. As I slide into the driver's seat and rev the engine, I glance back to see them both standing on the porch, bewildered.

It's not a victory, not really. But as I speed off, the tears spill, and for the first time in my life, they feel like tears of freedom.

CHAPTER 47

N ATE

~

"You're a better model than your father," Richard says, beaming with what could only be described as … pride. He shifts toward the edge of the seat and grabs one stack of signed contracts from my desk.

"What's that supposed to mean?" Getting glowing feedback from my Dad's trusted advisor and attorney for Bell Capital is unexpected, to say the least.

"Your father was still working on closing these five deals when he had his stroke. You know his style. It's effective, but …"

"Slow."

"He schmoozes and butters people up to get what he wants out of the deal," Richard says, then shrugs. "While you, on the other hand …"

"I … what?"

"Make folks realize you're the smartest man in the room and the deal you're offering is one they shouldn't refuse. But take too long, and it will be gone." He whistles under his breath. "It's direct, ruthless, and equally, if not more, effective," Richard pushes another contract across the desk for me to sign.

"Think so," I say, as my fingers cramp from signing the pages. "Why don't you accept electronic signatures?" I glare at Richard, tossing the pen onto my desk.

"Oh, I do. Your father just prefers to sign everything old school."

"Of course he does. The next round will be different, got it?"

"Absolutely." Richard grabs the pages and lays them neatly into his opened briefcase. "How's the quarter looking?"

"Record earnings. Half Dad, half me. Good sign to the investment community that we're still a worthy partner," I say, more than pleased with the results of my first three months running Bell Capital.

"I'm impressed and not surprised. There's a reason your father identified you as the only person he wanted to step in if he had to take a leave of absence," Richard explains.

"I'm sure he set that up long ago and forgot to change it."

"Are you crazy? You do know David Bell, don't you? We review and update that document every quarter. He makes all kinds of changes but never to the person he trusts the most to lead his company."

"Is that right?" I say, unable to hide my shock.

Susan knocks on my door, then barrels inside. "You're two o'clock is still waiting in the board room." Disdain is heavy in her voice.

"I'm sorry. I've been talking your ear off. Let me get out of here." He rises, then extends his hand to my side of the desk. I shake it as he says, "Excellent job, Nate."

If only I could hear those exact words from my dad. With everything I've accomplished, it has to be coming soon.

As Richard leaves my office, I tell Susan, "Send him in."

Moments later, Javier de los Reyes walks with confident purpose into my office. I greet him with a hug, then lead him to the couches arranged in the corner.

"I'm surprised to see you," I say.

"No, you're not." He gives me a look. "I'm here for Sybille Organics. I should've known better when we talked a few months ago. Bell Capital swooping in to get a controlling interest in the company put all of us on notice. With the massive success of the Herbal Root Essentials line, my execs are on me to bring it into our portfolio. We can't take a chance that you offload it to one of our competitors."

"It's not for sale," I say. Sybille Organics is the crown jewel of our quarter and is shaping up to have a more significant impact for the rest of the year. Leela has far exceeded everyone's expectations, extending the contract with GrabHub, closing on more deals with retail stores in the US, and revamping the production processes. When she suggested that we use the automated facility for the less complex parts of the product development and then ship the base to our main factory for blending in the delicate ingredients, like the calyxera root, none of us knew how much of a game changer that would be. It tripled our production capacity almost overnight.

"But you're in the business of flipping companies once you make them a success, which you've already done for Sybille Organics. Why not cash out now?" Javier persists.

"Trust me, you can't afford what I'd want for it."

Javier takes a page from his portfolio and places it in front of me.

The purchase price on the deal sheet makes me do a double take.

"Is this some kind of joke?" I ask, glaring at Javier.

"That's the low end of a range approved by my board of directors," he says, then leans back in his chair. "I'm only telling you that to show how serious we are about acquiring the company." Javier looks too pleased with himself. "Imagine announcing this as a subsequent event in your quarterly release. The whole world will know Nate Bell has emerged from his father's shadow as the most formidable player in private equity. Isn't that what you want?"

I take a deep breath and stare at the number again.

Javier isn't wrong.

Taking this deal would prove to Dad that he didn't make a mistake trusting me with his business—not only did I close on his open deals, but I sought out investments he never would've given a second look and got a massive ROI from them.

This is a private equity firm, after all.

It's what we do.

There's nothing more I can do for Sybille Organics.

Maybe I should set the company free so that Leela can blossom even more without me.

Who am I kidding? Closing on a deal would secure my father's respect once and for all. Just because I was the one he trusted most to hand the reigns of the company over to doesn't mean he thought I'd be more successful at it than he is. But that's what I've done. This deal proves it more than anything else.

I drum my fingers on the desk. "Our agreement with Sybille Organics includes a buyback clause …"

"A standard Bell Capital buyback clause, I presume?"

"Yes."

Javier knows firsthand what that means and how to eliminate it as an issue in closing a deal. He grabs a pen from his pocket and leans over the desk. He scribbles a number that increases the proposed purchase price by twenty percent. Exercising the buyback clause is nearly impossible now.

I exhale loudly. I'd be a fool to turn down this deal, so why am I hesitating? Leela is a businesswoman. She'll understand, and it won't impact the twenty percent she still owns. In fact, her net worth would skyrocket because of the value now placed on her company.

It's a win-win for both of us.

I ask, "What would happen to Leela?"

"We'd offer her the same per unit value for her interest," Javier explains.

"So, a complete buyout? She wouldn't be involved in the company afterward?"

"We'd offer her a role as the Chief Brand Officer. I'd love for her to remain the face of the products while we get more experienced executives to take over running the day-to-day," Javier says. "My board won't go for an executive with just a high school diploma running the company. Not when we have highly qualified business school grads clamoring to run their own division. This purchase helps with some of the strain on our succession plans."

"You shouldn't be so quick to push her out. I promise she'll surprise you with what she's capable of. No one knows this industry or the company better than she does. Her instincts are stellar, and decision-making is flawless," I say, hoping to change his mind.

"That's high praise coming from you," Javier says. "I'll float it by our executive leadership team, but no promises."

"And if she refuses to sell?"

"Then she wouldn't have a role in the company going forward. She'd be a passive investor."

"A very rich passive investor," I say, stroking my chin.

Javier grins at me. "So, Nate. Do we have a deal?"

CHAPTER 48

L EELA

~

I SQUINT AT THE VARIOUS COLOR FLAGS DOTTING THE LUSH green lawn of Bell Park. Each flag denotes the pathway to a clue about the town's history. I'm kicking myself for agreeing to this. But I can't back out now.

"What is going on out here?" Nate's deep voice breaks through my concentration.

My heart makes that silly leap whenever I see him for the first time during the day. Not that I was expecting to see him at all this afternoon. I whirl around to face him, then suck in a breath. The sun's golden light warms his handsome face, and I can't help but smile. He walks toward me with one hand shoved into the pocket of his perfectly pressed khakis, the other holding a to-go cup of espresso from Brewed Awakening Coffeehouse. He looks casual and at ease, sleeves rolled up to reveal the muscular forearms I find myself wrapped in all the time.

I'm not sure how much longer I can keep the truth from him.

I want him to know how much I love him, but I also don't want to scare him away. After yesterday's debacle with my parents, Nate is the only consistent and supportive person in my life.

Pushing the thoughts away, I press my hands on my hips and respond, "Do you remember before we went to Hawaii, I was talking to Mrs. Wilkerson in the park?"

"No." He tosses back the espresso like a tequila shot. I wince, hoping it doesn't scald his throat, but he looks fine after swallowing.

"Well," I start, motioning vaguely toward the dozens of flags as if they explain everything. "She thought Sybille Organics would be perfect to pilot the new Kimbell Scavenger Hunt. It's more expensive than I thought, but I've learned a few things about the town and your family."

Nate tilts his head, his brow furrowing. "About my family? Like what?"

"Like how your great-great—uh, I don't know how many greats— grandmother Kimberly Bell owned the first hair salon in town."

He blinks, his lips twitching as though he's holding back a laugh. "That's wrong."

"Mrs. Wilkerson told me all about it," I counter, but uncertainty creeps into my voice.

"She's wrong. Trust me." Nate tosses his empty cup into a trash can, then stops within inches of me. The heavenly scent of his cologne washes over me, and I can't help but relax.

A mixture of amusement and exasperation spreads across his face as he tucks strands of my hair behind my ear. "Bells grow up hearing folklore about our family from the time we can crawl," he explains. "It's one of the family's favorite pastimes—keeping our history alive by passing on the stories."

"I wonder how she got it so wrong," I muse.

"Kimberly Bell," he begins, with the patience of a man correcting an overactive child, "who preferred to be called Kim, not Kimberly— which I've told Mrs. Wilkerson many times—wanted to help out a hairstylist who moved to town. She was the woman's first client, which got other people to trust her and use her services. Otherwise, her business never would've taken off. But Grammie Kim never owned the salon."

"Grammie Kim?" I sputter as a giggle escapes her lips.

"That's what Bells call her, affectionately, of course."

"Of course," I nod, caressing his arm. "Well, Mrs. Wilkerson wasn't entirely wrong."

His lips quirk up in a half-smile. "The salon failed within the year. The woman was horrible at styling hair. Grammie Kim wore a bonnet for months until her hair grew out."

"Oh, that's terrible." I wince sympathetically. Grammie Kim and I have more in common than Nate realizes.

"That's business," he replies, shrugging lightly. "So, when is this scavenger hunt?"

"Next week," I say. "You should come by."

He nods thoughtfully, his eyes narrowing. "I think I will to fact-check the information Mrs. Wilkerson is spreading about my family."

"I'm sure she'll love that," I tease, rolling my eyes. "Come on, let's head over to the gazebo. I have something I want to talk to you about."

Nate hesitates, glancing at the octagonal structure shaded by massive oak trees. The string lights sparkle, casting faint shadows over the glossy white wood. "Let's talk somewhere else."

"Don't tell me you believe the gazebo is cursed, too?"

"Mrs. Wilkerson told you about that?"

"She also said the gazebo was only a few good experiences away from improving its reputation." My heart races with anticipation of sharing my news. "What I want to talk about is all good, so humor me."

"Fine." Nate gives in, slipping his hand into mine. We walk along the stone pathway to the gazebo. The faint smell of freshly cut grass lingers. Like the perfect gentleman, he keeps me steady as I walk into the structure.

We cross the planks, creaking from our steps. Nate sighs, then says, "I have some news, too."

"Ladies first," I say quickly, brushing away his interruption. My pulse flutters nervously as I sink onto the bench. I glance up at him. "I got a call from my banker this morning. They've agreed to loan me enough money to buy back part of the interest in Sybille Organics."

Nate stiffens. His knuckles graze the edge of the bench as he sits beside me, leaving a careful amount of space between us. "How much are we talking?"

"Enough to give me a fifty-one percent ownership," I explain, leaning forward as the excitement bubbles up in me again. "I'll have real control over my company again. And, once I prove that I can make regular payments on the loan and the sales of the new product line continue to be strong, they're open to giving me another loan to buy back the rest of Bell Capital's interest. Isn't that wonderful?"

Silence.

It's heavy and crushing as it lingers between us.

"Nate?" I prompt. "What's wrong?"

His shoulders rise and fall in a measured breath. "Did you review the terms of the buyback clause?"

"Yes, I did," I reply, sitting up straighter. "My lawyer, Olivia reviewed them, along with the lawyers from the bank. We all went through every line and made sure that the amount we calculated met the terms."

"How did you determine fair value?" His voice is calm, but there's an edge there, the kind that makes my skin prickle.

"Come on, Nate." I wave my hand dismissively, though anxiety begins to curl in my chest. "The fair value of my company hasn't changed drastically in the four months or so since you invested in it. Companies don't have wild swings in valuation. We agreed to use your investment amount to determine the buyback value."

He exhales, rubbing the back of his neck. "I received an offer for our interest in Sybille Organics."

The string lights above us dim, casting long shadows inside the gazebo. "What are you saying?"

"Your company is worth much more than what Bell Capital invested." Nate leans forward, resting his elbows on his knees as he stares at the floorboards. "It's our business model working how it was designed. We invest in companies we believe we can improve the valuation of and then sell them."

His words hit me like a gust of icy wind. "How much has the valuation changed?"

He runs a hand through his hair, a gesture I recognize as a sign of discomfort. "That brings me to my news."

CHAPTER 49

L EELA

~

I STIFFEN, BRACING MYSELF. "I'M LISTENING."

Nate exhales slowly, his shoulders sagging. "The offer is from Primewell Industries."

"Are you serious?" I ask, stunned. Primewell owns several top-selling haircare brands in the U.S. I can't believe my products are on their radar.

"Very. They set an enterprise value of twenty times what we invested for our eighty percent interest."

I blink, his words hitting me like a blow to the chest. "Twenty times?" I echo, my voice faint.

He nods. "They believe in the growth potential of the products and the brand you've created. Our investment in infrastructure is a part of that, but this is a testament to you."

"That's nice." My voice trembles as I try to decipher what he's saying. "But I guess that means we have to agree on the new valuation for the company. One offer can't drive the number that high. Wouldn't we need to see what a few other companies are willing to pay? That could lower the amount to something more palatable for my bank."

Nate shifts uncomfortably on the bench, running a hand over his jaw. "It doesn't matter what your bank will loan you."

The pit in my stomach grows colder. "Why not?"

His eyes dart away for the briefest moment before coming back to mine. "Because I had to move on the deal."

I sit up straighter, my spine going rigid. "Move on the deal? What does that mean?"

"It's a great deal for both of us. One that doesn't come around often," he says, like it's just another business decision. Like he's explaining a market trend and not ripping my heart out.

The world tilts for a second. I grip the bench tighter, needing the solidity beneath me to stay grounded. "You already agreed to the sale?" I ask, my voice sharp and brittle. "It's a done deal?"

"Yes," he says, his voice low. "And they want to buy your interest, too. You're going to be a very wealthy woman. Of course, they still want you to be involved—"

"Let me get this straight," I interrupt, cutting him off with a trembling hand. "They want to buy my entire company out from under me and then hire me as their employee to run it?"

Nate's jaw tightens. "Not exactly."

I shake my head, letting out a short, humorless laugh. "What exactly, then?"

"You'd be their Chief Brand Officer and the face of the company," he explains carefully, as if picking his words might soften the blow. "I've also insisted they put in a non-negotiable role as CEO for you for one year. If you impress them, you have a shot of keeping that position."

"A shot?" A mirthless laugh escapes my lips. "And if I don't?" My voice wavers as the weight of his words presses down on me. "They'll use me for marketing, but I won't have any say in future products. I won't be running the company."

Nate flinches.

Well, that's as clear an answer as I can get.

"Okay, so what if I refuse to sell?" I challenge, leaning forward, my eyes boring into his.

"Then you won't have a role in the company at all," he says, his voice hardening. "Which I know doesn't work for you. That's why I'm forcing them to add the language to keep you on in a provisional CEO role."

I let out a sharp breath, staring at him in disbelief. "Am I supposed to thank you for that?" My voice is tight, barely masking the wave of anger crashing inside me.

"This is good news, Leela." He leans closer, his hand brushing mine as though trying to comfort me, but I jerk away, standing abruptly. "You'll have enough money to embark on your next corporate adventure."

"That's your dream, Nate. Not mine," I snap. "You love gobbling up companies, playing around with them, and then selling them off as you move on to the next shiny object. I don't. I only want to run my haircare line. But because of you, I've lost any chance at running the company I created!"

"It's business," he says simply, standing now, his height towering over me but not enough to diminish my fury. "You know how these things work."

I stand, blinking at him as tears prick the corners of my eyes. "I know how these things work?" I repeat, my voice rising. "No, I didn't know. But you're teaching me one of the hardest lessons of my life." I stand and face off against him. "You're unbelievable. I thought I knew you, Nate. But you did this. You signed that agreement to stop me from having any chance of buying back a controlling interest in my own company!"

"You never told me you were working with a bank to get funding," he counters, his voice growing sharper now. "I didn't know."

I scoff, folding my arms tightly against my chest. "Would it have mattered?"

Nate looks away.

"I didn't think so."

"Leela ... " he starts, his voice softening.

"Don't you dare Leela me!" I snap, cutting him off. I push past him, but he grabs my arm and jerks me back to him. I bump into his muscular body as he holds me close.

"Don't go."

Pushing him away, I say, "Congratulations, Nate. You got what you thought you'd get from this relationship. You destroyed us just like you warned me you would."

"It doesn't have to be like this," he pleads, stepping closer.

I let out a shaky breath, the words spilling out before I can stop them. "God help me, I thought you'd prove yourself wrong. That we would survive and thrive as a couple." I shake my head, my voice breaking. "Turns out I'm the fool." I take another step back. "You did the one thing that could hurt me so much that I'd never forgive you," I whisper. "The one thing that would convince me to walk away from you for good."

Nate's voice catches, then turns hard as stone. "Is that what you're doing? Walking away ... after everything? After all we mean to each other?"

I swallow hard, forcing myself to meet his gaze even as tears blur my vision. "What can I say? You were right. You told me not to fall in love with you. Stupid me—I did it anyway. So now I'm here with no company, and my heart obliterated into ashes. Hope your return on investment keeps you warm at night."

He opens his mouth, but I hold up a hand, silencing him. "I'm going to be a lot more like you now. Straightforward. So, here's your answer. Yes, Nate Bell. I am walking away from you for good. We are totally over. Don't even think about ever speaking to me again."

The silence that follows is deafening, drowning out the faint hum of children's laughter as they frolic on the playground and the distant murmur of traffic from Main Street.

Nate's dark eyes are as cold as they were the day we first met … in the elevator. I was right about him back then.

Without another word, I push past him and rush out of the gazebo. The ashes of my heart blow away in the wind with every step.

CHAPTER 50

Nate

~

Rolling out of my sleeping bag, I stare across the rolling hills as the sun peeks over the tree tops. I hiked for hours most of the night, weaving in and out of the dense trees until sleep clawed at me. My mind raced about how I could've told Leela the news differently in a way that didn't leave her running, not walking, away from me.

There was a time when I would've let her go.

But that moment has come and gone.

"You're a hard guy to track down."

I don't have to turn around to know it's Luke.

"Let me guess. Willow sent you an SOS. Begged you to do a search and rescue to find me," I say, glancing over at my best friend. He thrusts a thermos filled with hot coffee in my face. I take it and sip the black brew.

"It was your mother. She's pretty intense. Telling her no is never an option," Luke says, sitting on the ground next to me. He grabs my tarp, discarded jacket, water bottle and flashlight, organizing them neatly into my backpack. "You scare folks when you turn the preserve cameras off."

"Sometimes, I don't want my every move tracked."

"Like after you've been dumped by the woman you love?"

"That definitely tops the list," I admit, then gulp more coffee. "Can you believe I fell in love? The earth must be spinning backward on its axis."

Luke laughs and grips the back of my neck, shaking me. "I kinda knew this was going to happen. Something in the water at the fire station."

"I blame Santos," I mumble. "He started this crap when he came to town. We were all happy bachelors before then."

"But we're much happier now."

"Speak for yourself," I groan, then look at the man who's as close to me as a brother since the first day of our freshman year at SMU. The only person I'd let be around me right now. "You know, as soon as I turned onto the grounds, I knew she was gone. I could feel that she wasn't at the lodge anymore. I'd gotten used to being there with her or picking her up and taking her back to my place. Our normal routine." I exhale loudly. "The house felt uncomfortable without her."

"I'm sorry you're going through this," Luke says, then punches me in the arm. "But it's your fault. What were you thinking?"

"I was doing my job." I don't understand why this crucial point is so hard for everybody to understand. I continue, "I made the best business deal for Bell Capital and Sybille Organics. One that's putting the investment community on notice that Bell Capital is in good hands with me. Maybe even better hands than if my dad was running things."

"And that was worth hurting the woman you love?"

"Whose side are you on?"

"Yours. I'm trying to get you to see what a big mistake you made."

"I don't make mistakes," I counter. "If I had to do it all over again, I'd do the same thing."

"Seriously?" He looks at me like I've sprouted another head.

"Before the investment by Bell Capital, Sybille Organics was nowhere close to a trajectory to make Leela a multi-millionaire. She would have had a successful company and a lifestyle in the upper middle class. But millions? It wasn't going to happen," I say, then snatch a blade of grass from the ground. "With one signature, I did that for her."

"You did that for yourself."

"Do you think I would've done a deal that wasn't a win-win for both of us? I can be cold and heartless, but not to her. Never to her."

"This deal ain't a win for her, Nate. She came to you to help save a company she dreamed of running herself. Making it a success because of her skills and abilities. Now, she won't be able to do that because of you."

"Yes, she will. With the money from the Primewell deal, she can start five or ten more businesses. Explore different interests all from a place of financial freedom. That's what she never had. She paid herself the smallest salary of all the employees before we took over. Pouring every penny of profit back into that business. Living at home with her parents. That's why running Sybille Organics was so hard and stressful for her. I took that stress away," I say, anger building inside me. "As soon as Leela realizes that, we'll get our relationship back on track. I just need to give her … space."

"You think it's that simple?"

"I know it is."

"How?"

I smirk. "Because she's in love with me."

"Did she tell you that?"

Luke doesn't believe me.

"She did," I insist.

"What exactly did Leela say?"

"She was going on and on, ranting about how I destroyed us and made a fool of her, then she says something like she was stupid for falling in love with me." I pause as the memory of her exact words wash over me.

You told me not to fall in love with you.

Stupid me—I did it anyway.

From the moment I heard those words, nothing else mattered.

I knew this was the woman I was going to marry.

I will get Leela back, and she will be my wife.

"Honestly, I wasn't surprised," I say, then add, "I was surprised she said it out loud. Deep down, I knew it. I felt it. But we never talked about it. I wanted her to have a chance to walk away if she needed to." I stare out into the horizon.

"So, if Leela hadn't fallen in love with you, you would let her go?"

"Absolutely. I can live with a broken heart, you know that. I've done it before. This time would be infinitely harder, but I'd do it again just to know that she'd be at peace without me," I say, stunned by the truth of my words. "But Leela isn't going to know a minute of peace without me because she loves me. Nothing will work in her life without me like it won't in mine without her. That's the idiotic way love works. So, I will get her back."

"Wow … this is worse than I thought."

"Worse? How?"

"We're talking about Leela here. This is the same woman whose reaction to you was always the opposite of what you expected. She stood up to you when others wouldn't. Succeeded when you threw obstacles in her way. Challenged you when others cowered. Told you the hard truths when no one else had the guts. Refused to back down when you pushed."

"Loved me when I was unlovable."

"Yeah, she did that, too."

"Love doesn't just vanish when you're pissed off. You know that better than anyone," I remind him. "No matter how much you lost when Kennedy was awarded your inheritance, your love for her never died. It grew more."

"So what? Are you going to stage a fire to get Leela to realize she doesn't want to live without you?" Luke chuckles under his breath.

"Of course not. I'm on a leave of absence from the fire station, remember? Plus, I'd never copy your romantic ending. Leela deserves better than a used love reunion."

"She also deserves better than a man who doesn't consult her on major decisions that would impact both your lives."

"Consulting her wouldn't have changed the outcome."

"You sure about that?"

"I worked my butt off for this win, and I got it. This deal with Primewell is the biggest return on investment in Bell Capital's history. The kind of success that my dad can't deny. I did it alone, investing in an industry he'd never touch with a ten-foot pole. I had to close the deal."

"And that could be why she won't be able to forgive you," Luke says, his words sobering me, chipping away at my confidence. "You sacrificed her happiness and goals for yours. She might be the one person who can love you and live without you."

His words settle like an anvil in my gut. Leave it to Luke to give me a dose of my brand of brutal honesty.

For a split second, I wonder if he could be right.

Did I go too far this time?

The answer screams back at me louder than ever.

I reach for my backpack and stuff the sleeping bag inside. "Well, if the extra zeros in her bank account aren't enough to make up for what I did, then I'll have to figure out what will. I'm not going to live my life without her, that's for damn sure."

"Good luck, my friend. You're going to need it."

CHAPTER 51

L EELA

~

Exiting the SUV, I walk toward Dillon Crockett as he jogs down the porch steps of Crockett Manor in Downtown Kimbell.

"Glad I was able to reach you," he says, then whistles. "Nice car."

"Thanks, it was," I pause, stopping myself from my usual response —it was a gift from my boyfriend. Because Nate and I are no longer a couple. He made sure of that when he sold Sybille Organics to Primewell.

At first, I wanted to trash every gift Nate had given me just like he'd trashed our relationship. Or at least sell them through one of those luxury goods consignment stores and pad my savings account with the proceeds.

But giving the gifts away wouldn't make me feel better.

Those gifts weren't a symbol of our end but a testament to the good things that Nate deposited into my life during our relationship.

The ways he helped me stand up for myself, see that I don't need to jump through hoops to make people like me, and believe that I'm a great leader even though I don't have the fancy college degrees other business owners have.

I don't want to forget any of that.

And I don't want to forget that the time we shared our lives was real and not some figment of my imagination.

Giving up the Lambo, the clothes, shoes, and purses would be too hard, anyway. Why heap more suffering onto my broken heart? Who knows? One day, I might feel detached enough to sell off these things. But not today.

"An impulse purchase? I've done a few of those over the years," Dillon says as he walks around the vehicle. He presses his face against the window, peering inside as his grin grows wider.

"You mentioned a room opened up?" I say, trying to get his attention from gawking at my SUV.

After Nate dropped his bomb on me, I headed straight to the Painted Lady Lodge and packed my things. I never want to see Nate or speak to him again after what he did. Staying at his guesthouse was the last place I wanted to be.

I drove around Kimbell, stopping at several bed and breakfasts sold out with tourists during the busy summer season. The owners were kind enough to give me other suggestions in the area, but when those didn't pan out, I spent the night at a roadside motel that had seen better days. I have no plans to stay there again.

"Sure did," Dillon says, beckoning me to follow him into the house. "One of the guests is moving out after a long-term stay, so I grabbed the room and set it aside for you. He and his fiancée are here right now, gathering up his things," Dillon explains.

The interior of the house is as decadent as you'd expect from the opulent, old-world charm of the exterior. Dark mahogany walls adorned with polished moldings exude a timeless grandeur. We walk past a music room with a large grand piano in the corner, then through the dining room with a table that seats at least twelve before turning into a lounge boasting an ornate, carved wood bar backed by an immense gilded mirror. Tufted leather chairs gather around tables bearing delicate stained-glass lamps.

Dillon slips behind the bar. "Our housekeeper, Alma, will need about an hour to clean the room once he's gone," he says, producing a sleek bottle of wine from behind the bar. I instantly recognize the brand. The dark glass gleams under the flickering lights of the vintage sconces on the walls. "In the meantime, you can relax with this, on the house. It's from a local winery and has won a ton of awards."

He grabs a wineglass and leads me toward a cozy nook tucked in the corner of the lounge. My steps sink into the plush carpet as the gentle strains of jazz play overhead. I ease into the plush armchair, its smooth leather enveloping me, as Dillon pours a generous glass of red wine. He sets the bottle down with a gentle clink.

"I'll let you know when the room is ready," he says with a polite nod, then leaves me alone in the lounge.

Swirling the wineglass around a few times like Nate taught me, I sniff the aroma but can't discern the complex scents. Nate usually helped me figure that part out, carefully focusing on each distinct smell until I could identify it myself. I shut my eyes and take a big sip. Even without knowing the flavors, I think it's good. On par with the expensive bottles Nate and I shared many nights.

Stop it. Stop thinking about Nate.

Taking a larger gulp of wine, I gaze out the window at the bustle of Kimbell's Main Street. But my thoughts are far from the happy people meandering in and out of the stores and restaurants.

There's so much to do now that Bell Capital is selling Sybille Organics. First up is breaking the news to the employees. An email from Susan made it clear that Nate is leaving those details to me. He's open to participating if I want him to. I don't. Then there's Javier de los Reyes from Primewell, who wants to meet to discuss his offer on my twenty percent interest in the company. Both things I had no clue I'd be dealing with twenty-four hours ago.

I blink back a sudden sting of tears and pour more wine into my now empty glass, hoping a second helping will coax me into calm.

"The Shiraz is more comforting than the Cab, in my opinion." A woman's voice, warm and sweet, breaks through my reverie. I glance up. She's standing a few feet away, a mix of grace and casual ease.

I manage a weak smile. "Well, since it was a complimentary gift from the owner, this one will have to do. Plus, I hear it's won a bunch of awards." I swirl the wine in my glass. "Tastes pretty good, I guess." I pause, quirking an eyebrow. "Although it is weird to drink wine made by my ex's ex."

"Your ex's ex?" Her eyes widen just a fraction, then she smiles faintly, her expression unreadable. "Wait. Are you Leela Jamison?"

I nod. I forgot I was in a small town founded by Nate's family. Of course, everyone here knows him. My fingers tighten around the stem of the wine glass. "Are you a friend of Nate's?"

She tucks a strand of copper-highlighted dark hair behind her ear, her eyes studying me with interest, and then says, "I'm Harlow-Rose."

CHAPTER 52

L EELA

~

"Oh ... well, this is awkward." My stomach drops.

"Doesn't have to be. May I?" She points at the chair on the opposite side of the table.

"Of course," I say, not entirely sure I want to commiserate with the only woman Nate has ever loved. He surely doesn't love me, or he wouldn't have sold my company without telling me.

Harlow-Rose sits, then beckons for Dillon to bring her a glass. She pours a small amount of wine into it and takes a sip. "I'm sorry things didn't work out for you and Nate."

"I'm not," I say, belligerence bleeding in my words. "He predicted this. I didn't believe him, but he was right. It is what it is."

She lowers her glass to the table, her gaze drifting to the ceiling. "Nate has this way about him—like he's completely unapproachable, untouchable, and that makes everyone want him. Want to be around him. Be his friend. Or more. So when you're the one he chooses, even for a while, it makes you feel like the queen of the universe. His universe. At least, until reality kicks in and reminds you that ... well, you're not."

I glance at her over the rim of my glass. "That's disturbingly accurate."

"I'm probably the only person who knows exactly how you're feeling right now," she says, her voice softening. "But Nate and I were so young—high school sweethearts. We didn't stand a chance. But it still took me a long time to get over him."

"Even though you were the one who ended things? Not him," I say, leaning forward.

Her eyes flick to mine, a faint crease forming between her brows. "He told you that?"

"He told me his side of the story." I recount the details of what Nate told me about their break-up. Harlow-Rose's expression shifts subtly, a mix of emotions flickers across her face.

"Well," she says when I finish, her voice measured. "All of that's true. I don't regret my decision. His wild days at SMU are still the stuff of campus legend. Besides ..." A small smile breaks through the tension in her expression. "If I hadn't ended things, I never would've met my fiancé, Santos. We have a connection I never had with Nate."

"I'm not so sure that's true," I say before I can stop myself.

Her head tilts, curiosity sparking in her gaze. "Why do you say that?"

I take another sip of wine, buying time to organize my thoughts. "Because he was in love with you back then. He would've moved heaven and earth to make you happy. Definitely would've stayed faithful to you through college, even with y'all being hundreds of miles away." The truth of it burns in my throat. "That's how important you were to him. Who knows? The two of you could be married now if you hadn't pushed him away. And that would've saved me from ..." I swallow hard.

"From what?" she asks, her voice barely above a whisper.

I clutch my shirt near my chest. "This horrible piercing pain where my heart used to be."

An apology lingers in her gaze as she reaches for my hand. "He told you all of that about me? Us? Our old relationship?"

"Yeah, but he's totally over you, so don't worry about any residual feelings," I say, hoping to clear things up. "Nate and I have this surreal ability to dig into each other's heads, to share every messy, unfiltered thought. It's terrifying, honestly. He knows things about me no one else ever will." I shake my head. "But Nate cares deeply when he lets people close. He just doesn't always make the best decisions for them. Some of those choices," I clear my throat. "They have consequences I don't think he intends."

"His parents taught him a lot of great things, but how to navigate matters of the heart wasn't one of them."

"That's for sure," I say, my voice sharp but not unkind. "He has this warped idea of himself—this version of who he thinks he's supposed to be. When he strays too far from that image, he self-corrects. But it's not about being better. It's about proving he's right. It's self-destructive. I won't let myself go through cycles of that with him. This first round was a knockout punch for me."

"I can't believe it, but Nate is totally in love with you."

Her statement hits me like a physical blow. "What makes you think that?"

"It's pretty obvious." A knowing smile plays at the corners of her mouth. She leans forward, her voice dropping to a conspiratorial whisper. "Nate never shared deep feelings with me. I doubt he even tells that kind of stuff to Luke or Willow. But he told … you. There's only one reason he would do that."

I freeze. "You can't know that for sure. The two of you have barely spoken since you got engaged, and he's torn up about that, by the way."

She points at me. "Something Nate would never share with anyone except someone who means the world to him."

I stare at her, my pulse pounding in my ears.

"You know Nate doesn't let people in easily," she continues. "But he let you in. You know him. You understand him in a way I never did. That's what was missing between us. That's what I have with Santos."

"That doesn't mean Nate is in love with me," I say, my voice cracking.

Are you asking me if I'm in love with you, Leela?

The rule was you could not fall in love with me. That hasn't changed. I had no rules about my feelings for you. So do you want me to answer your question or not?

My hand trembles as I set the glass of wine back on the table. What if I had answered his question differently? What would Nate have responded? And would that have changed what happened between us? Changed how I feel about what he did?

I push the what-ifs from my mind because it's pointless.

"Yeah, it kinda does." She observes me like she's scrutinizing the impact of her theory on me. "Do you love him?"

The wine weighs heavily in my hand. A war of conflicting emotions erupts inside of me.

"It doesn't matter!" My voice rises sharply, drawing a curious glance from Dillon at the bar. "He sold my company without telling me. Without giving me a chance to buy it back."

"He did what?" Harlow-Rose asks, confusion clouding her face.

I yank the bottle from the table and fill our glasses. "I spent years building that company from scratch. Late nights, early mornings, all my savings—everything I had, I poured into it. And he just … took it out from under me. Signed the papers, made the deal, and didn't even have the decency to consult me."

"Unbelievable." Harlow-Rose grabs the glass and takes several gulps. "Just the thought of losing my business—it makes me feel sick. When you build something from nothing—"

"It stops being about the money," I finish for her, my voice quiet but resolute.

She nods. "It's the journey. The creativity. It's—"

"Breathing life into your dreams," I say softly. "And then dreaming again and breathing life into those too."

Her eyes meet mine, a flicker of understanding passing between us. "And he took all of that away from you," she says. "He's such a fool," Harlow-Rose announces, a tinge of anger in her tone.

"I'm the bigger one." The admission is bitter, so I chase it down with lots of red wine. Wiping the liquid from my lips, I ask, "Why did I fall for him?"

She reaches for my hand and gives it a gentle squeeze. "Because love doesn't play fair. Just remember that you're much stronger than you feel right now. You'll get through this." Her gaze lifts to something behind me.

I turn to see a handsome Latino leaning against the bar. His honey-colored eyes are full of concern as he watches us.

"That must be your Santos," I say, pulling my hand away. "Go, I'll be fine."

"You sure?"

I nod, wishing I'd never opened up to Harlow-Rose about me and Nate.

"Take care of yourself." She leans over and hugs me.

"I will," I say, then watch as she heads out of the lounge with the love of her life.

I thought I had a shot at that kind of love with Nate but I don't.

Not anymore.

CHAPTER 53

L EELA

~

S TARING AT MY EMPTY EMAIL INBOX, I BREATHE A HEAVY sigh.

I survived the week.

By far the toughest I've ever experienced since creating Sybille Organics. The only bright side was the revolving door of employees in my office, which kept my mind off Nate and his betrayal.

I'm looking forward to getting away from Kimbell for the weekend. Out of the blue, I got a call from my parents with surprise tickets to Harold's concert in Dallas. My brother was touched by the gratitude angel and arranged for a private jet, a hotel room near the concert hall, and front-row tickets to his show. Unsurprisingly, my parents were overjoyed with this opportunity to see him perform live for the first time in years. But the bigger surprise was that they apologized to me for our argument the last time I was in Houston. I was deeply touched, and it meant the world to me. I came close to telling them that I was on the verge of losing my business to Primewell but thought better of it. They deserve a weekend of happiness with Harold, and I need the distraction.

Logging out of my computer, I grab my purse from the bottom drawer. I have just enough time to drive to the private airfield in Houston for the trip to Dallas. My bags are packed and in the back of the SUV. I can't wait to get some distance from this town that reminds me of Nate at every turn.

The break couldn't come at a better time since next week is the team-building scavenger hunt to learn all about Kimbell's history, aka all about Nate and his family. But I'm not going to dwell on that right now.

A soft knock raps at my door. I look up to see Faye, Mischa, Sade, and Precious poking their heads in.

"Hey, can we talk to you before you head out?" Mischa asks.

"Of course," I say, waving them inside. "What's on your mind?"

Sade clears her throat. "We wanted to thank you for your honesty and transparency about the sale of the company to Primewell. It's not what we wanted, but knowing what to expect has helped us feel less anxious."

"I'm glad. This is not easy for any of us. I'm feeling all the same anxiety that y'all are," I admit.

"We get that," Faye says. "We're all worried about our jobs, but the reality is, we can find new ones. The retention bonuses will definitely help. But you can't get your company back. You are Sybille Organics, and that's been taken away from you."

"Yeah, it has. I'm still trying to come to terms with that."

"Especially since your man was the mastermind behind this disaster. I get keeping business and personal separate but come on!" Mischa says, rolling her eyes.

"Nate is not a bad guy," I say, the words tumbling out of my mouth. "He is the CEO of one of the most successful private equity firms in the country. He flips businesses like folks flip houses. It's what the company does. He has no control over Primewell's actions or the potential layoffs." I take a deep breath, waiting for the anger and pain to wrack through my body, but it doesn't this time. I'm not just trying to convince my managers of this. I know it's true. I just wish I'd gotten a bank to give me the loan earlier. I could've avoided this situation or at least delayed it.

"You're seriously not mad at him about it?" Precious asks.

"Being mad only hurts me. I'm working through it," I say.

"Well, no matter what happens in the future, we also wanted to tell you that working for you has been the best experience of our careers. There's so much we've learned from you. You are an amazing leader, and we appreciate the time we all spent working together," Mischa says.

"I know y'all didn't come in here trying to make me cry!" I shout, shaking my finger at each of them.

"That's why we picked Friday. We could drop this mushy bomb, then send you on your way," Sade says.

"Have a great time in Dallas," Faye says.

"Thanks. I'll see y'all on Monday," I say as they wave and exit my office. I will miss working with them … almost as much as I miss working with Nate.

How can I be so disappointed in him and want him at the same time? I must be losing my mind. Thank goodness he's had the good sense to do as I ask and keep his distance from me.

I lock up my office, a strange sense of finality settling over me as I hear the click. It's not just the end of a long week but the end of a chapter I didn't want to close. Heading out into the stifling humidity of the Texas late afternoon, I shield my eyes from the bright sun and crank the engine of the SUV.

CHAPTER 54

L EELA

Two hours later, I pull into the parking lot of Hooks Airport in North Houston and race onto the waiting Gulfstream G5, gleaming under the soft glow of the hangar lights. It's not my first time boarding a private jet, but the surreal shine of wealth hasn't worn off, no matter how much I pretend otherwise. The chilly air of the cabin wraps around me, a stark contrast to the hot evening air. Mom and Dad are already seated, the picture of contentment.

"Traffic was horrendous. Some kind of accident on Highway 290, so I had to detour to FM 1488 and cut across to get over here." I wave at the flight attendant and drop into the nearest seat, the tension in my shoulders refusing to loosen. "I'm so sorry y'all had to wait for me."

"It's fine. Take a deep breath," Mom says, beaming at me as she lowers her novel to her lap.

"Danielle, please get my daughter a glass of wine to relax her frazzled nerves," Dad says, patting the seat next to him.

I glance back at Danielle, who gives me a warm smile. "Would you like red or white?"

"Just water, thank you."

"Suit yourself. This plane is stocked with great wines and even some hard liquor if you get nervous about being on small planes," Dad explains.

Mom adds, "I had a small sip of cognac. Not too much. It was divine and made me feel a lot better."

"Well, you two certainly look ready to enjoy the weekend," I say, glancing back and forth between them.

"Not every day you get to fly on a private jet!" Dad says with boisterous laughter. "But I know this is nothing for you, right? You flew on the Bell Capital private jet to Hawaii."

"I did," I say, not bothering to clarify that it was Nate's personal private plane and that his 747 makes this G5 look like a toy. "It was nice of Harold to arrange this trip so we could see him. I can't remember the last time we were all together as a family. It's going to be nice."

"You're thanking the wrong man for this weekend getaway," Mom says, then gives me an exaggerated wink.

"What do you mean? Didn't Harold have his team set this up?" I ask.

Dad squirms in his seat as Danielle brings me a glass of water and a small plate of chocolate-covered grapes.

"I remember you liked having those before," she says politely, then walks away.

I stare at the grapes for a beat too long. A memory flickers—Nate introducing me to the unusual combination, one of his favorites, on the flight back to Kimbell from Hawaii. The richness of the dark chocolate mingled with the sweetness of the grapes, an unexpected but immensely enjoyable combination. Just like the man.

When Danielle disappears into the galley near the cockpit, I ask, "Who arranged for this trip?"

Mom breaks into a huge smile. "Well, your boyfriend stopped by the house looking for you."

"My boyfriend …"

"Don't be coy, sweetie. Nate visited us, and I must say, I was impressed with him," Dad says, nodding at me. "Good man, with a good head on his shoulders."

"And very charming, too. He definitely cares deeply about you," Mom adds.

"Nate?"

They nod at me enthusiastically.

"You met Nate, and you like him?" I ask, desperate for clarity.

"What's not to like? He's amazing and devilishly handsome," Mom says.

"Not the typical stuck-up, pretentious billionaire either. Down-to-earth and a straight shooter. That's a rare combination," Dad says.

"Let me get this straight. Nate visited you at the house and arranged for this trip to Dallas to see Harold?"

"Sweetie, he came to the house looking for you. He told us about your lover's spat," Mom explains.

"Lover's spat? And did he say what was behind it?"

"He was vague about it, don't worry. All he said was that he made a decision about your company and didn't consult you like he should have. He feels real bad about it and wanted to apologize," Dad says. "But we told him you hadn't moved back home."

"I told him you were staying at some fancy bed and breakfast in Kimbell, and he seemed to know the place. Did the two of you meet up?" Mom asks.

"Now, don't go trying to get into her romantic life. That is none of our business," Dad says. "But as he was leaving, I thanked him for supporting the not-for-profit that sponsors Harold's concert tour and how we planned to drive down for the performance in Dallas."

"And he immediately stepped up and told us not to worry about driving. He'd have a jet fly us there and arrange everything we needed. He's so thoughtful," Mom says.

"Thoughtful?" Sarcasm drips from my words, but something more complicated swirls around me. A cocktail of irritation, disbelief, and something else I can't pin down. Gratitude? No. Never that. But a part of me—a small, infuriating part—feels a flicker of warmth at the thought of Nate going to all this trouble. For me. I shove the feeling down, locking it away with the other tangled emotions, then blurt out, "Well, Nate and I broke up because he sold my company without telling me."

"But you said they only bought part of the company," Dad says, frowning. "How could he do that?"

"Okay, he sold his stake in my company."

"Well, he's a businessman." Dad shrugs. "If he got a good deal because your shampoo is flying off the shelves, why shouldn't he sell? That's just smart."

My mouth falls open.

"Exactly!" Mom chimes in. "And if your company is worth more, that must mean your share is worth more, too, right?"

"Well, technically, that's true—"

"So it's good news for both of you! Congratulations, sweetie." Dad beams.

"And we get to celebrate this good news with your brother this weekend!" Mom exclaims. "This is just wonderful."

I drag a hand down my face. "Yeah … wonderful."

The biggest problem is that what Nate has done is wonderful. He's reconnected me with my parents, mended our rift, and set us up for a much-needed family getaway.

How can he hurt me so bad and still do the sweetest things for me?

Nate

~

Clutching my cell phone to my ear, I search the crowd, hoping to talk to Leela before the team building festivities begin.

"This is a bad idea," Willow tells me for the third time.

"I'm not disagreeing with you."

"Leela hates you for good reason, and she wants nothing to do with you."

"She does not hate me," I snap, pushing my way past the ribbon cordoning off the park for the employees of Sybille Organics.

"Fine," Willow concedes. "But she wants nothing to do with you. Showing up at the park to crash her team building event won't change that. So, why are you doing this?"

"Because," I say, ignoring the pain in my chest. "It's been eight days, Willow."

"I know, and I'm sorry. Seriously, my heart breaks for you even though I wholeheartedly support both decisions you made," Willow says.

The sale of Sybille Organics coincided with the creation of Bell Naturals, my solely owned company, which was created to source rare natural ingredients for use in beauty care. It's a deviation for me, but a path I was inspired to take because of Leela.

When we made the deal in Hawaii, I decided at the last minute to buy the land from my personal funds—partly to protect the calyxera root from Dad, who has no interest in the industry, and partly because owning something that matters to Leela is important to me. I wanted to do everything I could to protect her from losing the supply of calyxera root ever again.

My sister continues, "Still, I'm not sure seeing Leela will make you feel better."

"You don't have to be sure."

As each day passed, my focus waned. I've become a mess at work, unable to think straight as I daydream about memories of when Leela and I were together. It's a miracle that I haven't screwed something up. The only prescription for this malady is to be around her again, even if she doesn't want to see me.

"Okay, but don't say I didn't warn you."

I stuff the cell phone in my back pocket and walk toward the elevated wooden platform set up as a stage near the train depot museum. I spot Mrs. Wilkerson and stop in my tracks as Leela emerges in the museum's doorway.

She's wearing a flowy sundress that sways around her legs with every step as she walks across the stage. Her thick hair cascades down her shoulders in gentle waves, framing a face etched into my memory. Those intoxicating hazel eyes shine with quiet confidence, just like the first time I ever laid eyes on her. Everything about her overloads my senses, reminding me how deeply she owns my heart.

My sister is wrong.

I'm definitely doing the right thing.

Leela and Mrs. Wilkerson stand in the center of the stage as the employees erupt into raucous cheers and claps. Leela beams as she returns the action, cheering and clapping for the employees, which makes them go wild.

After several minutes, they settle down, and she grabs the microphone.

"What a wild ride we've had!" Leela says, smiling at them. "We've endured every challenge and obstacle thrown at us and continued to come out on top because we came together and worked as a team." She saunters across the stage, making eye contact with several in the crowd. "The thing that I'm most proud of is how well we've handled change, and boy, we've had a lot of change over the past few months. Through it all, we maintained our focus and commitment to the vision, delivering on our contracts and providing excellent products to the women who rely on us for stellar hair care."

The employees whoop and holler.

"Tomorrow holds a lot of uncertainty with the Primewell acquisition of our company. But today, I want us to focus on having fun and learning more about this charming town that has welcomed us," Leela says. "Now, I'll turn it over to Mrs. Wilkerson to explain the scavenger hunt details."

I'm moving before I realize it, running onto the stage. I wrap an arm around Mrs. Wilkerson as I ease the microphone from her hand. She smiles.

"Before that, I want to speak to everyone. I haven't gotten a chance to since the announcement of the sale," I say, then sneak a glance at Leela.

She looks surprised and not … disgusted … to see me. It's not a figment of my imagination. I swear a hint of excitement dances in her eyes like she's happy despite her anger. Our gazes lock, but it's short-lived as boos grow loud from the employees.

I'm not surprised. I knew selling Sybille Organics would make me the bad guy to every single employee of the company. Just when they were settling into a new normal, I changed the game. There's a huge question mark around how many employees will be given job offers under the new ownership, creating stress and strain throughout the company.

Leela yells over the boos. "Wait, guys! Let's not do this!" She reaches for the microphone, and I relinquish it to her. "Come on, Nate deserves our respect. We wouldn't have made it this far without his tireless efforts. He brought on the second factory, secured a supply of calyxera root, and closed on several international retail contracts for our products. We owe a lot of our success to him and should hear him out."

The crowd reluctantly stops booing.

Leela doesn't look at me as she hands the microphone back to me.

"I'll keep this brief. Don't want to stand in between you and a day of fun," I say, but don't get any laughs for my joke. I press on. "In business, change is inevitable. It's easy to feel like something different than what you've known will be bad instead of good. I've known many people on Primewell's leadership team for years. They're good people, and I wouldn't have signed off on the sale if I wasn't sure they'd take good care of y'all," I explain. Murmurs of skepticism ripple through the crowd. "That being said, Primewell has the first option of selecting the employees they want to extend offers to. Once they've identified those individuals, anyone not selected will be given jobs at other businesses owned by Bell Capital. None of you will be unemployed."

"What?" Leela whispers next to me. "Are you serious? You're going to make sure everyone has a job."

"Every single last person," I say into the microphone, but my gaze never leaves hers. She looks genuinely touched by the unexpected offer. But it was a decision that had the full support of my executive leadership team.

Claps and cheers ring out again amongst the employees as they high-five each other.

"Enjoy your event today. All of you deserve it," I say, determined not to be any more of a burden to Leela. Just seeing her for this short time has done wonders for my mood.

Mrs. Wilkerson grabs my arm, stopping me from walking off the stage. "Not so fast, Nate. I'm sure everyone would love it if you stuck around and participated in the scavenger hunt. Isn't that right, everybody?"

The crowd cheers in response. Leela's smile tightens as she looks away.

"Especially since the theme of the scavenger hunt is our founding mother, your great-great-great-great-great grandmother, the amazing and industrious Kimberly Bell!" Mrs. Wilkerson says. "What do you say? You and Leela could be a team."

I don't respond. Just look at Leela.

"It's up to you," I mouth toward her.

She hesitates, then nods.

"It's settled. Leela and Nate will compete with all of you to win the scavenger hunt!" Mrs. Wilkerson declares.

Leela waves her hands, then beckons for the microphone. "But we won't be eligible for any prizes. We'll play for bragging rights only."

The employees like that response.

I step to the side next to Leela as Mrs. Wilkerson explains the scavenger hunt details.

"That's extremely generous, guaranteeing everyone a job," Leela whispers. "How did you get the board to agree to that?"

"It made good business sense. You develop high-quality employees. We'd prefer not to lose them to other companies. It's as simple as that," I say, dismissing her gratitude.

There's something more important I need to know from her.

I lower my voice and ask, "Are you ok with doing the scavenger hunt … with me?"

CHAPTER 56

L EELA

~

"No." I cross my arms over my chest and stare into those dark orbs that made me fall in love. This is a horrible idea. "But it would look weird if I didn't agree after your amazing offer."

"Understood," Nate says, mirroring my pose. He just looks infinitely more sexy standing that way than I ever could. I inhale a deep breath as he steps closer to me. "I know we technically can't win the game, but it would look terrible if I lost a scavenger hunt based on my family history. So, we need to tap back into that stellar teamwork we used to do and wipe the floor with these other teams."

"Well, when you put it that way, let's look at the first clue," I say, unfolding the paper that Mrs. Wilkerson handed to each of us. Based on the scavenger hunt rules, we were all randomly given clues in a different order so teams wouldn't stalk others to find them. The goal is to be the fastest pair to collect all seven golden ribbons hidden at each clue's location. I read our clue to Nate. "Kimberly taught her son to read in a small red building where children take heed. A bell once called young minds to grow. What place still echoes from long ago?"

A frown creases his face as he looks perturbed. "This is problematic already. Is she just revising my family history to suit her needs?" He seems genuinely offended.

"What's wrong with the clue?"

"The answer is obviously the old schoolhouse where Grady Smith's antique store is located."

"The clue can't be wrong if you know the answer." I scan the storefront names until I see the antique store in the distance. "There it is. Come on." I head down the sidewalk toward the store, and Nate falls into step by my side. He's wearing a new cologne. The one I picked when I surprised him for lunch one day in Houston. After a decadent meal, we passed through the men's section of Niemen Marcus, where the scent caught my attention. I made the mistake of telling Nate, and he bought it on the spot.

"The clue is wrong. Kimberly taught her son to read in a small red building where children take heed. That's pure fiction. Grammie Kim wasn't a teacher and she definitely didn't send her kids to the public school. No member of my family has ever gone to public school. Grammie Kim hired private tutors to live with her and teach her kids. The whole clue needs to be redone. It's ridiculous."

I stifle a laugh. "Got it. Public school isn't good enough for the Bells."

"That's not what I'm saying. But the truth is that we all attend private school as a matter of … tradition."

The next two clues have us hiking from the antique store to Bell Park, where we snag ribbons at the old oak tree and the clock tower. Nate's mood grows more sour as he laments more errors by Mrs. Wilkerson.

Apparently, Kimberly Bell did not give a memorable speech at the old oak tree. Her granddaughter did that sixty years after the town's founding. The clock tower wasn't erected after her death to pay homage to her dream of having one. She loathed the idea, so the town waited until she died before creating it.

"I'm not sure I want to read the next clue. These have all been farces." Nate walks up to the paper tacked onto the brick of the clock tower.

"I'll jot down these corrections and give them to Mrs. Wilkerson after we get through all the clues. I'm sure that's the only mistake she's made. What does the next clue say?" I ask.

"Where Kimberly's Bible was the first to arrive. A place where books helped the town to thrive. Its shelves hold tales from days of yore. What building still guards stories and lore?"

"That's got to be the Kimbell Library? Right?" I ask, tugging at Nate's arm.

He scoffs. "Most likely. But if you want to find Grammie Kim's bible, it's in the Bell Family library on our estate. The book she donated was a Boydell edition of Shakespeare's Works. It's illustrated and was a highly sought-after collector's edition even when Grammie Kim bought it. Unbelievable."

"Okay, so Mrs. Wilkerson is zero for four. I'm sure she thought her research was sound and didn't realize the mistakes she was making," I say.

Nate's jaw clenches as he searches the park for Mrs. Wilkerson. When he finds her helping a group of employees with one of the clues we've already gotten, he levels her with a stare that could melt steel.

"Nate ... "

"Yeah, let's get to the library," he says, slipping his hand in mine as he leads the way. His touch is so natural and perfect that neither of us realizes what he's done until we're several steps away.

His hand stiffens in mine. "I'm sorry," Nate says, stopping in front of me. "I didn't mean to make this awkward. Old habits, you know?"

"Yeah, don't worry about it. How far is the library?" I ask, dodging any attempt to talk about our failed relationship. I don't trust myself to have the conversation without becoming an emotional wreck. Plus, talking about it won't change anything.

What's done is done. There's no way we can come back from what he did to me.

Nate points ahead, and we fall into an uncomfortable silence until we reach the library. He opens the door, and I follow him inside.

The woman behind the counter blanches as we enter. Worry clouds her dark brown eyes as she fidgets with the strands of her wavy black hair. "How angry are you?" She asks, ignoring me and directing all her attention to Nate. She's more than pretty and knows him well. Jealousy rises within me, but I force the feeling away.

"What do you think?" Nate retorts, then turns to me. "This is our librarian and famed author of the Larry Llama children's books, Odalis Cruz. Odalis, this is Leela Jamison, owner of Sybille Organics."

"Technically, I'm not the owner. Haven't been for a while," I say, with more edge in my voice than I wanted. I don't look at Nate, although I can feel the heat of his gaze on me.

Odalis picks up on the tension and thankfully changes the subject back to the scavenger hunt. "When Mrs. Wilkerson dropped off the clue, I didn't read it right away, or I would've corrected her. I swear."

"So what are you telling folks when they come in?" Nate asks, leaning against the counter.

"You two are the first. Congrats," Odalis says, handing us our fourth gold ribbon. "But my plan is to tactfully correct the clue and give them insight into the book of Shakespeare's Works and why that was the book Kimberly Bell chose to donate to start the library." She turns to me. "Would you like to see it? It's well protected in a glass case down that hallway."

"No, we need to get working on the next clue. Nate can't come in second place on a hunt based on his family," I explain without mentioning that the last thing I want is to gaze at romantic sonnets with Nate by my side.

Odalis grins, then motions for me to turn the ribbon over. "Good luck." She turns her attention to a pair entering the library searching for their gold ribbon.

I tug at Nate's arm, pulling him toward the entry to the library.

"Don't worry, okay? I've written down this one, too. Mrs. Wilkerson shouldn't have a problem fixing these before doing another scavenger hunt."

"She should have had someone, anyone, from my family review these stupid clues. We all could've helped her fix them. I doubt she got anything right in the rest of them," Nate pouts.

The despair in his face is so real and so adorable. All I want is to wrap him in my arms and make it better for him. But that's what a girlfriend would do, which I'm not. Anymore.

"Only one way to find out," I say as I turn away from him. "Let's find the next clue."

CHAPTER 57

L EELA

THE NEXT TWO CLUES PROVE NATE WAS RIGHT.

We meander over to the location of the first general store, where Grammie Kim traded flour, not gold, for eggs and milk, as the clue stated. Then, over to the old saloon, which now houses Baker Bros BBQ, where Grammie Kim never broke up a fight between two men vying for her heart. Instead, the duel ended when one suitor shot the other, and she found out about it the next day.

"Was the guy killed?" I ask, mortified by this turn of events.

"No, but since he lost the bet, he was the one who left town."

"And Grammie Kim and the other man were able to start a relationship?"

"Of course not. She sent him packing. She wasn't the type to let anyone make decisions for her, kind of like someone else I know," Nate says, giving me a wink.

I ignore him and look at the last clue. "Here's Mrs. Wilkerson's last chance to get a clue right." I read the text from the index card tucked in the window of Baker Bros BBQ. "Kimberly danced with a new love on a planked, sturdy floor. A festival night she cherished and more. Over the water, it spans with care. What crossing holds the night's memory there?"

"Let me see that." Nate reaches for the index card.

"Over the water has to be some kind of bridge. But I haven't seen a creek or bridge anywhere as we've crisscrossed all over downtown Kimbell," I say, stopping to turn around in a full circle. My gaze canvasses the area.

"Old Stony Bridge. It's behind Elm Street Brewery, several blocks away if you stay on Main Street. But I know a shortcut to get there in about five minutes." He points to an alleyway beside the restaurant that leads to an overgrown forest.

"Let's head over, and you can tell me what Mrs. Wilkerson got wrong about that clue."

Nate is quiet as he leads me through the brush, pausing to push aside overgrown limbs and swipe away cobwebs as we meander through the downtrodden path.

"Let me guess," I say. "Grammie Kim didn't dance with a new love. She danced alone. Or she didn't dance on the bridge at all. Somebody else who looked like her danced, and the story got muddled." I laugh as the myriad of possibilities multiply in my mind. I glance over at Nate, and his face is pure stone. He doesn't even crack a smile at my joke. "Nate …"

"The bridge is right here," he says, steering me behind the charming brewery, a mission-styled building with white brick walls and elegant arched windows. The stone bridge emerges ahead—a marvel worn by time and covered with moss is stately with intricate carvings of intertwined ivy and blooming roses along its grand balustrades. "Harlow-Rose's family owns this brewery. One of the stipulations when we sold the land to them was that this bridge could never be torn down. Mr. Robinson keeps it maintained and true to how it was all those years ago … when Grammie Kim danced with Rhett Deveraux."

"Wait …" I reach a hand out to grab his arm. "The clue is … right?"

"Yeah, she got this one right. Rhett was a gigolo. Self-taught in gentlemanly graces, he was a grifter who crafted his persona—part scholar, part seducer—to slip into the town's high society and steal Grammie Kim's heart. But everyone knew he was a fraud. Because of Grammie Kim's standing in the community, she could never marry a playboy. But they had a not-so-secret love affair until the day she died. He was no good for her, but she loved him anyway." Nate levels me with an intense stare that takes my breath away.

I look away and push past him, desperate to get some distance. Walking over the bridge, I caress the limestone railing until I'm standing in the middle where Kimberly Bell danced under the moonlight with the secret love of her life. A soft breeze rustles through the trees, blowing strands of my hair across my face.

Nate's hand gently brushes the tresses from my eyes, then caresses my face. Time stops for me, and I'm lost in him. His dark eyes are full of passion and desire. The closeness of his body to mine. For a moment, I think he's going to pull me into a romantic dance. But I couldn't be more wrong. The magnetic pull draws him closer and closer to me until his mouth claims mine.

The kiss is intense, raw, untamed, desperate, and hungry. Every thought within me screams to resist and stop him, but I can't. It feels too good to stop. Every ounce of love I have for this man keeps me from pushing him away. His arms encircle my waist, pulling me into him as my arms dangle at my sides. I can't hold him. I won't. I'm only letting myself have this last kiss with him as a goodbye. His hands roam my body until they are entangled in my hair, pressing my head into his. He deepens the kiss, and my knees feel weak, followed by my resolve to stay away from him.

I can't let this continue, no matter how much I love the way it feels.

How right it feels to be with Nate. We could've been so perfect together if he hadn't ruined things.

I try to pull away.

Nate holds me tighter, his mouth dancing over mine.

I shake my head and shove him, but he doesn't budge. Turning, I wriggle a few inches from him, then slap him.

Hard.

His arms fall away from me.

Instantly, I miss his touch.

The closeness of him.

But it's not real.

Nate isn't just this sweet, passionate, attentive man. He's also brusque, self-centered and unapologetic. That part of him will always disappoint me. And I won't live my life like that. Not for him. Not for anyone.

My breaths are coming hard as we stare at each other without speaking. I don't even know what to say. Telling him to keep his hands off me sounds ridiculous since we just spent the last several minutes kissing like our lives depended on it.

A smirk plays on his lips as his hand touches the red mark on his face where I slapped him. His eyes dance with mischief as he takes one step away from me, then another.

"I'm sorry …" I push the words out. "I shouldn't have slapped you. I just—"

"Love me?" Nate says, his smile morphing into the sexy version. "It's okay. I love you, too."

My mouth gapes open as my heart thuds in my chest.

Did he say he loves me?

"I love you, Leela," he repeats as if he read my mind. "I'm in love with you. I'll always love you. That will never change." Nate grabs our last golden ribbon from a hook at the end of the bridge and hands it to me. "We should head back to the Train Depot and turn our ribbons in." He raises his hands in mock surrender. "I wasn't joking when I said I need to win this scavenger hunt."

He turns and walks away, leaving me with confusing thoughts rattling in my brain.

For the first time, I realize getting over Nate Bell will be much more complicated than I thought.

CHAPTER 58

L EELA

~

AN ARM WEIGHS HEAVY AGAINST MY WAIST, HOLDING ME
tight as I wake. I don't open my eyes as I caress the strong hand. My
fingers glide lightly over the taut muscles of the arm that has held me
so many times. A feeling I've memorized—

My eyes fling open.

"Nate …" His name tumbles from my lips as I glance over at his
dark hair, rumpled from sleep. He's staring at me like I'm the only
thing he wants to look at for the rest of his life.

"Morning, Beautiful," he says, then leans over to trail kisses along
my neck.

I clench my eyes shut. This cannot be happening.

I open them again, and he's still here, peppering my skin with light
kisses.

"What are you doing here?" I force the words out.

"We won the scavenger hunt, remember?" Nate murmurs against my neck as he turns me toward him, pulling me tighter into his arms. He's shirtless, revealing a chest that would make any woman salivate. Thank goodness I'm wearing pajamas, but I'm shocked that I have no memory of how we got here … in my bed at Crockett Manor.

"Yes, that was important. But I don't know how … why … you're … here."

"Because you love me," Nate says as if it is the answer to all life's conundrums. "And I love you. We're supposed to be together. You know that."

I swallow and stare into his dark eyes. The love reflected at me makes my heart yearn for this man. But he's wrong. Isn't he? I have not forgiven him for what he did to me. I can't believe I don't remember—

"Leela, you love me, right?" Nate prods.

My heart thuds in my chest.

"Say it," he demands.

"How I feel about you doesn't matter."

"It's the only thing that matters," Nate says, caressing my face. "You think when we are old and gray, either of us will care about how many haircare products you sold and how many companies I took over? We're not going to care about that at all. The only thing that will matter is that I love you with every part of me. That's what you'll cherish, and I'll cherish the fact that …" his voice trails off.

But despite every warning bell going off in my brain to not admit this to him, I can't withhold the truth any longer. "You'll cherish that I love you more than I ever thought was possible to love anyone."

The smile that spreads across his face is enough to wipe away all my anger and disappointment from him selling my company behind my back. It's intoxicating to know that I make him this happy. I want to keep that smile on his face, but at what cost? How many more disappointments will I suffer if I try to have a future with Nate? I don't trust him to take care of my heart.

"But I can't be with you. A relationship between us just doesn't work," I say, although it pains me. "I can't get over what you did."

"I'm going to make it up to you. You'll see," Nate says, then leans forward and gently kisses my lips.

"How?" I ask.

His response sends a shiver through me. "I will not lose you."

A sharp knock on the door jolts me awake. I jerk up in the bed, look around frantically, and then exhale a long sigh. It was a dream. A tortuous figment of my hyperactive imagination.

I slam my fists into the mattress, pummeling it with punches until I'm out of breath.

"Leela … everything okay in there?" Alma, the housekeeper, asks, her voice wafting in from the other side of the door. "You missed your wake-up call, so I'm checking on you."

"Wake up call?" I whisper, then spot the empty bottle of Tito's vodka on the nightstand. Memories flood my mind of what happened after Nate, and I returned to Bell Park with the ribbons from the scavenger hunt.

He was a perfect gentleman like he hadn't kissed my breath away on the bridge. Mrs. Wilkerson acknowledged us as the fastest to complete the scavenger hunt, which Nate responded to with a smirk of pride as he shoved my notepad full of corrections that needed to be made to the clues in her face. Mrs. Wilkerson turned red with embarrassment as she fumbled excuses for her faux pas and promised to fix things before another group did the scavenger hunt. Satisfied with that response, Nate gave his goodbyes, leaving me alone to wrap up the day with the employees. After the last of them had left the park, I walked back to Crockett Manor, swiped a half pint of vodka from the bar, and holed up in my room, drinking the memories away.

Something I don't plan to do ever again.

A key jostles in the door, and it pops open.

Alma peeks inside and looks relieved to see me staring back at her.

"I'm sorry, I was worried. You're usually punctual in the morning and out of here by now. When you didn't pick up the phone for the wake-up call or grab breakfast, I wanted to make sure you were okay."

"I'm here," I say, then sigh. "I don't know about being okay."

Alma pauses, her gaze going from me to the bottle on the nightstand. "Man problems?" She asks.

"How'd you guess?" I ask, shaking my head.

"I've been there with the love of my life. God rest his soul," Alma says with a small smile. "Men can be so frustrating. Do you want to talk or to be left alone?"

"Might be nice to talk … if you have time," I say.

"I have time and breakfast," Alma says, walking inside with a tray on one arm. She closes the door with her foot and walks to the other bedside table. "If that's all you had for dinner last night, you need to eat. How's your head?"

"No hangover, just crazy dreams."

"The crazy kind of dreams where the fantasy of everything you want is playing out in your mind? Those crazy dreams?" She giggles.

"Exactly! It felt so real, but it wasn't."

"Maybe not, but I'm sure it was still special to get everything you wanted, even if only in a dream. My Tito passed away almost three years ago. I miss him terribly. The more time passes, the less he shows up in my dreams."

She looks disheartened, and my heart aches for her. I reach for her hand and gently squeeze it.

"As much as that man frustrated me, I'd give anything to have him back," Alma says. "But you didn't invite me in to talk about my sad story. Here, drink some orange juice." She shoves the glass into my hand, and I take a long sip.

"Who messed up? You or him?" Alma asks.

"He did. Big time."

"And you think you can't forgive him?"

"Right."

"Do you love him?" She asks. From the look on her face, I know she'd see through me if I lied.

"Yes."

"And he loves you?"

"He says he does."

She frowns. "You don't believe him?"

"I believe him," I'm quick to answer. I have no doubts about Nate's love for me. I question whether he can make the best decisions for our love or continue to do things that hurt it.

Alma nods, then shoves a plate of scrambled eggs with cheese and chorizo onto my lap. "Eat. The grease will help soak up the alcohol."

"Okay," I say, loving her logic, whether accurate or not. I shove a forkful into my mouth and groan with pleasure. "This is divine."

"Thank you," Alma beams, then her face grows serious. "People sometimes get tricked into thinking it's easy to find love. Like it's right around the corner, waiting for you whenever you want to look for it. But the reality is that it's a lot harder to find love, to fall in love, than people think. And when you do find it, it must be treasured like the precious gift it is. Because sometimes, too soon, it is taken away from you, and you can't get it back."

Her words are sobering. I push the eggs around the plate as her message sinks into my soul.

Alma touches a finger to my chin, forcing me to look at her. "There's just one more question you need to answer."

"What's that?"

"Do you want to live without him?"

N ATE

GWEN'S COUNTRY CAFE IS BUSIER THIS MORNING THAN usual. I recognize a few locals crammed at tables. But the rest are unfamiliar—tourists descending on our town like vultures for the summer now that Lake Lasso is developing into a premier vacation spot.

Lucky for me, Gwen always has a table or two held back for her regulars. I squeeze past a group who'd been waiting for a while and ease into a seat at a bistro-sized table, then glance up at Gwen.

"Those folks are going to be pretty upset you let me skip the line," I say, then skim the menu.

"Well, they can head over to that new fancy coffee spot if they get tired of waiting. There's not enough money in the world for me to turn away the folks who've kept me in business long before Kimbell became the hot new vacation destination," Gwen says, wiping sweat from her hairline. "What are you in the mood for this morning?"

"Omelet with bacon and bell peppers," I say, then toss the menu back on the table.

"Your pretty girlfriend not joining you today?" She asks.

"Nope. She's pretty upset with me right now," I say, refusing to acknowledge that Leela broke up with me. Not when I'm still wracking my brain for something to do that will make up for selling her company.

"Well, my money is on you, Nate. You'll find a way to make things right. Y'all make a beautiful couple," Gwen says. "I'll make that omelet for you myself. Coffee, too? Black, right?"

I nod, then watch as she scampers back to the kitchen.

"I agree with Gwen. Definitely a beautiful couple."

I look up and see Harlow-Rose gripping the chair opposite me. The diamond on her left hand is better than I thought Santos could afford but not lavish enough to suggest Harlow-Rose helped with the cost. No doubt he put his foot down and took months to scrape together enough money to get that ring. Something to be admired, I suppose.

"Congrats on your ... engagement," I say.

"Thanks. I owe you an apology," Harlow-Rose says.

"Don't bother. I'm over it now," I admit. I'd give anything for the days when all I had to be upset about was Harlow-Rose letting me learn about her engagement through the grapevine.

"Not just about not telling you myself about my engagement," she says, then motions for the chair.

"I'm meeting someone," I say, in no mood to have this conversation. The only happily in love person I let myself be around these days is Luke. I don't have the capacity for anyone else's joyous love while the woman I love has kicked me out of her life.

"Okay, then I'll be quick. Leela told me how you felt when I broke things off after our high school graduation. I know it was so long ago, and none of that matters anymore, but I wish I hadn't dismissed your feelings so easily. Wish I'd been able to see you and know your heart like she does," Harlow-Rose says, then takes a deep breath. "What I'm saying is that I didn't realize I hurt you back then. I'm sorry for that."

Leave it to Leela to defend me to Harlow-Rose even when she's doing everything in her power to live without me. Moments like these reinforce what I know in my head and my heart. I have to fight to get her back.

"Apology accepted," I respond, then glance at the door as Javier walks in, looking ragged. "Anything else?"

"No, I guess that's all," Harlow-Rose says, a frown crinkling her forehead. "Nate, are we ok?"

I give her a reassuring smile. "We'll always be okay, Harlow-Rose. Nothing will ever change that."

She looks relieved and smiles.

"Sorry, I'm late," Javier says.

I stand and do quick introductions. Harlow-Rose excuses herself to leave us for our meeting.

"This morning has been full of surprises," Javier says, an edge of anger in his tone. "Why didn't you tell me that the supply of the critical ingredient of Sybille Organics' new line is on land that isn't owned by Sybille Organics or Bell Capital?"

"It wasn't pertinent to the negotiations," I say.

"Yes, it was!" Javier yells, banging a fist on the table. "Especially since a long-term agreement for the calyxera root hasn't been negotiated. There's only enough supply to cover the extension with GrabHub. That'll get us to the end of the year but doesn't come close to meeting the demand we'll have to enact our expansion goals," Javier continues his rant. "Nobody seemed to know who the supplier was. Everybody kept saying check with Nate, so I'm here to check with you. Who do I need to negotiate with?"

"You're looking at him."

"Bell Capital doesn't own the land. Why would I need to negotiate with you?"

"Because Bell Naturals bought the land in Hawaii with the calyxera root growing all over it. A newly formed entity owned solely by … me." I lean back and grin.

Javier's shoulders relax as he shakes his head at me. "You Bells are a force to be reckoned with. I must admit, it's a brilliant move. An untapped market that is only going to get bigger."

"You don't know the half of it," I say. Calyxera root isn't the only rare natural ingredient gaining popularity in beauty care products. Over the past weeks, I've been buying up land around the world where other natural ingredients are sourced to expand and diversify our inventory. And more importantly, I've instituted strict rules to ensure we're giving back and supporting the communities where the ingredients grow. This won't be a come in and take what we need, leaving nothing behind for the communities. I'm committed to partnering with them and funneling back portions of the profits to help better the places where we cultivate the ingredients.

That was Leela's vision for the land purchase of the calyxera root and how she convinced the landowners to sell to us in the first place. I will honor that model and roll it out worldwide as we seek to sustainably provide the ingredients while protecting them from over-harvesting and extinction.

"Don't worry. I'll give you a good deal to keep your expansion plans on track."

"That's good to hear because the negotiations with Leela took a nosedive this morning," Javier says, shaking his head. "You were right about her. I underestimated what a savvy businesswoman she is. I think she may have stolen several negotiation tactics from your playbook."

I tense, sitting up straighter in my seat. "What happened?"

"She's playing hardball, and I'm scrambling to protect our interests," Javier says. "She refused our generous offer to buy her twenty percent interest and declined to be employed by Primewell after the deal closes."

"She did ..." I say, unable to hide my surprise. I never imagined that Leela would sit idly by as a passive investor in the company she built from the ground up.

"I wish that's where it ended, but it gets worse."

"Do tell."

"She's not going to hold onto her interest in the company. Instead, she's decided to seek offers from others and will sell to the highest bidder. Primewell will have no say in who we'll be sharing ownership with," Javier says, throwing up his hands. "Can you believe that?"

A laugh escapes my lips. "Kind of like the situation we forced her into, don't you think?"

"How can you laugh at a time like this? Do you know how many of our competitors would love to jump in on this deal? Get insight into how we run things. This could be very bad for us," Javier says. "And the lawyers tell me there's nothing we can do to stop her."

"I tried to warn you," I say, feeling proud of Leela. I might be getting soft, adopting some of her style, but she's sharpened her edges and took on some of mine. It's why we're perfect for each other. "What's your plan?"

"There's only one thing we can do—try to buy the interest from whoever she sells to," Javier explains.

I whistle. "That's going to be expensive."

"Tell me about it," Javier says.

My cell phone buzzes in my pocket.

Grabbing it, a text message from Mom pops up on the screen.

> MOM
>
> Your father wants to discuss the quarterly results today. He expects you to meet him in fifteen minutes.

A buzz of excitement flows through me. It's my first chance to hear what Dad thinks about everything I accomplished while he's been out. A meeting that can erase the horrible one that led to his stroke. I'm surprised at how much this means to me. How much I've been hoping for the chance to change his mind and make him proud.

I type quickly on the phone.

Tell him I'll be there.

CHAPTER 60

NATE

I'M NOT PREPARED FOR WHAT'S ON THE OTHER SIDE OF Dad's door.

Dad sits propped up in the hospital bed, stiff and defiant as ever, surrounded by standing monitors displaying various financial statements and reports. His laptop rests on the overbed table, its screen casting a cold light against his pale skin. I hear his voice before he sees me—sharp, deliberate, as he barks commands into the air.

It's surreal. His speech is slower now, but the tone is unmistakable: strong, cocky, and commanding. If I close my eyes, I can almost forget the slack side of his mouth and how his body betrays him with every slight movement.

I listen, stunned. He's dictating an email to the Bell Capital lawyers with surprising precision.

"Did the doctors clear you for work?" I ask, stepping into the room and crossing toward him.

His head jerks up, startled, and—for a split second—I catch a flash of joy in his eyes. It disappears as quickly as it came.

"We reached a compromise," Dad says, the right corner of his mouth lifting in a crooked smile while the left remains slack. "Those speech exercises they put me through? Child's play. If I'm going to get back to normal, I need realistic practice."

He attempts to lift a hand toward the monitors, but it shakes violently halfway there. Frustrated, he lets it drop. "Dictating emails and reports—real work—that's what's helping me get better at talking. I'm not allowed to send them out yet, though."

Pulling the rolling stool next to his bed, I sit down. I wonder how many of his dictated reports critique my performance as interim CEO and whether they are filled with praise or more criticism. "Your progress is impressive," I say.

"Don't look so shocked," Dad fires back, leveling me with a sharp, shrewd stare. "Or disappointed. Taking over as CEO is temporary, Nate. Don't get too comfortable in my position—or my office."

"I never moved into your office," I admit quietly.

He blinks, caught off guard, then shrugs like it doesn't matter.

"Mom said you wanted to talk about the quarterly results," I say, shifting the conversation. This is my chance. I've spent months proving I can lead Bell Capital, but everyone else's praise means nothing if I don't get his.

Dad grunts, his gaze unreadable as he studies me. "You did what I expected you to do."

I tense. I know that tone too well.

"You handled the low-hanging fruit. Closed the deals I had teed up before I left. The terms were fine. More favorable—but not as strong as they would've been if I'd still been there to nurture the relationships."

"Understood," I say tightly. I feel ten years old again, desperate for a scrap of praise and getting nothing but criticism in return.

"You realize Patty or Karl could've done the same thing, right?"

Dad continues, his voice cutting. "But I didn't leave them in charge. I left you in charge because I expected more."

I fight to keep my voice even. "What about the new deals I brokered?" I ask, almost afraid of his answer. I'm proud of my foray into haircare with Sybille Organics, but I already know what's coming.

"That," Dad says, a glimmer of grudging respect in his voice, "was a surprise. The only bright spot."

Hope flares in my chest—until he keeps going.

"Ballsy move to go into an industry we've never touched. I'll give you that. And flipping it so quickly to Primewell was smart. You got out before you realized you were out of your element."

Out of my element? Unbelievable.

"But it was a small win," he adds, unimpressed. "We're a multi-billion dollar company, Nate. Deals in the hundreds of millions get lost in the rounding. You know that."

"The deal was after the quarter. The impact will show next quarter," I counter, trying to keep my frustration in check. "It positions us to exceed our targets, even without factoring in the rest of the organization's results."

"And what's coming after that?" Dad demands.

"What?"

He narrows his gaze. "You wasted all your time on your little haircare business, so there's nothing else in the pipeline. That's the real problem. As CEO, you can't get so caught up in one deal that you stop thinking ten or fifteen steps ahead. You just don't get it, Nate—and I'm not sure you ever will."

His words are daggers. Everything I've done—months of sacrifice, grinding, torching my life—has been for nothing.

I swallow hard. My voice is tight. "I gave up everything to secure that deal. I worked nonstop for months to prove to you that I could keep your company thriving."

"Stop being dramatic," Dad says dismissively.

"Dramatic?" I push up from the stool, the words pouring out before I can stop them. "I'll show you dramatic. I fell in love with an incredible woman who owns that 'little' haircare business. I worked beside her and discovered parts of myself I didn't know existed—parts you stifled for years. She made me a better man. But I threw it all away. For you. For Bell Capital. For a shot at your approval."

Dad's face shifts from confusion to anger, but I don't care.

"She doesn't want me anymore because I sold her company out from under her—to secure a deal to make you proud," I continue, pacing the room. "I've lost the woman I love, and you still think I'm a failure. You want me to do something you don't expect? Fine. I quit. Find someone else to mold into your image because I can't be that person."

"Why am I not surprised you're a quitter?" Dad spits. "What are you going to do? Jump ship to one of my competitors just to stick it to me? Let them use you to piss me off? That's pathetic."

I stop pacing and face him. "I'm shocked you'd even care. But no— I'm not joining another private equity firm. I've started my own business. A company that specializes in sustainably sourced natural ingredients for beauty products. The focus isn't just on profit but on giving back to the communities we source from. Something you never bothered to think about."

I turn for the door.

"Wait!" Dad's voice cracks behind me. "Don't go … son."

I freeze. Did I hear him right?

"Please," he says softly. His right arm extends toward me. My gaze drifts to the tattered braided leather bracelet still on his wrist.

He says, "Come here."

Slowly, I turn back. His face is wet with tears, and something deeper glistens in his eyes.

"I have never been prouder of you than I am in this moment," Dad says.

"You're proud of me?" I whisper, barely believing it. I move quickly across the room, standing over his bed as he looks up at me.

"Stepping out on your own takes courage. Fortitude. It's what I always hoped for you. I didn't want you living in my shadow, carrying my legacy. I wanted you to forge your own branch of the Bell family tree—your way."

"All this time, you wanted me to leave Bell Capital?"

"I wanted you to choose your path," Dad says, his voice softening. "You finally decided you wouldn't let anyone test you anymore. You know who you are now. That's all I ever wanted."

He squeezes my hand—stronger than I expect. "I love you, son. I always have."

"I love you, too, Dad."

"And I'm happy you've found a woman to love. You've got to fix things with her. Get her to take you back."

"I know." My voice drops, the shame settling in my chest like lead as I sit on the stool. "I've been trying to figure out how to make it right, but I'm coming up empty. She won't forgive me."

Dad raises an eyebrow, his expression turning sharper. "Come on, Nate. You're one of the best dealmakers I've ever seen. You tell me: what's the first rule of fixing a bad deal?"

I frown. "You undo it."

"Exactly," Dad says. "A good dealmaker knows how to close. A great dealmaker knows when—and how—to open the door again. This isn't about business anymore. It's about love. Real love. And that matters more than any bottom line."

I blink, startled. "Even if there's a cost to Bell Capital?"

Dad snorts, shaking his head. "What do you care? You don't work there anymore." He looks at me, his eyes steady. "If this woman means as much to you as you say, fight for her. Show her you're willing to sacrifice something for her this time. Show her she matters more than any deal or approval—mine or anyone else's."

I stare at him, his words settling into the cracks I didn't know were still there.

"You think it's that simple?" I ask quietly.

"No," Dad admits. "But nothing worth having ever is."

I let out a slow breath, the weight of everything starting to shift.

For the first time, I see something I never thought I'd get from my father: understanding.

"Thanks, Dad."

I stand, feeling a renewed sense of purpose.

"Go get her," Dad says, a small smile tugging at his mouth. "And don't mess it up this time."

"I won't," I promise.

CHAPTER 61

L EELA

~

Twiddling the pen between my fingers, I stare at the latest offer to purchase my interest in Sybille Organics. The response from the market is beyond my expectations, with lucrative deals exceeding what Primewell offered. As much as it hurts to walk away from the company I built, I can't help but swell with pride that so many companies and private investors see the value in the products I created. It just stings that I won't be around to shepherd the company to more significant success.

It didn't take long to realize that working for Primewell wasn't in my best interest. Taking my ideas and letting some big conglomerate reap the benefits and money from them sickened me. I also didn't want to be locked into a non-compete agreement with them for the next five years, which was one of the sticking points in their agreement. I'm not sure what my next step is, but I know it won't be working for someone else.

I'll create something new and fresh and bring it to market myself, like I've done in the past. Maybe haircare, maybe something entirely different. With the dollars being waved in my face, I'll have the financial security to take my time and figure it out.

I just wish that figuring out my personal life was going as well as my professional one.

Alma's question from a week ago is still niggling in the back of my brain.

Do I want to live without Nate?

The rational part of me sees how he concluded that selling off Sybille Organics to Primewell was a win-win for both of us. But my heart can't get over that he did it behind my back. He didn't consult me or seek my input or thoughts before he made the decision. A decision that had far-reaching effects on my life more than his. If he loved me, why would he do that to me? I don't have an answer to that question.

Just like I don't have an answer to Alma's.

Life would be so much easier if I hated Nate for what he did.

But it's impossible for me to hate him.

I miss him more and more every day that passes.

The memory of our kiss on the bridge comforts me, but not as much as when he told me he loves me. I suspected he felt the same about me as I did him, but hearing him say the words touched me more than I believed they could. In the moment, it was easy to hold onto my anger and disappointment. But now, I'm not sure that standing on that principle is worth losing the man who loves me.

And leave it to Nate to start respecting my wishes and stay away, when I don't want him to. Maybe that's my answer?

"Arghhhh!!!" I scream, covering my face with my hands.

"Having a bad day?" A woman's voice floats into my office.

My gaze jerks toward the door to see Willow Bell standing there with a smirk.

"I think I have something that will make it infinitely better," she says, then saunters in.

"Willow, hi, I wasn't expecting to see you ..." I say, trying to pull myself together.

"There's been a shake-up at Bell Capital. I wanted you to hear about it from me before it goes public," Willow says, easing into a chair across from my desk. "Nate is out as interim CEO, and Alona Kalinskaya, our mother, is in."

"I don't understand. Why isn't Nate the CEO anymore?"

"My brother had the good sense to resign and go on to bigger and better things." She grins.

"He resigned. Where is he going?"

"He started his own company. Going to be his own boss out of the shadow of our dad, and he'll be back volunteering at the fire station soon. I swear, I've never seen him happier." She pauses, then says, "Except when he was with you."

"I don't even know how to process all of this. It's so unexpected." The urge to call Nate and discover the story behind his abrupt departure from Bell Capital is strong. Willow has no reason to lie to me, but I'd much rather see for myself that Nate is in a better place with this change.

I've wanted to contact Nate for days, and this is the perfect excuse since I definitely needed one. Telling Nate I'm calling because I miss him and want to talk to him, but I'm still not sure if I can forgive him wasn't a viable option. Now I have one.

"Not entirely unexpected. You know Nate has always felt this pull to contribute more to the community around him than what Bell Capital allowed him to do. It's why he put in all the extra hours to protect his role as a volunteer firefighter for all those years. Now, he's building his legacy. A company focused on sustainably sourcing natural ingredients for beauty products that gives back to the communities where the ingredients are from."

"That's his new business?" I ask, remembering our discussions around that exact vision after purchasing the land in Hawaii with the calyxera root.

"Sounds familiar, doesn't it? Shows what a big influence you are on my brother's life in many ways. You're good for him."

"In some ways, he was good for me, too."

"And in others, he was a huge disappointment," Willow says bluntly. "But, he's made a major move to fix things for you. One our family wholeheartedly supports."

"Fix things … how?" I have no clue what Nate could do that would change the past, but surprisingly, I'm open to hearing what Willow has to say.

"When y'all negotiated the deal for the calyxera root, Nate purchased the land with his private funds. Not Sybille Organics' and not Bell Capital's. The Hawaiian land is the foundation of his new business—Bell Naturals," Willow explains. "That also makes him Sybille Organics' most critical supplier for the Herbal Root Essentials line."

"Because we purchase the root from his company," I say, getting the connection, but not sure how that matters.

"Unfortunately, Sybille Organics and Bell Naturals didn't close on a long-term supply agreement before the pending sale of Bell Capital's interest in the company to Primewell."

"Okay, but I'm sure Nate will negotiate that deal now, won't he?"

"No, he won't. He's told Primewell that their aggressive expansion of the new product line would deplete too much of the natural calyxera root in Hawaii, and he's not entering into any deals with them for it."

"But that means we'll run out of inventory for the new product line before the end of the year."

"Exactly," Willow says, then gives me a wink. "Without that critical ingredient available for the product, Primewell has pulled out of the deal with Bell Capital to buy our interest."

"They did?" My mouth falls open.

"Bell Capital gets a modest termination of agreement payment from Primewell and retains ownership of Sybille Organics. Nate explained that you'd lined up a bank to loan you money to buy back a controlling interest," Willow says. "Bell Capital is happy to accept the terms of the original deal if you're still interested."

"If! If! Of course, I'm still interested!" I say, jumping up from my chair. "Wait before I get too excited. You're telling me that you'll accept a much lower amount than you were going to receive from Primewell?"

"That's the beauty of a family-owned business. We get to decide when the best decision for the company is one that puts the company first or family first." Willow laughs. "Nate wanted you to have your company back, and he made it happen. All you need to do is get with your bank and start the ball rolling."

"He did this for me?"

"There's nothing my brother wouldn't do for you. Despite his prickly exterior, he's the most loyal, loving, and caring person I've ever known. He will always do what's right, especially when he knows he made a mistake," Willow says. "That's what makes him the best. So, should I tell my parents we have a deal?"

I'm trembling as I fall back into my chair. "Yes. We have a deal."

CHAPTER 62

L EELA

~

IT'S BEEN TWO WEEKS SINCE NATE ARRANGED FOR ME TO regain control of my company. Days filled with nonstop meetings with bankers, lawyers, and the Bell Capital executive team, hammering out a fair valuation for Sybille Organics in light of the latest sales projections and finalizing my first buyback of interest from them. I'm now the proud owner of fifty-three percent of Sybille Organics. Additionally, we've agreed upon a two-year plan to buy back the remaining interest owned by Bell Capital, giving me the best of both worlds. I'll have access to their top-notch teams to support our global distribution expansion while retaining control over the vision and strategy for the future.

But Nate wasn't around for any of this.

When Willow stopped by my office to tell me the news about the Primewell deal falling through, Nate was on a flight to Hawaii to oversee the harvesting of calyxera root at his new company, Bell Naturals.

I must have picked up my phone hundreds of times over the days, starting texts to him and deleting them. Almost dialing his number, then putting my phone away. Telling him how much his sacrifice meant to me over the phone or in a text felt wrong.

I want to look him in the eyes when I thank him for everything he did for me. For putting his professional reputation aside, risking the ire of his family, and burning bridges with Primewell to make things right.

Because he loves me.

And I love him.

I don't know if we'll find our way back to each other now.

But it's what I want. I have to believe that Nate wouldn't have gone through all this trouble if he didn't want a chance to recapture our relationship and our future together.

Still, his absence and silence have left me rattled. I don't understand why he wouldn't check in and see what I thought about what he'd done.

Or maybe he's made things right to move on with his life, leaving me behind with this chapter of the old him.

But I'm done second-guessing and speculating.

No matter what, I want him to know how I feel and that I still hope for a future for the two of us, even if it looks a lot different than what we thought it would.

I was overjoyed and nervous when I heard from some of the employees that Nate was seen having lunch with the other firefighters at Baker Bros BBQ yesterday. But now that I'm standing at his front door, I feel at peace and calm—mainly because there's no sneaking up on anyone at the Bell Estate. I went through security, who no doubt called him and got approval to allow me onto the grounds.

Nate knows I'm on the way to see him, and he's allowed it.

I raise my hand and knock on his front door, but the force pushes it open. Startled, I take a tentative step inside. The house is eerily quiet as I enter and close the door behind me.

"Nate ... " I call out, walking through the foyer, past the music room and library, until the room opens into the towering ceilings of his living room. The draperies are drawn closed, blocking the morning sun and casting the room in a dreary darkness.

Across the room, Nate lays crumpled on the couch in a wrinkled SMU t-shirt and jogging pants. His hair is a tousled mess. A few days stubble covers his jaw, and his eyes are dark and haunted, but he's the most handsome man I've ever seen. The man I love with all my heart.

"Hi," I say, as he drinks in the sight of me. I flush with heat under his intense gaze. Feeling self-conscious, I tug at the bright yellow halter dress hugging my curves.

"Hi?" His voice is a low growl. "Is that what you came to say to me?"

"Well ... no ... I ..." My words stick in my throat. I never expected him to be upset with me.

"I waited two weeks for you to call or text or ... something. But you never did," Nate hurls the words at me. "You didn't reach out at all."

"I know, and I'm sorry. I did think about it, but it felt wrong to have this conversation over the phone. I wanted to talk to you in person ... but then Willow told me you were out of town on business, and I figured it might be better to wait until you were back—"

"I would've dropped everything to come back here to you. All you had to do was say the word," he snaps. "It was pure torture, Leela. Not knowing what you were thinking or feeling. Not hearing your voice or being close to you." He rakes a hand through his hair. "I did everything I could to fix things, but—"

"You did more than I thought was possible. More than I could've ever dreamed. Words aren't enough to thank you for everything." I walk over to the couch, stopping a few feet from him. I want to tell him how much his sacrifice means to me. But I can't seem to get the words out.

He looks up at me with a fleeting hope in his eyes. "Do you forgive me?"

"Nate, you gave me my company back," I say, as if that explains everything.

He stands, closing the distance between us. My breath catches at how close he is to me. "That's not an answer to my question."

He's right. I take a deep breath and pour my heart out to him. "The truth is, you didn't have to blow up the deal with Primewell. When you made that deal, I was blindsided and hurt. But there's no way you would've closed that deal if it hurt me. You gave me financial freedom even if I didn't like how it happened. I know that now."

"But money isn't everything, is it?"

"No, it's not."

"And giving your company back to you isn't enough for you to forgive me …" His words drip with pain and regret.

"Nate …"

"I'm still glad I did it. I needed to make things right. Prove to you that you're more important to me than any business deal or pat on the back from my dad—"

"I love you," the words slip from my lips.

"What did you just say?" Nate asks.

"I forgive you, and I never ever stopped loving you. I need you to know that even if you hadn't made this huge sacrifice for me, some kind of way, I was going to find my way back to you," I say, reaching for his hands. "I know that in my heart."

The sexy smile plays on his lips. "Could you maybe have started with that … put me out of my misery?"

I laugh and throw my hands around his neck. "Good point. I'll keep that in mind for the future … if you still want one with me."

"You are my future," Nate says, kissing me. The touch of his lips against mine is like a firework exploding, igniting every nerve in my body with pleasure and longing. In that moment, everything else fades away, and all that matters is us, together again after what feels like an eternity apart. A rush of emotions floods me as I am reminded of how good it feels to be in his arms, cherished and loved by this man. How could I have ever thought I could survive without him?

Nate breaks the kiss too soon for my liking and stares at me with a hint of mischief in his dark gaze. "Now that you've come back to me, we can get married."

He grabs my hand and pulls me toward the dining room.

"Get married?" I ask, unable to believe my ears.

Nate points to a stack of documents on the table. "The pre-nuptial agreement is here, already reviewed by me and my lawyers. Your lawyer will be here in two hours to review it with you and propose any changes you want." He pauses, then glances at me. "But I think you'll find the terms to be fair and protect both of our respective businesses. In the meantime, there are wedding dresses in the guest room for you to choose from. Yolanda French, who owns the bridal boutique in town, will be here in about thirty minutes to do any alterations on the dress you choose—"

"Nate! What? I don't understand." I fumble with my words, trying to make sense of things. "What is going on?"

"We're getting married tonight," Nate says, a smirk playing on his lips.

"You and me?"

"Yes."

"Tonight."

"That's what I said."

I take a step back as the room spins around me. I open my mouth and close it several times.

Nate crosses his arms over his chest. "Do you need me to get down on one knee?"

"You want to marry me?"

"I will be marrying you ... tonight ... on my yacht floating across Lake Lasso at sunset. Before the day ends, you'll be my wife, and I'll be your husband. Forever."

"Is this a dream?"

"No, it's as real as it gets. A wise woman once told me that sometimes we prepare ourselves too much for what can go wrong that we're blindsided when something goes right."

His words trigger the remnants of a memory, but I can't place them.

Nate reaches into his pocket, but instead of pulling out a ring box, there's a stuffed butterfly in his hand. I choke back a sob as tears spring to my eyes. He reaches for my hand and places the toy in mine.

"The elevator ... you remembered me from the elevator." I can't believe it.

"I knew from the moment we got stuck inside that elevator that you would change my life. I just didn't know it would be this good."

"I bought this for Mr. Sabra's daughter. I told him about it, and then I couldn't find it. You had it all this time?"

"I liked having something of yours with me every day. But I don't need it anymore because I'll have you forever. Once you agree to marry me," Nate says, giving me an exaggerated eyebrow raise for forcing him to go through the formality.

Tears spill down my cheeks as he makes a theatrical move of sinking to one knee.

"I didn't know love until I met you, Leela. I've never wanted to share every part of myself with someone until you fluttered into my life like that stuffed butterfly. Each day with you opened up a new perspective and way to see the world, changing me for the better. You made me want to be a better man, not for you, but for me. Only true love does that. I can't imagine my life without you. I don't want to. Will you honor me by becoming my wife?"

I can barely respond as I collapse down into his arms, my yes coming out in a blubber of tears.

His fingertips gently brush away my tears. He stares at me with eyes filled with desire, pulling me closer to him until our faces are mere inches apart. His lips press against mine with urgency and tenderness, sending waves of bliss coursing through me. A sweet storm of longing fills every touch for the days we were apart, engulfing me and leaving me breathless.

We pull away, gasping for air and smiling through our tears. Nate looks at me with so much love that my heart aches at disappointing him. Holding him tightly, I say, "But we can't do this today. I want my parents and my brother to be with me—"

"They'll be on the boat tonight. Peter was instructed to find out everyone important to you and ensure they were here today for the wedding. Let me know if he missed anybody, and I'll fire him."

"You can't fire Peter. He's like family to you."

"Fine. I'll figure out some other suitable punishment for him."

"How were you able to do all of this?" I ask. "You didn't even know for sure that I would come to see you today."

"I hoped you would once you knew I was back in town."

"And if I didn't show up?"

"I would've found you," Nate says with a confident wink. He glances at his watch. "Now, I need to go. The rings and my tuxedo are being flown in from Paris. The plane is landing in thirty minutes, so I need to head over there. I'll text Willow to come over and help you get ready. Peter is on call for anything else you need. Get used to using him, will you?"

"Okay," I say, feeling like a princess in a fairytale.

"I love you," Nate says, kissing me again. "See you on the yacht tonight."

CHAPTER 63

NATE

FIVE GLASSES FILLED WITH AGED SCOTCH EXTEND TOWARD mine. I stop and glance at the faces surrounding me, realizing how lucky I am to have these guys by my side today.

"Another one bites the dust!" Wiley proclaims, clinking his glass against mine before tossing back the shot.

"To be honest, I'm not sure how I got invited to this party," Santos quips, swirling his drink instead of downing it. His lips twist into a smirk.

"Me either," Darren mutters, though he taps his glass against mine and offers me a small smile.

Having Darren and Santos in the same room was risky. The animosity of Darren and Jasmine versus Santos and Harlow-Rose has mostly been avoided. But with us all settling down, that will be a lot harder to do. Plus, I trusted Darren could put his feelings aside, temporarily, for me.

For some reason, having Harlow-Rose's fiancée around to help me celebrate felt like something I needed to do. She's one of my oldest friends. Even though things were rocky with us lately, inviting her soon-to-be-husband into our merry band of misfits was the best way I could show her that all is truly forgiven.

"We're all glad you can be part of this, Santos," Luke says. My best friend, ever the peacemaker, squeezes between the two enemies, just in case. "You'll have to get used to hanging out with all of us going forward, not just Ronan."

"He has a point, brother," Ronan says, tilting his glass toward Santos.

"I'm alright with that. You guys are good people," Santos says, giving Darren a conciliatory glance. The tension in Darren's jaw loosens as he tips his chin toward Santos in what is likely as close as we'll ever get to a truce between those two.

"Who of us would've ever put money on Darren and Nate being the first of our crew to get married?" Wiley asks, laughing as he reaches for the bottle of scotch.

"Well, none of us knew about Darren's secret love for Jasmine but you, Wiley. No way, we would've guessed they'd elope in Vegas on Valentine's Day." Ronan shakes his head. "But I'll say that's a romantic way of doing it."

"No offense, Nate, but you being next is a huge surprise," Darren says.

"Massive surprise ..." Ronan adds.

"Unbelievable, actually," Santos says.

"The last thing I would've guessed," Luke chimes in. "All your talk about you and love not mixing and how you don't do love was just a farce."

"If I remember correctly, dear friend, you didn't believe me back then. Even told me that the right woman would get me," I remind him.

"So, you're saying that I should be gloating and saying I told you so," Luke teases.

"It's the least I deserve," I say.

"And the most you deserve is an amazing woman like Leela," Wiley says, his boyish joking turning serious. "I get how you felt, Nate. None of y'all thought I could snag someone as smart and brilliant as Zaire, but look at us now."

"That's for sure," Ronan says. "Still don't see what she sees in you."

Wiley punches Ronan in the arm, then exhales. "There are days when I don't either. But real love has a way of lifting you up and supporting you when you don't think you deserve it."

I'm surprisingly impressed by Wiley's insights. "Leela does that for me. Every day. That's why I don't want to waste another minute not being married to her."

"Not that taking your time about getting married means you're wasting it," Luke chimes in, glancing at Ronan, then Wiley. "We all have our own timetables."

"That's true, brother," Ronan says, then rakes a hair through his hair. "But boy, do I wish I could get Mya to set a date. We were the first engaged, and at this rate, we'll be the last to get married."

"Can you blame her for wanting her wedding day to be perfect for her? That just looks different for every woman," Darren says. "For Jas, that was a kitschy Vegas chapel with an Elvis impersonator and hair ties for rings."

"You got the crap end of that deal," I say, then add, "You gave her your Super Bowl ring for her wedding band."

"There's no crap end of a deal with Jasmine. She's all I need," Darren says.

"Well, fellas, this is turning into a mush fest, and we're all losing testosterone at a rapid pace," Santos quips, leveling us with stern stares. "How about one last toast before this man walks down the aisle."

"Good plan, but we need to do this Kimbell style. None of this thousand-dollar scotch for our real toast," Ronan says. "We gotta toast with none other than …" he pauses, looking at me.

The answer is obvious.

"Elm beer," I say as I smile. "Peter should've put some bottles in the mini-fridge."

Wiley opens the fridge door. "Bingo!" He grabs them, tossing one to each of us.

Popping the tops, we stand in a circle as quiet settles over us.

"As Nate's best friend and best man, I'll do the honors," Luke says, then turns toward me. "Over the past few months, I've seen a big change in you … for the better. You stopped chasing others' definition of success and embraced your true self and what's important to you. Leela's presence in your life was the catalyst for this change that was so overdue."

"I wasn't that bad," I say, rolling my eyes.

"Dude, you worked nonstop and barely made time for anything other than trying to prove to your dad that you were worthy of following in his footsteps," Wiley shouts.

Luke says, "But not anymore. You're prioritizing what's important to you—firefighting with your closest friends, running a business that gives back to communities, and spending your life with Leela. The only woman who dares to put up with you."

The guys erupt into laughter.

"I'm proud of you for realizing what you had before it was too late," Luke says. The sincerity in his voice and the supportive gazes from the guys catch me off guard. Their support for me and this next phase of my life is more than I could've ever asked for. "And we all wish you the best for a life with Leela filled with understanding, compassion, and unconditional love."

"Hear, hear!" The guys shout in agreement.

"Thanks," I say quietly. "That means a lot."

Wiley sips his beer, then says, "And I hope married life doesn't turn you into a total softie. We've got a reputation to maintain, after all."

"Ain't that the truth, brother," Ronan adds, clinking glasses with each of us.

"And we'll all hold each other accountable to keep it up. That's for sure," I say, then raise my bottle to them—these guys who are my family. The only ones I want standing by my side as I marry the woman I love.

CHAPTER 64

LEELA

~

THE SCENT OF LAKE WATER AND ROSES WAFTS IN THE breeze as I step on the deck of the yacht. Everything feels like I'm in a dream I never dared to imagine for myself. The sun hangs low in the sky, painting the horizon in strokes of gold, orange, and lavender. Crystal-adorned string lights twinkle overhead, crisscrossing above a long aisle lined with white rose petals.

Beyond the aisle, our closest friends and family gather near the altar, beaming back at me with smiles and quiet excitement.

Willow appears at my side, adjusting the flowing veil cascading down my back.

"You sure you want to marry that guy?" She teases, but there's a tremor of emotion in her voice. "He's a handful."

"More than anything." I laugh softly, gripping the bouquet in my trembling hands. "I can handle him."

She snort laughs. "I'll remind you in a year that you said that."

As she smooths a strand of hair from my face, I look at the woman who, in a few moments, will be my sister-in-law. Part of my new family.

"Don't you dare cry. That makeup team costs a fortune, and you can't ruin their masterpiece. Not that you needed much makeup, which annoys me," Willow says.

"I'll do my best," I whisper, though tears are already pricking the corners of my eyes.

Willow stares at her brother for a long moment, then turns to me and says, "You make him happy, and that makes me happy. Thank you for loving him."

"I thought you didn't want me to cry," I say, swiping at a wayward tear.

She squeezes my hand. "Welcome to the family, Leela."

I mouth a thank you, then watch as she walks briskly toward the seats where the guests are waiting for me to walk down the aisle.

A complex melody rises from a piano in the distance. The first chords send my heart into a gallop. Harold beams at me as his fingers fly across the keys, playing a stunningly beautiful melody for me to walk down the aisle.

My parents emerge from the room, flanking me on each side.

"You ready, sweetheart?" Mom asks as she loops one arm in mine and kisses me softly on the temple.

Dad raises my hand to his lips. "We are so happy for you."

"Thank you … for being here. For walking me down the aisle," I say, emotions clogging my words.

"There's no place we'd rather be," Dad says, then pats my arm. "Come on, Nate looks impatient to make you his wife."

"Let's not keep him waiting any longer," I say, taking my first step down the aisle toward my future.

CHAPTER 65

ATE

~

W̲HEN SHE STEPS ONTO THE DECK, EVERYTHING ELSE FADES
away.

Leela.

She looks radiant in a flowing white gown that shimmers faintly in
the golden light. Her hair is swept back, the veil framing her face like a
halo. And those gorgeous hazel eyes—bright and filled with so much
love—lock onto mine as she walks toward me.

I forget how to breathe.

Luke leans in from his place at my side. "You good, man? You look
like you're about to pass out."

"I'm fine," I whisper, though my voice is thick. "I've never been
better."

Willow gives me a thumbs up, then sits beside our mom. I glance
at my dad, sitting in a wheelchair in the shadows, away from the other

guests. He insisted on coming, even though he didn't want to be seen or interact with anyone. The fact that he pressed his way to see me marry the woman I love means everything to me. We lock eyes and happiness washes over me. I did what he told me to do—I fixed things and got the girl.

Leela's brother moves to the piano and plays a melodic symphony perfect for the occasion. The guests rise to their feet as Leela, flanked by her parents, makes her way down the aisle.

She stops a few feet from me and hugs her mom, who's crying boatloads of tears. Then, she turns to her dad, who kisses her on the cheek and whispers something in her ear. She laughs. A sound that tickles my ears and makes my heart swell with love.

"I'm not telling him that," Leela whispers. "You'll have to do that yourself."

I step toward them, eager to pull her into my arms.

"I'm all ears," I say to her father.

"Take care of her, Nate," her dad says, then adds, "And don't let her boss you around."

"Too late for that," I say, laughing. "We both know who's in charge in our relationship. I like it that way. And I promise to take excellent care of your daughter. Always." A storm of emotions swirls within me as I say the words.

Leela smiles up at me, and in her eyes, I see everything—her strength, courage, and the love that blossomed through every challenge we faced.

"You're everything I've ever wanted," I whisper, squeezing her hand. "I love you."

Her lips curve into a shy smile. "I love you, too."

"Ready to get hitched?"

"Let's do it."

CHAPTER 66

L EELA

~

"DON'T YOU FEEL EVEN A TEENY WEENY BIT GUILTY?" I ASK, tipping the champagne glass to my lips and finishing the bubbly.

"What do you think?" Nate asks, staring at me like I've lost my mind.

"We abandoned all of our guests right after the wedding," I say, hoping everyone is still having a great time on the yacht.

"Trust me, they're being treated to the best party of their lives. We stayed long enough to take pictures, do our obligatory first dance, and cut the wedding cake. We checked all the boxes to allow us to start our honeymoon," Nate says, nuzzling his face into my neck.

"I am Mrs. Nate Bell," I say, still stunned. I'm a married woman. I stare at the custom-designed diamond about to blind me on my left hand. "How many carats is this?"

"Eight-ish," Nate says, tapping a finger on the emerald-cut

solitaire. "The band adds another three. Near flawless. It was the closest I could get to … you."

"You say the most romantic things to me," I laugh, sliding my arms around his waist and tugging him to me. "Who knew a random encounter in a broken elevator would lead to this?"

Nate laughs. "You know my dad is trying to take all the credit for our meeting."

"How? Because I attended the conference the week before?"

"No, that would be a better thing for him to bring up. But instead, he insists that his having a stroke is the reason why we met, and I owe him for having you in my life," Nate says, groaning. "Hard to say he's wrong since I was there to meet with the lawyers about who would take the reins of the company while he recovered."

"That's who you were meeting with. I didn't know. Well, we can't argue with your dad on that point."

"And he loves to take credit for every success, even mine. I'll let him have it this time. Especially since he pushed me to figure out how to break the deal with Primewell and get your company back."

"Now, I have to negotiate with you to secure a supply of calyxera root for my product line," I say, kissing him softly. "I hope you won't play hardball with me."

He raises an eyebrow, giving me a salacious look. "I'd love to play hardball with you, but we'll get to that later."

I giggle. "I'm sure we will."

"I'll give Sybille Organics whatever it needs at a fair price. I happen to be very fond of the owner. She's my favorite person on the planet," Nate says. "I'm looking forward to collaborating on more deals in the future."

"I'm so proud of you and the new business you created. You always downplayed the side of you who loves contributing to the community. I'm happy you're embracing that now with Bell Naturals," I say. "Who knew that was the one thing your dad wanted for you all along?"

"And because of you, I had the courage to do it. Walk away from what I'd been striving for my whole life, even though it didn't make me happy. You freed me to go after what would make me happy, and at the same time, I earned my father's respect and admiration. You're my lucky charm."

"Speaking of lucky charms, I can't find the stuffed butterfly. I meant to bring it to the wedding, but I must have laid it down somewhere," I say. "You'll help me look for it when we get back from our honeymoon?"

Nate scrunches his face, leaning away from me.

"Husband … did you steal my butterfly again?"

"Maybe." He reaches into the pocket of his tuxedo pants and pulls out the small toy. "I told you I like having a part of you with me when we're not together. I needed it more than you did today."

"Fine. Let's agree to share it," I say.

"Deal."

I lean back against him, exhaling a satisfied sigh. The butterfly clutched in my hands. "You never said where we're going on our honeymoon."

"To an island in the Caribbean," Nate says, his voice low in my ear.

"Am I supposed to guess which one?"

"No, but you should give it a name …"

"Give the island a name?"

"It's yours. You have to name it."

I flip over and stare at him. "You bought an island."

"Happy wedding day, darling," Nate says.

"You seriously bought us an island?"

"I bought *you* an island. Turnkey property, fully developed with water and electricity. Part of the British Virgin Islands. Reminds me of Kauai, which you loved, but much closer to get to."

"I don't even know what to say …"

"Try something like, 'Oh Nate, husband of my dreams, this is the best gift you could've ever gotten me!'" Nate says, mimicking my voice.

"You do a good impression of me," I say, swiping at the tears falling from my eyes. "But the island is the second-best gift you've ever given me."

He looks intrigued. "And the first?"

"Your heart."

Want more of Nate and Leela?
Get their swoon-worthy bonus story delivered straight to your email inbox!
https://BookHip.com/BZQVHWX

Next up in Kimbell, we revisit two couples, Darren & Jasmine and Wiley & Zaire, who learn that happily ever after sometimes requires love to defy the odds.

Check out the next book in the Kimbell Texas Sweet Romances …
DEFYING ODDS!
https://amzn.to/40Ex6tu

About the Author

Angel S. Vane never imagined she'd stumble into becoming an author. An avid fan of books her whole life combined with an active imagination were the right ingredients to embark on a single goal of completing one book.

Now she's written several books and has tapped into her love of Jane Austen novels by writing her own brand of satisfyingly sweet romances.

Learn more at Angel's website: subscribepage.io/angelsvane.

- facebook.com/satisfyinglysweetromance
- tiktok.com/@satisfyinglysweetromance
- amazon.com/stores/Angel-S.-Vane/author/B09TXDSNLB

About the Publisher

BONZAIMOON BOOKS

BonzaiMoon Books is a family-run, artisanal publishing company created in the summer of 2014. We publish works of fiction in various genres. Our passion and focus is working with authors who write the books you want to read, and giving those authors the opportunity to have more direct input in the publishing of their work.

For more information:
www.bonzaimoonbooks.com
info@bonzaimoonbooks.com

facebook.com/BonzaiMoonBooks